PRAISE FOR A
RUTH LOGAN HERNE

"The author exudes warmth and grace and love on each page of this novel, and the set-up for the next book leaves readers hungry for more."

Romantic Times reviewer Carrie Townsend for 4½ Star Top Pick
Home on the Range

"*Back in the Saddle* is an uplifting and heartwarming story about two wounded people using the power of faith to find the courage to change. A dramatic ranch setting, rich characterization, and a beautiful love story make this a book to savor. This is a strong beginning for what promises to be an exciting trilogy. Ruth Logan Herne is my new favorite author!"

New York Times bestselling author Karen White

"Heart and hope combine in Ruth Logan Herne's sweet tale of old wounds and ties that bind. Where faith and forgiveness are present, old scars can be healed and new love can bloom. Sometimes, you really can go home again."

Lisa Wingate, national bestselling author of *The Story Keeper* and
The Sea Keeper's Daughters

"From the first pages, readers will be drawn into the community of Gray's Glen, the amazing cast of characters, and the lives of the hero and heroine. Angelina and Colt fill the pages of *Back in the Saddle* with a romance that will have readers wanting to know their past, their future, and the story that intertwines their lives. Ruth Logan Herne takes us on a journey that we will want to continue!"

Brenda Minton, author of the Martin's Crossing series

Welcome to Wishing Bridge

ALSO BY RUTH LOGAN HERNE

Love Finds You in the City at Christmas
Refuge of the Heart
More Than a Promise
The First Gift
Try, Try Again
Running on Empty
Safely Home
Longing for a Miracle
Saved by the Sheriff
Home to His Heart
His Beloved Bride
The Pastor Takes a Wife
Second Chance Christmas
Second Chance at Love
A Town Called Christmas

Welcome to Wishing Bridge

RUTH LOGAN HERNE

Waterfall
PRESS

Text copyright © 2017 by Ruth M. Blodgett
All rights reserved.

No part of this book may be reproduced, or stored in a retrieval system, or transmitted in any form or by any means, electronic, mechanical, photocopying, recording, or otherwise, without express written permission of the publisher.

Published by Waterfall Press, Grand Haven, MI
www.brilliancepublishing.com

Amazon, the Amazon logo, and Waterfall Press are trademarks of Amazon.com, Inc., or its affiliates.

ISBN-13: 9781542046695
ISBN-10: 1542046696

Cover design by Rachel Adam Rogers

Printed in the United States of America

This beautiful story is dedicated to my wonderful daughter, Sarah, a woman who has worked hard to set the bar high, while helping others near and far. Sarah, I love you and am so proud of you! Congratulations on your achievements and your grace. Both are noteworthy.

CHAPTER ONE

LETCHWORTH STATE PARK
MOUNT MORRIS
WISHING BRIDGE
EXIT 1 MILE

Don't do it.

Kelsey McCleary stared straight ahead as the wipers slapped thickly falling snowflakes from her windshield. If she'd left midday as planned, she'd be below the Lake Erie snowbelt and into the Pennsylvania hills, en route to Harrisburg, but the car repairs had taken longer than expected . . . and cost more than anticipated, of course. She'd skirted a major accident and tie-up on I-81, heading across I-90 to its intersection with I-390 outside of Rochester. Avoiding that snowy, tangled mess near Syracuse had brought her here. Now. This close to Wishing Bridge.

The temptation to take the exit thrummed through her veins.

Her mother's family might live there. Vonnie McCleary had mentioned the town's name a long time ago, the kind of town name a person never forgot. At least that's how it had been for Kelsey.

Wishing Bridge.

The name alone raised an inviting image. Kelsey imagined a stone passage, arching over water, and people tossing wishes into the air.

She'd never had family other than Vonnie, and that relationship had left little to celebrate. But what if she did have family here? She'd searched the name "McCleary" and "Wishing Bridge" together years before and come up with a big, fat Internet zero. Of course a search was only as good as the keywords used, and Vonnie McCleary was never known for honesty. But Kelsey wasn't on a heritage-trail mission now. Her current path lay in a very different direction.

The baby kicked hard, then stretched, having long since outgrown its constrained space.

Kelsey couldn't think about the baby and the choice she was about to make. She didn't dare consider other options because she needed to put this infant's needs above her own desires. She'd grown up knowing the exact opposite of that, and she'd vowed to never make that mistake herself.

She slowed the car more as the snow intensified. She'd been teaching in the Adirondack region for several years and was accustomed to driving in the snow, but as the squall deepened, her resolve faded.

Should she take the exit and find shelter until the snow diminished? Or push through, knowing that lake-effect squalls off of Lake Erie were dense but sometimes narrow?

Her back wheels lost traction.

The car swerved right, then left, even at her reduced speed. Thick slush tugged her tires, and it wasn't as if they were anything to brag about. She'd been glad when they'd passed the state inspection earlier in the fall, but right now she was wishing for the thick-treaded version she had seen advertised throughout November. In the commercials, the cool, caring dad bought the pricey wheels for his coming-of-age daughter because he loved her. Because she was worth every penny. The nine-hundred-dollar price tag had put them out of Kelsey's budget, but the thought of driving a safe, solid vehicle had become a goal.

No one had ever offered to buy her good tires. Her traction and safety hadn't meant much to anyone in her past, but she had every intention of making sure her precious child was the apple of someone's eye. *Your baby can be the treasured child these barren couples have been waiting for.*

The Pennsylvania adoption agency blurb had caught her eye, and while she hadn't signed any papers, or chosen prospective parents, the phrase had kept her moving along.

Treasured child . . .

She'd longed for that. Prayed for it. All her life she'd dreamed of being someone's heart's desire.

It hadn't happened. Not back then. Not now. There hadn't been one person who had ever looked at Kelsey McCleary and described her as precious and meant it, including this baby's father.

The baby squirmed again, decidedly uncomfortable, and Kelsey shared the feeling. Her due date was closing in. Soon this little gift from God would be beloved and cherished and any other marvelous descriptor used to describe the love a parent has for a child.

LETCHWORTH STATE PARK
MOUNT MORRIS
WISHING BRIDGE
EXIT ½ MILE

The new sign appeared in her headlights.

The snowstorm intensified.

Wind gusted across the hood. The snow swirled in tornadic fashion, wedding-veil whirlwinds obliterating her view.

Whiteout conditions.

Kelsey bit her lower lip, gripped the steering wheel firmly, and signaled for the exit, not because she wanted to, but because she had no choice. If it was just herself, she might have risked continuing down the highway. But it wasn't just her, and her child's safety dictated the choice.

The baby moved again, as if commending her decision.

Kelsey urged the slipping tires up the exit ramp. They spun one way, then another, but gripped long enough to get her to the top of the fairly shallow incline.

Left or right?

She stared into the blinding snow, uncertain, then cranked the wheel to the right. When she got to the first country crossroads, snow-covered farm fields lay in every direction, leaving her with no guidance and yet another turn, another bend in the road.

Should she pull off and wait?

The thought of a mammoth snowplow burying her car nixed that idea.

She peered through the flakes, looking for signs of life, but if they existed, the storm obscured them.

Maybe she should have stayed on the highway.

Headlights appeared in her rearview mirror. Empowerment buoyed her, knowing she wasn't the only one on the road, but then the head-lights turned and disappeared up a long driveway she'd just passed.

Home. That other driver had just arrived at a destination she'd never known. A home.

Emotion steamrolled her. She swallowed it down.

The storm was messing with the signal on her phone, and she hadn't bought a map because she had a GPS, so why spend the extra money?

She turned left, hoping a town or village lay in that direction.

Leaning forward, she saw a light in the distance. It disappeared, but as the wind calmed for a quick second, a pinprick reappeared, red, then green.

A traffic light.

Then it was gone again, but the glimpse offered hope, and Kelsey aimed for it, resolute.

The baby stretched again, pushing up, then down, pressing against her bladder and every other imaginable organ, but if there was a traffic light, there must be a town with a convenience store or someplace she could find refuge while the squall blew itself out.

As she eased around a curve, she realized the light wasn't really on this road. It lay west of the north-south two-lane.

Did she dare turn again?

Her heart sped up. The light had been the only sign of life worth pursuing, unless she took her chances on a random driveway, but she'd read too many thrillers to even consider that option.

She turned right.

The road dipped and curved.

The dip took her by surprise, and when the back tires did a crazy dance, she overcorrected, sending the car into a full spin.

The combination of the incline and the spin launched her into the road's curve, but instead of easing left, the car careened off the road.

God save me.

The car skipped over a bump, then hurtled into a field, finally coming to rest with the front tipped into some kind of ditch. The back of the car was thrust up, and through the rear window her taillights cast twin beams of red into the falling snow.

Dear God . . .

Quick tears slipped down her cheeks. She wasn't a praying person, never had been, but the two words echoed in her brain. *Dear God . . .*

She grabbed for her phone.

Dead again.

She pried the back cover off, swiping tears with her hand while she fiddled the battery loose. She reinserted it, reattached the cover and held the "On" button until a happy whir indicated it was powering up.

She reached down to ease the seat back to allow her and the baby more room, but the awkward angle and her bulk fought her.

The phone lit up.

She grabbed hold of it and hit 9-1-1.

Nothing happened.

She stared at the phone and repeated the maneuver.

Still nothing.

Her heart lurched as the storm howled around her.

No reassuring bars appeared in her display. Not one.

No service.

She'd gassed up before she left and tried to remember what the local meteorologist had advised. The fashionable young woman had been wearing an adorable skater dress showing off her perfect shape, while Kelsey had felt more like a doddering cow the last few weeks.

Run the car and heat for fifteen minutes every hour.

She stared at the key, torn. If she turned off the car, she didn't dare keep the lights on and risk running the battery down. But if she left the car running, how soon would she run out of gas?

Snowy darkness pressed against the windows. Swallowing hard, Kelsey reached out and turned the key.

The sudden silence defined the storm's wrath. She sat, staring out, letting the tears fall.

She tried the phone one more time, holding it up to the window, then aiming it back toward Rochester. *9-1-1.*

Nothing.

Her belly tightened in a convincing Braxton Hicks contraction.

"Don't even think it." She put hands of comfort around the swell of her unborn child. "You hear me?"

The contraction eased, and the baby stretched.

Three minutes. She'd had the car off for three full minutes and already the windswept cold was seeping in.

Ten minutes every half hour, she decided as she begged the storm into submission. That should get her through the night.

And then someone would be sure to notice her come morning, wouldn't they?

Hopefully. And if not, she'd get out and walk for help once there was daylight.

No one will know you're missing.

She couldn't dwell on the emptiness of her life. She'd think about her second graders and how sweet they had been as they'd presented her with last-day tributes. Baby clothes, two coffee mugs, three boxes of chocolate, a baby blanket, and two monster-sized boxes of diapers.

She'd pretended joy.

She'd smiled through it all.

They thought their long-term substitute teacher was going back to her home state of Pennsylvania to have her baby and start a new life with her newborn child. That wasn't the plan, but she had smiled her way through because they didn't know that. No one did.

She would donate the baby items to charity. Some young family, down on their luck, would appreciate them, especially at Christmastime.

Ten minutes had passed.

She leaned her head back and closed her eyes, wishing things were different, wishing she could make a home for herself and her beautiful baby in a place where folks still loved one another, but as she rested her eyes, Kelsey was pretty sure that place didn't exist.

~

"Jeb! Jeb, did you see that?" Maggie Tompkins pointed north as she hopped out of her favorite chair. The chair's seat had grown slack over time, and she sank too low to rise up quickly, but the flash of distant light had her up in a hurry now.

"I saw nothing but the print in front of my eyes, Maggie, 'til you came leaping out of that old chair in need of replacing about five years back." Less excitable, her aging husband peered at her over the rims of his close-up glasses.

"The chair's fine," she insisted, then crossed to the window, drew back the lace curtain, and waved. "I saw lights, Jeb, like a car in trouble, over on Perchance Road." Tucked in an upper corner of the trapped-in-time town of Wishing Bridge, New York, the Tompkins house allowed a great view to the northwest from the broad living room. A mix of evergreens and deciduous trees blocked their summer view from this angle, but winter's bare branches afforded them greater insight.

Jeb rose more slowly. A bad hip made getting up and down tougher for him these days, especially at night. He moved to her side and peered through the storm. "I don't see a thing, Maggie, and I don't expect you did, either, the way that storm's carrying on."

"That way." She pointed again, but the heavy snowfall played with her eyes. "I think, anyway."

"You think you saw it, or you think it was that way?"

"I know I saw it, you old fool, and from where I was sitting, it should be right around the curve."

He sighed, his gaze following the direction she indicated. "Well, that's a stupid piece of roadway from the get-go, and we've got old-time folks to blame for not straightening it out when they had the chance. Best call it in, don't you think?"

She glanced his way, hesitating. "What if I'm wrong, Jeb? What if I'm pulling someone out into this storm to search for nothing?"

"Well, they're sheriffs, and they get paid to watch out for things." Common sense marked his tone like it always did. "Besides, if it's Hale Jackson on shift hereabouts, he's got a rare wisdom for a Jackson. If there's something to be found, he finds it."

Maggie waited a few more seconds, then picked up her landline and hit 9-1-1, glad she'd ignored friends' suggestions to save herself forty bucks a month and ditch it. On nights like this, when her cell-phone bars disappeared, she was mighty glad to have a working phone. It was her forty dollars and her peace of mind and well worth it to boot.

~

"Hale, you sure you don't want to put some of this chocolate creamer in that coffee? Plain, black coffee is about as unimaginative as you can get when the good Lord put temptations like this in front of us." EMT Lita Szabo raised the bottle of holiday-themed choco-mint creamer she'd just used in the compact firehouse kitchen. "There's plenty."

"I'm all right. Thanks, Lita. Do you guys need help getting anything else ready?"

Five members of the Wishing Bridge Volunteer Fire Department were manning the firehouse during the predicted lake-effect snowstorms stretching their way off Lake Erie. The wind-generated storms guaranteed wretched travel conditions and most likely a white Christmas in a few days' time, if Lake Erie's generosity followed the predicted accumulations.

She shook her head as she sipped her coffee.

"I think we're good. We've got food, heat, coffee, and water if we have folks who need shelter," added Brian Teague.

"All the comforts of home."

"The ones we can control, anyway." Brian added a bowl of semi-cooked barley to the ginormous kettle. "Soup will be ready in about half an hour, Hale. Have some with us."

The soup sounded good and smelled better. He was just about to accept the invitation when his shoulder radio cut in.

"C-34, a report of a possible car in trouble on Perchance Road, west of the intersection of County Road 27 and Perchance Road."

"Near the curve?"

"Affirmative. According to Maggie Tompkins the lights were there, and then they weren't."

If it was anyone else but Maggie, he might be skeptical. Visibility was down to single-digit feet right now, but Maggie wasn't one to ask for help lightly, although how she could see Perchance Road from her village home was anyone's guess. Hale keyed his reply as he grabbed up his thick gloves with his free hand. "C-34 responding."

"C-18 will rendezvous." His cousin Garrett chimed in from someplace near Mount Morris. As boys, they'd talked about being policemen one day. Hale's path to the blue uniform had seen more turns than Garrett's, but here they were in their early thirties, facing a squall-filled night shift together.

With conditions like this, Garrett would be smart to stay put unless needed. Hale spoke quickly. "C-18, let me scout first, then I'll call for backup if needed."

"No can do, C-34," Garrett responded. "I'm going stir-crazy watching the snow come down. A little adventure is just what I need, and why waste a great hat?"

They'd been issued new fur-lined Yukon hats, perfect for a night like this, although the style wasn't anything to turn a woman's head. These days, warm ears were more important than a dashing profile, anyway.

Hale waved to the fire crew, pushed through the heavy firehouse door, and trotted to his running cruiser parked alongside the firehouse. In stormy weather, on-duty officers left their cruisers running to ensure quick response times to emergency calls. The cruiser's warmth quickly melted the snow along his shoulders and boots. He scattered the coating on his head with a quick brush of his hand.

Brian had cleared the walk and the parking lot a quarter hour before. Already it was filling with fresh snow while wind-fed drifts formed mounds around the north and south corners. The mounds curved and stretched toward the middle from both ends of the classic brick building. He eased onto the road and headed north, then east, then north again.

Don't think.

Act.

He understood Garrett completely. Inactivity drove him crazy, too. Standing around, waiting for something to happen, watching the snow pile up . . .

Even if this call turned up nothing—and he hoped that was the case—he'd rather be out in the elements, proving his worth, than caught inside, steeped in thoughts of long cold nights and empty chairs around a festive holiday table.

CHAPTER TWO

The snow obliterated most of the town's holiday lights, casting nothing but a faint glow here and there, but as Hale pulled around Wishing Bridge's miniature version of a town park, the wind shifted momentarily. Ground lights illuminated the Nativity scene facing the roadway: a loving father, a caring mother, and a newborn babe, laid in a manger.

Hale deliberately shifted his gaze, eased into the turn, and aimed down the slope leading toward Perchance Road.

No visibility and a steep grade meant he kept his speed reduced. As he made the turn, he paused, glancing up. The Tompkins place faced north, but could Maggie really have seen anything over a mile away in these conditions?

No.

But it wasn't his duty to question. It was his job to follow orders, so he made the turn and progressed north at a crawl.

It took him nearly fifteen minutes to navigate an area that would have taken two minutes in normal conditions. He approached the curve and stopped.

A monster drift banked southeast from northwest across the lower part of the curve. Even in an SUV, there was no way to blast through the wall of rapidly growing snow.

He stared through the wipers and saw nothing. He'd have been a liar if he said the thought of heading back into town hadn't occurred to him, because the rapidly deteriorating conditions weren't the least bit inviting, but he shoved temptation aside as he settled the fur-lined, ear-flapped hat into place. He drew the outer zipper up snug on his thick wool jacket, and tugged his work-issued gloves over his fingers. He climbed out of the cruiser, leaving it running, the lights pointed toward the deeply sloped side of the almost ninety-degree curve.

He drew his weapon, hit the flashlight switch, and swept a wide arc left, then right.

Nothing. He moved forward and swept the arc again more slowly this time.

Piles of pristine white snow formed miniature mountain ranges along the shoulder, angling across the road. He aimed the light toward the base of the hill.

The snow wasn't as rounded there. Along the rest of the road, the mounds hop-skipped in a pattern, but the pattern broke at the base of this slope.

Why?

Maybe the natural reaction of the snow to the incline, maybe something else. He pushed through the narrowest base of the big drift, while he put a call out on the private channel for plows to be dispatched to the area ASAP.

"C-34, plowing has been suspended until the worst of the snow falls per county commissioner orders."

"Unsuspend it. I'm staring at a death trap."

The dispatcher sighed. "You sure, Hale? Because you know that's going to bring a heap of trouble down on your head."

He knew that.

He didn't care.

He'd grown up here. He'd become a man in a town that looked after its own and a whole lot of other people's troubles, too. If the power-hungry county commissioner didn't like his request, he could take it up with him, and Hale had no doubt he'd do just that. "Make the call, Brenda."

"Consider it done."

He waved the arc slowly again, sure that if something had happened here, evidence couldn't have been obliterated in such a short span of time. A wicked blast of sharp west wind said otherwise.

Garrett had said he was coming. The horrible conditions might have slowed him or stopped him, but he and his cousin had one thing in common: they didn't make promises lightly.

Hale scanned the area one more time, seeing nothing out of place. He crossed the road and slowly walked the north side of the curve. Whirling, whipping snow stung his cheeks and landed on his eyelashes. He was pretty sure his eyebrows were frozen as his breath puffed out then slapped back into his face with the force of the wind. When Hale was a boy, Maggie Tompkins had told a story of how dairy and beef farmers used to have to go out in the middle of the night to run the cattle. The bovines' hot breath would melt the ice crusting their faces so they wouldn't suffocate in bone-chilling cold and snow in the north country. He hadn't believed it then.

He believed it now as ice formed along the planes of his face.

The warm cruiser called to him, but he strode past it to check the west side of the hedgerow, a line of brush and young trees just thick enough to obscure his view. He trudged along, peering through slanted snow that swirled in the V-shaped swath of light.

Nothing unusual appeared. Not one thing. He hesitated, studying what he could through the blanket of white. Torn, he glanced upward, not afraid to seek heavenly help because right now he had nothing but a gut hunch to trust Maggie's report. And that wasn't enough to call out extra help during life-threatening conditions.

He clicked off the light and crossed back to the cruiser, anticipating the thawing temperature. As he pulled the door of the cruiser open, he turned for one last look.

Thick white snow beat against him, but as he lifted his right leg to climb in, a thin, rosy ribbon appeared above the snow.

He stared, swiped his eyes, and stared again.

Nothing.

But he'd *seen* it. He was sure of it.

He sighed, shut the door in the face of warmth, and strode back to the road's edge. Gust after gust battled him. As he rescanned the area, he was about to declare himself mentally unstable or, at the very least, visibility challenged, when the ribbon of light reappeared.

Not pink.

Red.

Taillights, tipped up, facing skyward, forming a silent cry for help.

Adrenaline burst through the cold. He barked a command into the radio. "Dispatch, on the scene of MVA on Perchance Road, just west of the curve, car off road, checking on occupants, full response requested."

"Roger that, C-34." A few seconds of silence followed as she keyed the proper response team. The Wishing Bridge call tones sounded, followed by Brenda's voice. "Wishing Bridge Fire Department, we have a report of a car off the road at the curve of Perchance Road, west of County Road 27. Sheriff's deputy on scene, request full response to curve of Perchance Road, north of the village and west of CR 27.

"Wishing Bridge, respond."

Brian's voice came back as Hale maneuvered through the thickly drifted snow. "Dispatch, this is Wishing Bridge, responding. On route to Perchance Road, west of CR 27 and north of village of Wishing Bridge, at the curve."

"Roger that."

Help was on the way, but how quickly would they arrive? And what kind of injuries awaited him ahead?

Hale plowed through the snowdrifts that formed deceptively innocent-looking lines of thick, heavy snow. Twice he nearly fell, but as he got closer, the twin taillight beams brightened, offering a focal point through the increasing fury of the first major winter weather they'd seen this year.

And then the lights were gone.

Vanished.

He peered through the snow and saw nothing but more snow.

He aimed the powerful flashlight beam forward, but the snow bounced the light back into his eyes, like high beams on a fog-filled night.

He swept the arc lower, cutting the reflection, and kept moving.

There. To your right.

Nose tipped into a drainage swale, the back end of a car rose in front of him, barely visible above the level grade.

He rushed to the front of the car and banged on the window then flashed his light.

Fogged windows. No movement.

Trapped inside and still breathing? He hoped so.

He wrenched the door, hoping it was unlocked. It opened into a narrow V.

He swept the light into the thin opening.

Pale gray eyes blinked up at him from a familiar face, although he didn't know this woman. And then it came to him.

She had Nora's eyes.

This woman was a younger version of Nora Hannon, his mother's old friend. So much like her that Hale had to look twice. Nora had moved to Florida years before, and had two grown boys. No girls, and no family around here.

The woman's eyes went wide, then blinked again before filling with quick, clear tears. "Thank you. Oh, thank you so much for finding me."

The wind should have snatched her voice.

It didn't. The reigning tempest took a moment to gather strength, and her words sounded soft and true in the winter night, in a slightly husky voice that brought Nora to mind again.

Hale moved in as much as he could, but the door's angle thwarted him. "Can you move, ma'am?"

She shook her head.

"Are you hurt?"

The wind picked up again, as if angry that it had ever stopped. The woman winced in uncertainty. Her eyes flicked down, then up.

Pregnant.

Hale's gut tightened. She was pressed between the seat and the wheel by a substantial curve of pregnancy beneath a short jacket, unsuitable for winter travel, and unfastened over the bulk of her expanded waistline.

Stuck.

Jaws of life?

Is there time for that? Think, man. You've got two victims here. "Is there anyone else in the car with you?"

She shook her head and shivered.

He needed to shut the door and have her warm the car. "Can you move the seat back to gain more room?"

"I can't." She looked miserable with good reason. "I tried. It won't budge. But I can't move enough to get a good handle on it, either." A shiver grabbed her again. Cold or shock, he wasn't sure which, but he couldn't risk either.

"I'm closing this"—he indicated the door—"and coming around to the other side. I want you to start the car and turn on the heater and warm things up now, okay? No need to worry about conserving gas, help's here. Nod that you understand me."

She dipped her chin and kept her left arm protectively over her stomach in a gesture he remembered well.

Too well.

He tried to close the door gently, but the wind snapped it from his hands and slammed it shut, shoving his protective instincts and his adrenaline into overdrive.

He circled the car's hood. The passenger side front door was wedged into the upward slope of the ditch along the hedgerow, blocking access. The rear passenger door was accessible, but at a difficult angle. He pulled open the door and carefully climbed inside.

Those familiar gray eyes met his in the rearview mirror. He leaned between the front seats at an awkward angle, and was able to shift the passenger seat back. It took three tries, but the seat finally clicked into place, leaving him uncomfortably tight in the confined space, but maybe allowing her some movement.

"Can you shift over here? If not, we'll see if they can pull the car back to give us access. When is your baby due, ma'am?"

"Two weeks. It was supposed to be a January baby, but it seems to be getting impatient. And cramped."

"Tight quarters, for sure." He aimed a smile of understanding her way. "Like his or her mother right about now."

She forced a smile, then grimaced, and Hale's heart hit pause, then jump-started. "Are you in labor?"

She breathed through what seemed to be a solid contraction, then puffed out a cleansing breath at the end. "It is distinctly possible." She glanced beyond him in the rearview mirror, but from this angle no oncoming help would be visible. "Please get me out of here."

Hale tapped the edge of her seat. "Try the seat adjustment bar one more time. I'm going to pull it from behind because gravity is fighting us."

"That and my size." She pressed her lips together and leaned as far left as she could. "Okay."

He shifted behind her and gripped the seat. "Go."

He felt the thrust of the mechanism near his feet, but the seat refused to move. "Hang on." He lowered himself to the floor and groped beneath her seat. Fabric met his hand. He took hold and pulled, but nothing happened.

He readjusted his position and stretched to reach around the seat. From that angle he could barely feel the material. He climbed out of the car and fought his way back to her door as the storm raged. He opened it and tried not to notice that she seemed to be in the throes of another contraction. He laid out low, along the swale's edge. Reaching in, his hand gripped the fabric this time. He pulled it toward him as the snow whipped his eyes and his cheeks, swirling beneath the barely open door as if seeking him out.

A thick, padded purse.

It flew into the snow once it came loose, and he set it behind him as he regained his footing. "I'm coming back around to help pull the seat back, okay?"

She nodded, making funny, little puffing breaths he remembered like it was yesterday. But it wasn't yesterday, it was five long years ago.

He shut her door more quietly this time, picked up the purse, and shoved through the snow again. If this maneuver worked, at least they could get her to the ambulance without taking time to cut into the car or risk jerking it into a towable position with her in it.

"Okay." He positioned himself behind her seat and sent her a confident look through the mirror. "You push, I'll brace."

She didn't look convinced or all that hopeful anymore, and he couldn't blame her. She stretched forward, then shifted to one side, the bulk of her middle not allowing much leverage. Seconds mounted. The wind howled, and the car's engine made a spit-noised protest as if unhappy.

"I've got it."

"Draw it up, okay?"

"Okay."

He braced back and pulled, helping her work against gravity. The seat jerked back, into his arms, not all the way, but enough, he thought. "How are we doing?"

"I'm free." Relief colored her voice as he worked to extricate himself from the now-narrowed space behind her, at the impossible up-tipped angle.

Good. The extra inches should allow the ambulance crew room to extract her with no extreme measures. "I'm going back to the road to direct them in to you, all right?"

"Don't go. Please." She turned. Her panicked voice commanded his attention. Once again he found himself looking straight into those familiar eyes. "Don't leave me alone."

Her face. Her voice. Those eyes, eyes he'd known as a child. An odd coincidence, of course, but her fearful expression called to him. "We'll get you out faster if they can find us. I'll be right back. I promise."

The engine stopped just then. It didn't cough, spit, or sputter, it simply died. What would have happened if he hadn't seen her and the car had refused to run through the long, dark, bitter night?

She studied him, as if weighing the possibilities, then popped open the door. "I'll walk."

She'll what?

He crawled out of the car as quick as he could at the impossible angle, and when he half fell, half jumped into the snow, she was standing across from him, shrugging as much of the jacket as she could around the broad curve of the baby. "You'll freeze."

"I can't stay there." She crossed a few feet with the snow and wind whipping around her, gripped his arm, and held tight. "I'm not hurt, and this baby has set its own timeline. Please."

She left him little choice. He removed his hat, settled it over her bare head and long, blond hair, pulled down the ear flaps, and let the chin strap dangle.

She looked ridiculous but warmer. He could live with that.

He grabbed her purse, took hold of her arm, and refused to think of how Brian and the crew would ream him later. She'd made a choice, and he was pretty sure he'd have made the same decision in similar circumstances.

He held tight, and by the time the ambulance and rescue vehicles drew close behind the commissioned snowplow, they were almost to the road.

Snow pelted them. The wind seemed to suck the air from around them, making talk impossible. Brian maneuvered the wagon, and Lita jumped out before he'd come to a full stop. She took one look at the woman, raked Hale with a scolding gaze, and then she and Brian helped the young woman to the back of Rescue One.

Garrett came up alongside him. "Your hat looks good on her, moron."

"She was freezing."

"She wiped out here?" Garrett flashed his light around, then motioned to Hale's cruiser. "Where'd she land?"

"Andrew's field, other side of the hedgerow, along the drainage swale."

Garrett swept the light across the snow-drenched corn lot and whistled softly because nothing in that snowy space suggested an MVA. "No one would have found her before morning. If then."

"She's pregnant and in labor. At least I think she is."

Garrett's jaw dropped. "Tell me you're lying."

Hale frowned. "You're acting stupid."

"I'm not acting, I'm fairly stupid, and I've got the former girlfriends to prove it, but that's a conversational topic for another night. The roads are closed, travel's suspended, and there's no way to get this woman to a hospital tonight."

"They could follow the plow."

Garrett shook his head as they fought their way through the snow to the rescue vehicles. "Not gonna happen."

Garrett couldn't be serious, but he looked serious, and that was a rarity in itself. Hale came around the back of the rescue wagon and tapped lightly.

Lita opened the door a crack.

"We need a plan."

"Got one. We're to transport to the firehouse and use bedroom one for an emergency maternity ward if necessary. Avis Washington is making her way down the block to be the midwife."

A moan echoed from the bed of the rescue vehicle. Lita pulled the door shut. "Follow or lead, your choice, but we're 'go' right now."

Hale climbed into his front seat while Garrett crossed the drifted snow to get into his SUV.

Hale turned his cruiser around, lights flashing, leading the way back to town. Rescue One followed his path, allowing the plow to move along the curved incline heading to County Road 27. Once the plow had gone through, Garrett curved through the narrow lane and followed the other rescue vehicles.

No hospital.

No doctor.

No medication.

Hale's gut wrenched. He'd stood by his wife's side when she had delivered their perfect and precious son, and he'd been humbled by what it took to bring a child into the world while a hapless man stood by, able to do nothing but offer words and ice chips.

When he weighed up what women endured, he considered his duties beyond lame by comparison.

Lights glowed from within the firehouse as Hale pulled into the adjacent parking lot. Road closings could render this the center of activity for the night, offering shelter to stranded travelers until the storm wore itself out and the roads were cleared.

Avis Washington trudged across the road, carrying a substantial bag. Hale moved to her side quickly as Rescue One maneuvered into place. "Can I help you with that, Avis?"

She thrust the bag at him. "Second floor. Just set it inside and I'll take it from there."

"Glad to, ma'am." He pushed open the door. Warmth met him full face, and it felt wonderful.

The scent of beef-and-barley soup laced the air, while the yeasty smell of fresh bread rode shotgun.

He took the steps two at a time and opened the door to Room One. The old firehouse had three stay-over units. They were rudimentary but warm and bright. He set Avis's bag inside the door, then grabbed a stack of extra towels and sheets from the closet adjoining the small upstairs bathroom.

He backed out, shoving memories aside.

This wasn't his personal emergency, it was his professional responsibility, and that's exactly what he'd cling to right now.

He went back down the steps, just in time to open the firehouse door for Lita, Avis, and the pregnant woman.

They made an awkward threesome as they moved up the metal stairs, but when they got near the top, the blonde looked back, over her shoulder.

Her gaze searched the growing crew of men below until her eyes met his.

"Thank you."

She mouthed the words, but it wasn't the words that grabbed hold of him and held tight.

It was those eyes, quiet and familiar, eyes he'd known from the time he could walk and talk, set in a face wreathed in pain.

But something else, too.

A hint of fear, as if caught out.

He nodded and held her gaze until she turned back around at Avis's urging.

Something wasn't right. It might not be absolutely wrong, but he was one hundred percent sure it wasn't quite right, and that meant he'd have some investigating to do. Starting with his mother and how much she knew about her old friend.

CHAPTER THREE

Thea Anastas peered at the unfamiliar number on her phone before she realized she wasn't wearing her glasses. She snatched them off the counter, put them on, and spotted two things right off. Kelsey McCleary's name and the code 9-1-1.

Memories flooded her. Images of Kelsey, standing firm against ill-meaning girls at John Marshall High School near Philadelphia. Kelsey, helping little kids in the high school psych class when the staff hosted a mock preschool event for local families. Kelsey, dreaming of being a wife and mother someday, the kind of mother she'd never had.

Thea called the number back immediately. Three girls had made a pledge twelve years before. A pledge that, if needed, they would post an SOS for help, and the others would come. A dozen years later, this was the first cry for help to come through.

Had it been that long? Really?

It had, she realized as the call took its own sweet time to connect.

Over a decade, and a lot of water had flowed under their respective bridges, but she'd vowed to never forget the two girls who had helped her find a path out of the darkness and into the light.

"Hello?"

The voice on the other end of the phone sounded nothing like her old friend. "Kelsey?"

"No, ma'am," the voice spoke softly, near a whisper. "This is Avis Washington here in Wishing Bridge, New York. Miss Kelsey is sound asleep right now, but she's been quite wound up, and when I asked her who we could call once her phone recharged, she said your name and number right away. Now that's a rarity in itself these days, young folks rememberin' phone numbers off the top of their heads without a smartphone to help, but she gave me two numbers—"

"Me and Jazz?"

"That is exactly right," the woman confirmed. "Can I have Kelsey call you when she wakes up? She's had a rough night of it, that's for certain, and in all my years of service, I don't think I've ever had a young woman who seemed so desperately alone. And that's just plain wrong, now, isn't it?"

"She doesn't need to call." Thea tugged a little-used rolling bag out of the back of her closet and set it on the bed.

"No?" Avis sounded a little disappointed in her reply. "Are you certain, miss?"

"No need to call because I'm on my way. Wishing Bridge, you said?"

"Yes, ma'am, I did say that." Avis Washington didn't sound one bit disappointed now. "In Upstate New York. Not too far off the 390 expressway."

Thea put Avis on speaker, hit the driving app, and punched in Wishing Bridge. "I'm in Pittsburgh, and you've had snow there."

"You can say that again!" The woman chuckled, and Thea found herself almost smiling because anyone who could laugh about snow was okay in her book. "Which is why we're tucked in the firehouse at the moment, but we're looking for a more suitable setting by later today. As long as today's forecast holds no surprises."

Surprises seemed to have been in full supply the last few days. First the announcement from the medical conglomerate that had taken over

Three Rivers Medical that her services were no longer needed, a kick in the head she certainly hadn't expected. Now Kelsey's SOS.

"I'll leave this morning, but it will take me a little while to get there. Hopefully by tonight. I don't dare take I-90 because that will drag me through the snowbelt, but that means country roads for most of the way. Have her call me if she'd like, though. I've got a Bluetooth connection in my car."

"I'll do that!" The sound of a baby fussing came through the phone. "I must go, but I'll look forward to meeting you later." Avis Washington's voice rang with soft strength, as if Thea had made the right decision. "Bye, now."

The other woman disconnected the phone on her end, while Thea processed what had just happened.

Then she decided to stop acting so OCD and get her stuff together. Kelsey needed her, and she'd made a promise years before. Since there was absolutely nothing keeping her in the bustle of Pittsburgh at the moment, she had the golden opportunity to hurry north and keep that vow. She threw a bunch of clean clothes in the big suitcase, glad she'd done laundry recently. She put the not-so-clean stuff in another bag, figuring they'd have a Laundromat somewhere. She emptied her bathroom of the meager essential products she used, packed her medical bag and laptop, and left her roommate a note. She stopped and grabbed a large coffee to go at a nearby convenience store and was on her way in under forty minutes.

Her phone rang as she headed north on Route 28. Only a few dozen people had her number.

How sad was that? Nearly thirty years old and fewer than forty people had her private phone number. She hadn't spent a lot of time thinking about that, but now she had time to think, unfortunately. Too much time.

She punched the phone button on the steering wheel. "Hello?"

"Thea? It's Jazz."

Jazz.

Tall, lithe, and so exotically beautiful that a plain girl like Thea should have hated Jacinda Monroe on sight. But when Jazz shared her dessert with Thea on a night when Thea's behavior had cost her the fudge-filled cake, she'd won a piece of Thea's cold heart. Hearing her old friend's voice, Thea realized Jazz had that piece of her heart still, despite the separation of years. "Hey, my friend. Did you get a summons, too?"

"I did, and I'm on my way. I'm flying in because it's been a long time since I drove a car on highways. Do you know what's up?"

"Not a clue."

"Well, then." Jazz's warm voice, with a tone that underscored her tall, copper-skinned beauty, sounded matter-of-fact. "I'll meet you up there. We'll have ourselves the reunion we keep promising one another, and about time, too."

"Can you break away from work?"

A pause marked the moment until Jazz spoke again. "It's Christmas," she said finally. "Not much gets done at the holidays."

"Which means January starts off with a bang, I bet."

"Always has," Jazz replied smoothly. "Oops, approaching a tunnel. Gotta go. See you later."

"Yes, and Jazz?"

"Mmhmm?"

"Safe travels, my friend."

Jazz gave a laugh that sounded a little forced. "The same to you."

Thea drove north, expecting bad weather, but the lake-effect storm had ended. Blinding sun reflected off of snow-covered hills and trees. Thick forests lined much of the roadway, with the occasional small town breaking the view.

Picturesque.

Driving through northern Appalachia was Christmas-card beautiful, as if serenity blanketed the area on a regular basis.

Too quiet. Too pretty. Too peaceful.

Thea was a get-up-and-go kind of girl, a medical professional, a person who hit the ground running from the moment she stepped out of bed until the moment she hit the mattress eighteen hours later.

And then she did it all again the next day, city girl to the max.

At least she had been until two days ago. Suddenly she had all the time in the world. She might appreciate that once she got over being tossed out of a job she did better than anyone else on staff.

She slugged her coffee, then reached for chocolate and found none. That wouldn't do. She'd pull off and stock up at the next small town. As long as there were coffee and chocolate on hand and a crisis to fix, she'd be fine.

Just fine.

~

"Well, hello, sleepyhead."

The smoky warm voice called to Kelsey as filtered light touched her face.

She blinked, yawned, and stretched before reality hit.

This wasn't her walk-up apartment. And this wasn't Harrisburg, Pennsylvania, where she was supposed to have her baby and quietly hand him or her over to understanding adoption officials.

Memories of the spinout and the snow flooded her. And then the pains, rhythmic and strong. She remembered strong words and gentle hands.

A tiny cry pulled her upright.

A tall, dark-skinned woman smiled at her. Avis, the woman had told her the night before. Avis . . . such a pretty name.

In her arms she held a wrapped-up, noisy bundle. "I figured when you heard her peeping, you'd wake up, and you did. It's a mother's way. And you did so well, honey! To give birth that quick, and with not a bit of carrying on. You must have been quite motivated to do that, and I was pleased to be on hand to help."

"I did well?" The previous night was blurred in some spots and crystal clear in others. "How is she? It *is* a girl, isn't it?"

"She is most assuredly a girl, and so pretty." Avis's voice cooed the words in the kind of lyrical tone people used around babies. "I'd say she looks like her mama, yes, she does! Wide eyes and a tiny frown nesting between them, like she's already worryin' about this or that." Avis aimed a frank look Kelsey's way. "I've been reassuring her that life is full of joyous times, and she'll find that out soon enough."

Kelsey formed the same W between her brows when puzzled or worried, but how could something like that pass down to a baby? Coincidence, of course.

"Shall we try nursing her?" Avis lifted the bundle to her shoulder and patted the baby's back while she jostled her lightly. "She sounds hungry, and while there won't be much milk for a couple of days, she can get some much needed practice on colostrum before the main event."

"Nurse her?" Kelsey stared at Avis, eyes wide.

She couldn't nurse this baby. She couldn't hold her and cuddle her and feel gentle tugs of satisfaction at the breast before giving her away.

Kelsey gripped the edge of the blanket so hard her knuckles went white.

Avis was watching her, probably wondering what kind of mother doesn't want to nurse their newborn.

How could she explain?

Her eyes filled again, and she was so tired of crying, so tired of overwrought emotions, and so mad at herself for making mistake upon mistake.

The baby squawked again, squirming.

Her body reacted to the sound. Her chest went tight, then loose.

Avis moved closer. "Not to fret, this is all normal emotional stuff when our bodies are riding what I like to call the Hormonal Express. It's not like they do us a favor and ease off over time, no, ma'am. That baby gets delivered and all that goes along with, and all of a sudden we're thrown into hormone stew." She spoke in a soft but firm voice, a voice you knew you could trust, no matter what. "I've gotten many a new mother through it, and I expect you and I will do just fine, Kelsey McCleary." She settled herself on the edge of the bed and didn't ask Kelsey if she wanted to hold the baby, she simply handed her over. "Here you go, little mama. Are you right-handed or left?"

"Right."

"Well then, let's settle her into your left arm, okay?" She tucked a couple of stout pillows behind Kelsey's back, then adjusted things for Kelsey's comfort. "Isn't she just a pretty little dolly?"

Kelsey had no choice but to look down.

She couldn't help it. She didn't want to, she was half afraid to, because if she looked at this baby, bonded with her, how could she possibly give her away?

The baby squawked and writhed, looking downright worried, which made two of them. Then she stuffed one of the tiniest hands Kelsey had ever seen into a rosebud-tinted mouth and peeked up.

It was a stern look she aimed at Kelsey, like she was wondering at all that had occurred, but then one tiny, almost invisible eyebrow arched, the left one, all on its own.

A move Kelsey made as naturally as breathing.

Her heart went still, then raced.

As if of its own accord, her free hand began to unbundle the wee girl. The overwhelming urge to see her beautiful baby took over her brain and her hands.

Avis sat nearby, smiling, and when the swaddling blanket came free, the tiny girl stretched and kicked, testing the new lack of boundaries.

She'd come through such change, being born. From dark, cramped circumstances she'd been brought into the light and the freedom of air.

She yanked her hand out of her mouth and let out a pleading cry. At that moment, Kelsey recognized what she had to do to procure the future she wanted for this beautiful child. She also knew what she needed to do right then.

With Avis's help, she arranged her shirt and the baby for nursing.

The adoption books agreed that she shouldn't do this, but then the books hadn't addressed a snowy emergency birth. This baby, her beloved daughter, would be fed as needed, and if that made Kelsey's moment of truth harder when she got to Harrisburg, so be it.

She'd promised to do whatever she could to make this baby girl's life as good as it could possibly be. And that would start with feeding her infant daughter.

CHAPTER FOUR

Warmth and sleep.

The pair dominated Hale's focus as the morning sun broke over the eastern hills. For now, the worst was over, but lake-effect snow was a funny thing. The morning calm could change quickly. If the winds picked up or shifted even slightly, the snowmaking machine known as the Great Lakes would run full blast once again. Wind direction would dictate who'd get buried under heavy white snow and who stayed clear.

This morning's respite allowed time for plows and businesses to shovel out before the next onslaught. He returned his cruiser to the lot behind the old town hall, signed out, and started the engine on his winter ride, a tough-as-nails aged pickup with not one fancy accoutrement in sight. The old four-wheel-drive was ugly as sin and ruggedly dependable. It kept his fair-weather rides safe from winter's wrath.

He swung into the firehouse on his way through town. "How'd you guys make out last night?"

"Seven stranded travelers, no medical emergencies among them, except for one six-pound, twelve-ounce baby girl born about an hour after you found her mama," said Lita. She tugged her hat and scarf into place as a new crew took over the kitchen. "Nice job, Deputy."

A baby girl, born so quick. He didn't allow himself to think of how close he'd come to driving away from that accident scene last night.

What if he had? What if he hadn't spotted that thin, rosy beam when he turned around? "What's her name?"

"Doesn't have one," Lita replied. "Weird, right? I had names for my kids before they were born. And I knew if they were boys or girls so I could be ready. Who doesn't find out the sex of their kid in this day and age?"

Avis came into the kitchen just then. She popped a pod into the brewing system and tsk-tsked Lita softly. "Not all folks are on board with this need-to-know-everything mind-set, Lita. Some like to know, some don't." She shrugged. "It's fine, either way."

"But no name?" Lita wasn't the sort that backed down or backed off, a trait that worked well in emergencies but not always in calmer venues. "Who has a kid and doesn't have a name picked out, Avis? It's weird. You know it. I know it."

"Different equates weird?" Avis stirred cream into her coffee and smiled. "Well, that levels the playin' field hereabouts, doesn't it?"

She was right about that. Wishing Bridge and Wyoming County had their share of distinct personalities, and every cop knew which ones to watch out for. Hale shifted his full attention to Avis. "Everything all right, Avis? No problems?"

"She was a trouper," Avis told him. "That's all I can really say, but what a wondrous thing to bring a perfect baby into the world under such natural circumstances. God is good, oh yes, he is!"

"I expect the good Lord appreciated the earthly help of your skilled hands," Hale noted, smiling. "Thanks for coming over. This town is real lucky to have you."

"And the reverse is equally true," she assured him. "I'm going to catch a quick rest while mama and baby do the same."

"Are they transporting her to the hospital today?" he asked. Avis surprised him by shaking her head.

"We've got a blood draw scheduled for baby and they'll run tests, but there's no insurance. Kelsey's fine, the baby's fine, so why run up a bill she can't pay? Depending on how long she's here, we'll get the baby hooked up with health care. Lord-a-mercy, folks have been having babies for a long time, and I am a certified midwife." She couldn't have missed Lita's doubtful expression if the EMT had tried to hide it, and she didn't try.

"It's not you I'm questioning. No insurance?" Lita rolled her eyes. "Curiouser and curiouser."

"When money's tight we pick and choose with care."

"What about checking out the baby medically?" Hale wondered. That had to be a must, didn't it?

"I've got that all arranged. The tests will be run, and Dr. Brandenburg is seeing the baby tomorrow. We do have to move her from here, though, and she's not fit to travel for a while. I'd like her tucked in somewhere safe and sound to recover for a week. Two would be better. But we'll see how that plays out."

No name. No insurance. An undependable car. No man in sight and no ring on her finger, and yes, he'd looked, wondering if there was someone they should call. The baby's father, perhaps.

"Do you need the sheriff's department to contact or find anyone for you? For her?" he added.

Avis leveled quiet eyes on him. Not judging. Avis wasn't the sort. More like . . . assessing. Then she shook her head, quiet-like. "I called her two friends once her phone was up and running a little while ago. They're on their way."

"And the strange factor just shot up exponentially." Lita moved to the door. "I'm not saying bad," she told Avis when the older woman sent her a look of caution. "Not enough to go on yet. But we're not talking an 'A plus B equals C' kind of life, from what I'm hearing."

"Not so uncommon these days, which makes rising above a beautiful thing." Avis moved toward the stairs as Lita let herself out the back door. "For myself, I'm moving straight to the romance of the situation."

"Romance?" Hale didn't mask his surprise at her word choice. "There is nothing romantic about a pregnant woman almost dying in a storm."

"No?"

He scoffed. "No. What a ridiculous notion, Avis."

She started up the stairs quietly, but halfway up she looked back and smiled. Just that. As if she knew something he didn't, and wasn't that a woman thing?

He went through the front door to his truck, disappointed and unsure why.

Lita's assessment niggled him. Not because she had called the new mother weird. She was too quick to judge, everyone knew that, so the locals put less weight on her assessments.

And yet, hadn't he gotten a similar vibe from the young woman?

He started across the freshly plowed parking lot, dead tired and ready to pack it in. He'd been cold for hours. And he wasn't always the most intuitive man on the planet, even when rested. It made no sense to try and puzzle things out on no rest and chilled limbs.

He would stop by his mother's place later. Talk to her about Nora. Right now, sleep was calling his name, but a woman approached him from the side lot of the firehouse. She held a microphone his way while a tall, lanky cameraman aimed a megalens at him.

"Deputy Jackson, are you the local hero who rescued a pregnant woman from the storm last night?"

Hale didn't like reporters. They had intruded on every aspect of his life, from his college sports career to his NFL fame, and then his crushing collapse back to being the hometown boy who'd had it all for just a little while.

"Actually, the 9-1-1 center dispatched a full squad to Perchance Road."

Her quick smile said she knew better. "Your humility is a wonderful thing, but it was you who answered the initial call, wasn't it?"

A part of him longed to keep on walking, but he couldn't, despite his misgivings about the media. This woman was doing her job, same as him. He didn't recognize her, so she must be from one of the smaller Rochester stations. "You seem to have me at a disadvantage." He breathed deep and smiled slow, a trick he'd learned at countless press conferences as a Philadelphia Eagle over the years. "You know who I am, but I'm not sure who you are."

"Catherine Kendall, YBNC."

Your Best News Channel, the cable news local. It was a solid, low-budget entity, and he'd never seen them smear a cop on purpose. That made talking to her a necessity, not a choice. "Yes, I went out on the initial call, with backup from Deputy Garrett Jackson."

"Sources tell us you performed a daring rescue in wretched conditions."

"They said that, huh?" He smiled again, at her and then the camera, playing it like a pro. "Well, I won't argue the conditions part of it. We were in the middle of a wild storm. And in all honesty, Catherine?"

She nodded and leaned the microphone closer.

"I came real close to *not* finding her. The wind and snow had obliterated all of her tracks, there was almost no visibility, and if her lights hadn't come on at just the right time, I might have missed her."

"Timing played a big part in the rescue, Deputy?"

"I'd go straight to timing and God," he told her.

Her eyes lit up. The camera moved closer. "You felt like God guided you?"

She didn't sound mocking like some might have. She appeared interested, as if his words made sense to her. "I'm saying that the odds were against that rescue. If Maggie Tompkins hadn't seen what she thought were spinning lights nearly a mile away in full-blown squall conditions, and if the driver hadn't turned on her lights at that specific moment, I would have called in a 'no cause' because there was nothing to indicate an accident had occurred. If that's not God's timing, I don't know what is."

"The light drew you to the car?"

Should he say that the first flash of pink made him reconsider? "Let's just say if I didn't see that flash through the blinding snow, we might be writing a very different story this morning. Temps dropped to single digits overnight, with a negative wind chill. I'm just glad we found her and got her back here in time to be properly cared for."

"Do you consider yourself a hero, Deputy Jackson?"

He refused to fall into that trap. Cops that got hero heads took a lot of grief on the force. "That designation goes straight to Avis Washington. We're really lucky to have a certified midwife right here in town."

The reporter took the subject turn in stride. "Gracious and brave." She offered a frank smile, no guile. "Deputy Jackson, thank you for your time. I expect you'd like to catch some sleep about now."

"You got that right." He smiled once more, reached out, and shook her hand. "Merry Christmas to you, both of you"—he included the cameraman and the camera in his look—"and to everyone at YBNC."

"We're good." She motioned to the cameraman to stop. "I meant what I said, Deputy," she called after him as he moved toward his truck.

"About the sleep?"

"About the hero. You did good."

He waved that off and drove to his rolling farm south of the village. He backed the truck into the garage, in case he had a call. His brother, Ben, had plowed the drives and the graveled yards in front of the two big barns. They'd partnered together on the beef farm when Hale had collected the insurance on his lost football career.

They'd dreamed of a place like this as kids, watching Westerns. In life's game of winners and losers, Hale's downfall had made their wish come true.

Stop thinking. Sleep. You're less introspective when you've slept.

He took the mental scolding to heart, shed his outer layers in the kitchen, and crawled into bed. When he awoke nearly seven hours later, it wasn't his plain, masculine bedroom he saw when he opened his eyes. It was the image of that young woman, catching his gaze in the rearview mirror. Reading the fear and something else in her eyes. Something inexplicable.

He showered, got dressed, grabbed coffee, and headed to his mother's, knowing Ben would have the farm work under control on his own. He was off tonight unless he got called in. A look west showed no clouds pushing their way, and the wind didn't have a lot of punch.

He pulled into his mother's driveway and climbed out of the truck, hoping for two things: a dinner invitation, because whatever she was cooking smelled real good as he walked up the back steps . . . and for her to tell him he was totally off base about this young woman and her nameless baby.

～

Thea and Jazz were coming to the middle of nowhere—literally—because Kelsey was in trouble.

Relief and guilt claimed Kelsey in equal measure. She climbed out of the low-slung bed to use the bathroom outside the door. The room spun. Her gut lurched as if she might throw up, but she hadn't eaten since the morning before.

She gripped the wall, then the corner of a plain, dark-brown dresser, willing the room to stay still.

"Oh, oh, oh." Firm hands took one arm, and the warmth and confidence in Avis's voice let her know she was all right. For the moment. "Bathroom call?"

"Yes. And I'd love to take a shower, Avis."

"I expect you would, pretty girl. Here's what we're going to do." Avis tucked Kelsey's arm through hers. "It's good for you to get up, but you lost a lot of blood after the delivery—not so much that I think we need to transfuse, but enough to go with caution for a week or two."

A week or two?

Kelsey's heart hammered.

There was no way she could stay here or anywhere for a week or two. She had a plan in place, a plan for her baby's welfare. Her best interests. And nothing could get in the way of that plan.

"Now I know that wasn't exactly in your plans," Avis went on, as if reading her mind. "But there's a great deal to consider directly after giving birth, and you and I will talk this out like the smart, educated women we are once you've had a shower and some food."

The shower sounded amazing.

The food did not.

"And you are not to worry."

Kelsey bit her lip, bit it hard, because that's all she'd been doing the last five months.

"Whatever the issues are, we can take care of them. And right now we'll deal with the immediate ones." Avis indicated the bathroom with the walled-off shower. "There's a railing in that shower. Use it if you get light-headed, and adjust the water first before you step in. I'll make sure Donny isn't running the dishwasher or anything downstairs so your water won't go to one extreme or the other. You take a shower, and I promise, things will feel better. And in a few days' time, they'll actually *be* better."

They wouldn't be. Kelsey knew that, but Avis's kindness offered a ray of hope. Maybe some way, somehow, they could recommit to the plan, because every time she looked down, into her daughter's tiny face, longing ate the edges of her resolve. "Thank you, Avis."

"You're welcome. You go have a nice, long shower and we'll talk after. Okay?"

"Okay."

Warmth. Caring. Compassion.

She read all those emotions and more in the older woman's face, a combination of strength and something indefinable.

Avis had called her intelligent. And educated. The words felt good, but was Avis guessing? Or just making uplifting small talk?

Kelsey didn't know, but when she stepped into the steamy shower and let clean, hot water sluice over her head and shoulders, the dizziness abated.

She kept her hand close to the railing, just in case, then didn't need to grab hold after all. As the fragrant soap and warm water cleansed her skin, her senses revived.

She'd gotten this far because she hadn't let the mistake of loving the wrong man ruin her life, or her child's. She'd finished the semester light in the pocketbook but with her goal firmly in hand.

The storm and the precipitous birth had changed the timing. Nothing else. Because no matter what happened, her baby girl's future would be secured the way Kelsey's never was. She'd make sure she stayed strong enough and focused enough to see her plan through.

Avis thought she needed to stay in town at least a week. Seven days could be a blink of an eye or a very long time, depending on circumstances. And with a brand-new baby in need of tender, loving care and a mother's love?

Kelsey was pretty sure that seven days would be more like a lifetime.

CHAPTER FIVE

"I'm not here to pester anyone." Maggie Tompkins brought a basket of fresh rolls and jam through the back door of the firehouse midafternoon. "But I thought I'd pop in, bring the lot o' youse a treat, and see how Avis is making out."

"Are these your homemade rolls, Maggie?" Ginny Chatham put her hand to her heart as she sniffed. "Oh, be still my heart. Food like this is never a bother and always welcome. Come on in, and I'll tell Avis you're here."

"Is she sleeping? Don't bother her if she's sleeping," Maggie warned.

"She's having Susan Bell step in for overnight to keep an eye on things once we figure where we can move this little mother and the baby," Ginny explained. "Firehouse regulations won't let us keep them here once the emergency is lifted, and that was hours ago. But we need them close by so Avis and Doc Brandenburg can look after them."

"We've got two clean, empty bedrooms at our place," said Jeb as he came in behind her. "Plenty of space to house them, and it would be nice to have a little one on hand, wouldn't it, Maggie?"

Would it? Maggie's hands shook slightly, like they'd been doing now and then whenever she thought about the blank slate of the upcoming Christmas holiday. "If we can be of help . . ."

"Sounds like we could." Jeb's voice stayed easy, but she couldn't miss the hinted hope.

"I think Avis would be over the moon to take you up on that. You're in the perfect location for Avis and the doc, and what a nice setting that would be for this young mother. If you're sure, that is?"

Was she sure? Maggie couldn't answer that honestly, because life had gone uncertain a long time ago when what seemed to be an act of charity had turned into a life-changing decision. A bad one. Then this year it took a ragged turn for the worse, after she and Jeb thought things had gotten better. Her pulse seemed loud in her ears. Jeb wasn't pushing, but she'd heard the raised note in his voice.

She knew one thing. She was tired of a quiet, empty house. So very tired of it. She turned to Jeb. "It would be nice to have a baby around, wouldn't it, Jeb? And help someone in need?"

He offered an instant, hopeful smile. "Nothin' like young voices and feedin' a baby to make Christmas seem like Christmas, Mother."

"Maggie, are you serious?" Avis came into the kitchen from the opposite door just then. "You and Jeb wouldn't mind giving up a room?"

"I've always wondered what I'd do if I was that Bethlehem innkeeper," Maggie confessed. "Would I find room for the needy or turn my back on them? Well, now's my chance to prove it."

"Can't say I've ever wondered that," Jeb drawled, "but it only makes sense for folks to be kind and openhearted when things go all catawampus."

"Jeb, I do love how you talk." Ginny giggled. "You ought to come down to the schools and tell the kids some of your stories. They'd learn a lot and be entertained all at once."

"He'd like that," Maggie exclaimed. "And it would get him out from under now and again. He misses going back and forth to work, and you know how winter is here. It stretches late in the day and stays too long."

"Woman, I can speak for myself. I'm not that old nor doddering yet." Jeb tipped his gaze down to Ginny. "I'd love it."

"Well, thank you for saying what I already said, Jeb Tompkins, and now we'd best get back to the topic at hand. This mama and baby. We'll need a crib for the baby."

"Ginny's daughter-in-law donated a bassinet for us to use," Avis said. "It will be fine for a few weeks. She sent over some bedding and newborn clothes, too. All freshly washed."

Maggie held up a second finger. "Diapers."

"There were boxes of them in the car when they towed it out, so we've got that covered."

"Is she nursing the baby? Or do we need a bottle setup?"

"Nursing for the moment." Avis hesitated, as if not quite ready to commit. "You know how that goes, Maggie. It comes naturally to some but not all, so I'll come up with a bottle system and formula. Just in case."

Maggie remembered that like it was yesterday and not three-and-a-half decades back. She bit back a sigh because she didn't remember getting old, yet she was staring seventy in the face. And she'd felt every inch of those years this past six months, but right now she felt young. "I've got the middle room freshly cleaned. We'll use that one, and if we need the other room, we'll run the duster in there when we get back home. Just think of it!" She clapped her hands together. "A Christmas baby!"

"Well, I'm not sure how long she'll be staying," Avis warned. "I've advised a week at least, and I'd prefer two, truth be known. But it *is* exciting to have such a happy ending to what could have been a dreadful tragedy. And we have you to thank for that, Maggie."

"Lucky you noticed those lights through that window. Otherwise—" Ginny's mouth pressed tight.

Maggie waved that off. "The sweet Lord put me in the right place at the right time and sent the perfect deputy out into the cold. I've never known Hale Jackson to give up on anything, though Lord knows he had reason to over the years. Things happen for a reason, Ginny. I'm not holdin' that luck had much to do with it."

"And since you're more often right than wrong, I won't argue."
Ginny set the basket of rolls on the counter next to the stove. "These
will be perfect with the pot of chili I made for supper."

"Maggie, I'm going down the hall to the firehouse office so I can
arrange transportation." Avis moved toward the connecting door. "Do
you and Jeb need any groceries at your place?"

"We'll stop at the market in Warsaw to make sure we've got the
essentials." Maggie tucked her scarf a little more snugly around her
neck. "And ice cream, of course. I don't know a young mother who
doesn't appreciate a dish of Perry's finest now and again. This time of
year they have that 'White Christmas' flavor we all like so well. I didn't
see much sense in buying a whole container for the two of us." Maggie
paused, amazed at how quickly things had turned around. Days of
dread might now become a time of expectation, and all because she'd
seen those lights sweep a three-sixty along the Perchance Road bend last
night. "We'll get stocked up and meet you at our place around four.
Does that work on your end?"

"It's perfect. I'll explain all of this to Kelsey when she wakes up.
And you're sure that having a baby around won't mess up your sleep?"
Avis asked.

"Hittin' seventy already took care of that," Jeb assured her. "We'll
see you up at our place in a bit."

A baby.

A baby!

She and Jeb had longed for a big family long ago, and the Lord
had seen fit to send them one child, a beautiful girl, their sweet Bonnie.
Such a wonder she was, sweet and kind and good. Always anxious to
please, a delightful child.

And then they'd opened their home to her cousin's orphaned kids
when Bonnie was six years old. Adam and Alexis were preteens in need
of a home when they lost their mother to cancer. A home of love and
faith, the social worker said, and Jeb and Maggie had an abundance

of both. They had opened their hearts and home to the pair, willingly making them part of the family.

But reality had reared its ugly head when the older kids hated coming north to live with Maggie and Jeb, and they had let the world know it. Maggie had never known a child to have a true mean streak. The very thought had seemed ludicrous. She'd brushed off the warning signs as her own inexperience with older kids, until the brother and sister duo caused trouble in school and in the town with their sneaky, mean-hearted behaviors.

And Bonnie, their sweet child, had borne the brunt of the teens' anger for almost two years before Maggie realized the full truth of the matter. Long enough to mess up Bonnie's self-esteem and instigate the eating disorder that had claimed her life earlier this year.

Guilt and remorse swamped her. Folks often said they'd never change a thing if given a chance.

Maggie didn't feel that way at all. If she could go back and change those decisions, she'd do it. Naïve and loving, she'd trusted too quickly and held the resulting grief in her hands and hers alone because she was the mother. She should have seen what was happening and curtailed it, and she hadn't.

Sadness had veiled the past six months, and truth to tell, she'd dreaded every single minute of the approaching holidays.

For the time being, that was about to end.

They waved goodbye and hustled to the car with more purposeful steps than they'd had lately. As Jeb steered the car toward the grocery store down Route 19, Maggie pulled a pad of paper from the glove compartment. She started a quick list of things they might need. Breakfast food. Cold cuts. Fresh veggies. A sudden thought made her pause.

What if the young mother was a vegetarian, like so many young folks these days?

"Let's get a samplin' of this and that and see what's what once she's at the house," Jeb advised as he paused for a traffic light.

"How did you know exactly what I was thinking?" She didn't say it scolding-like, and that was a change because she'd been doing her share of scolding lately. She reached over and patted his leg. "We haven't had anyone at the house in months, Jeb. Just the thought has my wheels turning."

"And when your wheels turn, my workload increases, but I can't say I mind," he told her. "It does me good to have something to look forward to, Mags. Especially this year."

"I know." She spoke softly because she knew the meaning behind the raw timing. "The good Lord giveth."

"And he taketh away."

"Blessed be the name of the Lord." She said the words but didn't feel them, and that was a conundrum because she'd always felt them . . . until last summer. You'd think half a year would make a difference, a big difference, but with twinkle lights shining and carols playing, her heart wasn't any better.

It was worse, actually. And that was cause for concern. But then a parent wasn't supposed to bury a child, though she'd stood at no small number of funerals for that very thing over the years. She just never expected it would be her child. Her daughter. Her beloved.

Jeb came around the car and took her hand. He hadn't done that in some time. It felt good. "Let's grab stuff and get home so we don't keep them waiting."

"We'll step lively!"

He laughed, and it was his old laugh, the one she had fallen in love with a long time ago. As they hurried into the busy supermarket, she felt something close to joy, so close that she almost felt guilty.

She quashed the feeling, seized a cart, and went around the well-outfitted store with more spring in her step than she'd had in a long time. All because of a baby.

~

"You want me to stay where?" Kelsey stared at Avis, then drew her brow in much the same way her newborn daughter did. "I can't possibly do that."

"Why?" The bronze-skinned midwife set a freshly folded set of towels on the laminated dresser top.

Kelsey splayed her hands. "I don't know these people."

"You didn't know me twenty-four hours ago, but that's come out all right, hasn't it?"

It had, but—"I didn't exactly have a choice, Avis."

Avis acknowledged that with a nod as she laid out the changing mat to freshen the baby's diaper.

"An emergency is one thing," Kelsey argued. "You're a midwife, and I was delivering a baby. This is different. It's like moving in with someone."

Avis sent her one of those kind, motherly looks she'd used in the heat of labor the night before. "Here's the thing. Maggie and Jeb are good people, and they don't have anyone at their house for the holidays, so having you and the baby around would be a great joy to them. They live in the village, right up on Wyoming Hill Road. It was Maggie who saw your car spin out of control last night. She called it in to the 9-1-1 center, and they sent Deputy Jackson to check it out. If Maggie hadn't trusted her eyes and made that call . . ."

Avis left the sentence open-ended, and Kelsey understood what she wasn't saying. She could have been trapped in that car, stuck in an impossible situation in the frigid cold as her baby fought to enter the world. "You don't think it's weird for me to move in with complete strangers?"

"Some places, maybe," Avis acknowledged with a shrug. "Not here. And not Jeb and Maggie Tompkins. They're the salt of the earth. The whole town loves them. I think it would be nice, honey." Avis lifted the baby, then settled her onto the mat as she motioned Kelsey over. "Your turn to do the honors."

"Don't good mothers have instincts about all this stuff?" Kelsey moved to her side and gazed down at the baby. A double thrust of love and fear broadsided her, but she bent and unfastened the drawstring at the bottom of the long gown. The baby kicked and fussed, clearly at odds with her mother's awkward maneuvers.

"Surprisingly, no. A point that has launched anthropological studies for a long time," Avis told her. She didn't laugh at Kelsey. She offered quiet advice as Kelsey took care of the baby, and when she was done, Avis showed her how to lift the tiny girl. "Keep this hand supporting her rump, and this one along her neck and head."

Kelsey stared down.

The baby stared up.

Her chest went tight. Her throat followed along. "Take her. Please."

Avis took the baby and grasped Kelsey's upper arm with her free hand. "Are you light-headed again?"

Kelsey shook her head.

"Feeling poorly? Or just scared to death, darlin'?"

Was it Avis's voice or the word "darlin'" that brought Kelsey to tears? Maybe a combination of both.

"Sit down."

Kelsey sat.

Avis took a seat in the chair alongside the small bed, then tucked the baby into Kelsey's arms. "There now. You hold your precious child and tell me what's going on."

"How much time do you have?" Kelsey lifted watery eyes to Avis but held tight to the squirming bundle. What if she dropped her? What if she couldn't hand her away when the time came? What if she absolutely, positively ruined this child's life because she'd messed up so thoroughly?

"I've got all the time you need." Avis's voice soothed like brown sugar syrup on French toast, and before she knew it, Kelsey was spilling her history—her recent history, that is—to the sympathetic woman facing her.

"Adoption." Avis laid a golden-brown hand against the baby's pale skin. "Such a noble thing, Kelsey."

"It wasn't one bit noble," she whispered. She swiped her right hand to her cheek, and when Avis tucked a stash of tissues into her hand, she used them, too. "I didn't have a good childhood. My mom was a total screwup, but maybe that was an excuse I used to pretend I wasn't making my own laundry list of bad choices. I made a lot of mistakes, but I straightened myself out and promised myself I wouldn't mess up. I went to school, graduated with honors, and got my teaching degree. And then I managed to backtrack all my goals because I believed the wrong person. What kind of stable adult does that?"

"Who doesn't like to hear the words of a sweet-talkin' man, child?" Avis rolled her eyes like that was a no-brainer, then she sat back. "There is a lot to consider here, pretty girl."

Kelsey didn't feel pretty, but Avis's kindness helped soften the ache clutching at her heart. "I wasn't going to see her. Or touch her. Hold her. Nurse her. And now I'm doing all of that, so how can I possibly hand her over to some stranger and entrust her to them? What if they mess up?" She shuddered, took a breath, then breathed out, purposefully.

"It took everything I had to pay for the prenatal care up north. Her father left me with nearly eight thousand dollars in credit-card bills before he took off, and I had to file police reports about identity theft in order to get them taken off my credit rating. But that meant anyone and everyone would know how gullible I was. My substitute-teaching job was over—the teacher is coming back after the holiday break—and how can you go for job interviews for a long-term sub or teaching position when you're nine months pregnant and unmarried?"

Avis held her hand.

Just that.

Head bowed, she kept her warm, slim fingers on top of Kelsey's hand, the one snugged around the baby.

Her lips moved silently. Praying, Kelsey realized, something she hadn't done in a long, long time. Awkwardness put a chokehold on her once again.

Tough-edged Mrs. Effel had promised to pray for her years ago at Hannah's Hope. Joan Effel was like the quintessential utility player for the foster-care group home. She didn't run the place on paper, but make no mistake, Hannah's Hope—a foster home for troubled teen girls— was *her* project. She unclogged sinks, cooked meals, ordered supplies, and offered free advice with a side of cryptic wisdom thrown in at no extra cost. And if you broke the rules—rules put in place to protect hardheaded teens like Kelsey—it was Joan Effel who called you on the carpet. In retrospect, Kelsey owed the tough-as-nails woman more than she could ever possibly repay.

"I will pray for your troubled soul, Kelsey McCleary," Mrs. Effel had told her one night when Kelsey had slipped out a second-story window to meet up with a group of weed-smoking teens outside the convenience store a quarter mile up the road. She stood waiting at the bottom of the fence Kelsey had climbed down in her escape.

She faced Kelsey straight on and held her gaze, nice and tight. "I will most assuredly pray for you. It might help, it might not, but I'm going to do it anyway because I want you to go through life knowing someone cared enough about you to pray for you. Every single day. And now you have a choice." She looked east toward the lights of the twenty-four-hour minimarket. "To head down the road to hang out with that sorry band of misguided souls, or"—she hooked a thumb toward the big, old, rambling house in need of repair—"you come inside with me and have some hot chocolate and a good night's sleep before school tomorrow."

Kelsey had stood there, staring at the older woman, wondering why she was being so nice. And then it hit her.

She was at a crossroads. Stay or go, the decision loomed much larger than she'd expected minutes before. Like life challenging death, her choice hovered in the narrow backyard of a crumbling structure. Stay with the wise older woman who accepted her for who she was? Or go off with a group of rule-breaking potheads determined to mess up their lives, a path much like her mother had taken years before. "Hot chocolate sounds real good, actually."

"Well then." Mrs. Effel had smiled. She'd looped her arm through Kelsey's, just so. "Let's go see about that."

Hearing Avis's soft words, Kelsey wondered if Mrs. Effel still prayed for her. And if she did, would she be disappointed in her now?

The baby yawned, stretched, and peeked one eye open. Then she shut it tight in sleep, as if trusting her mother to make the right decisions. Just like Mrs. Effel. "I'll stay at the Tompkins house."

Avis finished her prayer and raised her eyes. "They'll be thrilled. And they will spoil you. And you will bring a light into their lives every moment you're there, so this blessing will go both ways."

A voice from the stairs interrupted them. "Avis. Turn on the little TV in there. Channel seven's got Hale on, talking about last night's rescue!"

"Well, we don't want to miss this, do we?" Avis clicked the remote. The small, flat TV flashed on. When she'd flipped to the right station, a tall, rugged cop dwarfed the woman reporter as he answered questions in a warm, friendly manner.

"That's him?"

"Deputy Hale Jackson, yes. He found you and saved your life. And hers." Avis didn't look down at the baby. She didn't have to. "He's a fine man, our Hale."

To-die-for handsome. Square jawed. Square shouldered. And the way he smiled at the reporter, and the camera, made Kelsey remember how he'd smiled at her the night before.

She hadn't been able to remember his face upon awakening. She'd tried a couple of times, but those hours were a blur of fear, pain, and activity.

But here he was, sweet-talking, humble, crazy good-looking, and thoughtful. "I'd like to thank him sometime. If that would be all right."

"I'm sure it would, but don't go overboard. You can hear him there." Avis indicated the TV as Hale praised her work as a midwife. "Hale doesn't do what he does for thanks. He does it because it's the right thing to do. Noble. Like you. Now let's get you packed up here, pretty girl, and have a little food, all right? Ginny made chili down below, but I'm not sure how that would go over on baby's tummy when your milk comes in. Gassy babies are not fun to be around. What about some oatmeal and toast? They've got the maple-and-brown-sugar kind downstairs."

Her favorite, and it didn't just sound good. It sounded delicious. "I'd love some oatmeal, actually."

"I'll bring it up. If she wakes up and gets hungry, just lift your top and offer her the chance to eat. Right now she's getting used to things. Just like you. It's all about practice. Learning to latch on is a big accomplishment these first days. I think we'll be able to get you settled in over at the Tompkins house before your friends arrive in a couple of hours."

Jazz and Thea. On their way here, to help her. Support her. Realizing that she'd gone and done exactly what they'd sworn they wouldn't do. She'd ended up pregnant, broke, and alone. "I shouldn't have bothered them, especially when all of you are being so nice to me. I wonder if it's too late to stop them? Tell them there's no need?"

"They're grown women, both of them?" Avis stood in the doorway, ready to head downstairs.

She nodded. "My age. We all graduated together from Marshall High outside of Philly."

"Then let them come," Avis advised. "Nothing like celebrating old times and new life to bring us full circle, darlin'."

Thea was a medical professional, a nurse practitioner. Jazz was a New York model who'd made the cover of all the biggest and best fashion rags. How could she face them, two successful career women?

The baby squirmed again. She looked worried.

So was Kelsey. But as Avis's footsteps retreated down the metal steps, the baby opened her mouth in a soundless cry.

Kelsey pushed worry aside. She needed to feed her baby. Her daughter. The rest would take care of itself, one way or another. She hoped.

CHAPTER SIX

A phone call interrupted her as Thea settled a fresh cup of coffee into the center console of her flashy little sports car. Yes, it was used, but it had suited her when she'd bought it eighteen months back. Now she'd have to land a job or an interim position fairly quickly to keep up with payments on that, her student loans, and her shared townhouse in the Lofts. She picked up the phone, and it was Jazz on the other end, calling from JFK. "Any chance you can pick me up in Rochester around five-forty-five? Save me a car rental?"

Save her a car rental?

An odd request from a supermodel, but Thea said yes quickly. "Glad to. Where can we stay when we get into this little town? Any idea?"

"Haven't done a little town in over a decade. Blank."

Neither had Thea. She'd finished her nursing degree in a small town, but after that it had been nothing but big cities, hefty loans, and pricey apartments. And now, when she finally felt like she was standing on terra firma, here she was, jobless and headed to an off-the-map spot in the snow-covered hills of Western New York. "I'll see if I can find something."

"Thanks. Boarding."

Picking up Jazz meant driving nearly an hour past Wishing Bridge, then an hour back, but that was all right. That hour alone would give them time to talk. Catch up. Compare notes.

The thought made her twitch. An out-of-work medical professional with megadebt facing off with one of Manhattan's most sought-after faces above a body that showcased fashion like Tiffany showcased gems.

You're not plain. You're normal. With glasses and a flat chest. Jazz is just off-the-charts gorgeous. Stop beating yourself up.

She hit the Bluetooth connection and called Kelsey's number. This time Kelsey answered. "Thea?"

"Kelse." She hadn't said Kelsey's name like that in a long time. Too long. "I'm detouring up to the Rochester airport to pick up Jazz, then we're heading back your way. Is there any place we can stay nearby?"

"I have no clue. Hang on, Thea, let me ask someone."

No clue?

She didn't have time to reason out why a smart woman like Kelsey was unaware of her surroundings before Kelsey was back on the phone. "There's a little inn not far from here, about five minutes south. It's on Old Woodsmoke Road, and the name is . . ." She paused, listening to someone. "Well, that's easy to remember. It's called the Woodsmoke Inn."

Thea was pretty sure the Woodsmoke Inn didn't make it into most travel brochures, but she'd lived life as a struggling college student for a long time. She could do anything for a night or two. She hoped. "I'll check it out. You hold tight, okay?"

"Yes. Thea, listen—" Kelsey's voice took a decidedly apologetic tone.

"No regrets," Thea ordered. They'd made a pledge a long time ago, and they'd made rules to go with the promise. "Rule one: we call for help as needed. That's why we made the pledge. Hey, I've got to get back on the road. See you tonight."

"All right."

Thea headed east, caught the interstate loop, and headed for Rochester. Whatever was going on with Kelsey, she couldn't have picked a better time to put out a call for help because Thea Anastas's schedule had recently become a blank page.

~

"There's the conquering hero." Jill Jackson crossed the kitchen and gave Hale a hug when he came through the back door of her cozy kitchen. "You hungry?"

"Starved and hoping you'd ask me to supper. And how'd you know about last night? Did you talk to Ben?"

"No need to run interrogation on your brother when you're all over the news, Hale."

The reporter. He sank into the seat, wondering how something as simple as beef stew could smell so good. "Just doing my job. Glad it came out all right, though."

"A scary business, to have someone just disappear off the road like that." She made a face as she dished up a monster-sized bowl of food. "And then to go into labor? What a night. Thank heavens for the kindness of strangers, that's all I can say."

"I actually get paid for my kindness," he joked, then read her expression and backtracked. "Except that's not what you meant. Is it?"

"Maggie and Jeb are taking that young mother in."

"They're what?" Hale sat straighter. "I go to sleep for seven hours and the whole town goes crazy? Let's back this up a little. When did this happen? We don't know this woman. Whose idea was this?"

His mother stopped stirring to stare at him, for good reason. He was overreacting. She gave him a funny look and went back to her saucepot before she answered. "I don't know when. About now, I guess." She glanced at the wall clock. "I heard it from Max Reichert. He met up with Maggie and Jeb in the grocery and stopped by here on his way home. They told him they were stocking up for their unexpected and most welcome company."

Maggie Tompkins was about the sweetest, kindest person on the planet. Jeb was a little tougher, but only by a slight degree. The thought of them taking in a stranger . . . He set down his spoon. "I don't like this."

His mother frowned.

"She's a stranger."

"Well. Yes. But they'll get to know her, and that baby, too, come the middle of the night."

"This isn't funny."

"Sleep deprivation never is, but what's come over you?" Her frown deepened. She came closer. "Is there something about this woman you're not telling me? Us? Anyone?"

"No. Well. Not really. It's just—"

She slipped into the chair across from his. "Just what, Hale?"

"Did Nora ever have a kid? A daughter?"

"Nora Samson? You know she didn't, she's got two boys, both in Florida with her. Why?"

He'd known the answer before he asked the question, so why did he ask it? Because it wasn't just this young woman's pretty gray eyes. It was her voice, too. A voice he'd heard daily the first ten years of his life. But that was preposterous, wasn't it? "This girl reminds me of Nora. That's all."

"And that's it?"

"Well. And a hunch that things aren't what they seem."

"A hunch."

She sounded doubtful, but Hale had trusted his instincts often in the past. He was willing to trust them now. "Yes."

His mother got up, crossed the room and busied herself at the sink. "Everybody's got a doppelganger. Don't they?"

"So I've heard."

"Some study group did a search for them online. For doppelgangers, folks that look alike. Did you know that?" She aimed a look his way. "And then they showed the pictures of the people side by side, with similar haircuts. Some of them looked enough alike to be twins. To fool their own mothers."

"Coincidence is an amazing thing."

"It is." She turned his way, more serious than she'd been moments before when she was lauding his heroic skills in the thick of the storm. "It all comes down to numbers, I suppose. The combination of genetics is like the lottery. Every now and again you get a real close match. With millions of people in the world, it's bound to happen."

She was right. He knew that, so why did it seem off?

The voice.

That's what he couldn't quite get past. Sure, folks could look alike in the accidents of genetic pairing. But looks *and* voice?

"This will be a blessing to Maggie and Jeb, Hale."

Her words held a warning he couldn't ignore, not after the Tompkins' loss that summer. "It was looking like a mighty lonely holiday over there, that's for sure."

She didn't have to remind him; he well understood that. He knew the truth of it, with every holiday and special occasion and each one of little Michael's birthdays. He'd given up his right to celebrate with the boy, thinking it was a noble gesture.

But when special occasions came around, it didn't feel noble. It felt harsh and stupid and empty. On top of that, he was pretty sure that last night's accident victim was low on resources. "I expect she can use the help, too. Her car died in the snow, and my guess is she's short on cash. The stuff I saw in the car wasn't exactly upscale. But it was dark."

"That makes you finding her and folks here helping even more important, especially now. At Christmas," she added.

He'd keep his concerns to himself, Hale decided as he ate his stew. His mother was right. Helping this woman was a nice thing to do, and if it kept Maggie and Jeb from dwelling on the emptiness of their house, he was okay with that.

But he'd keep his eyes open. Ears, too. Instincts had kept him at the top of his game during his football career. He could read other teams and their plays. Their body language. Those same instincts had kept him alive and earned him regular commendations on the police force, so he wasn't about to ignore his misgivings. He'd explore them, but he'd do it quietly because he hadn't only seen mistrust in that young woman's eyes. He'd seen the kind of hurt he saw reflected in the mirror every morning before he blinked it back and put a smile on his face, and he couldn't help but wonder why. It was a sorry way to live, and he knew the truth in that.

~

Fear gripped Kelsey's midsection as Avis pulled her car into the driveway of a classic old home on the upper side of the village. A wraparound porch offered an invitation to sit in nicer weather, and the windows shone bright with the lights within, but the house seemed subdued among its more festive neighbors. There were no Christmas decorations outside or behind the Priscilla-style curtains, though other houses along the road had gone all out.

The big, old house sat quiet, as if it didn't have the energy to dress up for the holidays.

The baby squalled in her car seat, desperately unhappy with her current state of affairs. Kelsey longed to do the same, but she didn't. She climbed out of the car, breathed easy and light as a cramp hit her, then circled the car for the baby.

"I'll bring her in, pretty girl. You head on up there so we can get you tucked into the room they've got ready for you. And if I know the neighbors here, they'll be by with treats and meals, all hoping for a glimpse of this precious child. There is nothing like the birth of a baby at Christmas to get folks in the spirit, is there?"

Kelsey had no idea. She'd never lived in a neighborhood where folks looked out for one another, unless police were involved. Low-rent apartments on a substitute teacher's salary had kept her in more transient areas, even after she'd earned her master's degree in elementary education. Not bad places, but not homey like this street. This village. For just a moment she wondered what it would be like to live in Wishing Bridge.

Of course, she couldn't.

Who knew what kind of history Vonnie might have had here, if she'd actually lived here at all? There was no telling what Kelsey's presence could stir up, so showing up out of the blue wasn't a real smart idea. The fact that it had been the only option wasn't lost on her, but as she approached the front door of the Tompkins house, she couldn't quell the clutch of fear. What if her mother had been telling the truth for once in her life? That she was from here, and that Kelsey's conception hadn't been consensual? That made her father a criminal, and possibly a criminal that still lived here.

She shuttered her thoughts as the door opened.

"You're here!"

A kind-faced woman held out a hand as if Kelsey were a long-lost friend. Then she took her arm and led Kelsey into one of the sweetest-smelling places she'd been in a long time. The older woman tucked her arm through Kelsey's. "Now, I've got you upstairs. It's a lovely room, but if the stairs are too much for you so soon after having the baby, we can switch up the office down here. You just let me know, all right?" She smiled at Kelsey, the kind of smile she'd seen in old-time movies, when folks played parts like real people.

"I think it will be fine."

"I'm Maggie. This is my husband, Jeb. Tompkins, that is," she added. "Welcome to our home, Kelsey."

The old woman's thoughtfulness eased the knot of fear in Kelsey's gut. "It's very kind of you to do this."

"It's our pleasure," Maggie told her and sounded absolutely sincere about it.

"It sure is because things were getting mighty quiet around here," Jeb added. "And that just don't do right for the holidays, now does it?" He pulled up a zipper on an old, gray hoodie. "I'm going to bring in the stuff from Avis's car while you ladies get settled."

"That sounds good, Jeb."

They went up the broad staircase together, one of those old-fashioned kinds that turned midway. Wide, too, not like new stairways.

"You okay?" Maggie asked as they drew close to the second-floor hallway.

"Yes, actually." The fact that she was fine pleased Kelsey. "Not too bad. I used to be pretty rigid about staying in shape, but there's something about the ninth month that kicks that notion to the curb."

Maggie laughed and led her into a big, broad, centered bedroom. Two open doors went off the hall to the left of this one. First a bathroom, old-fashioned and quaint. Then another bedroom, just as big as this one. To the right, at the end of the hall leading into the clever extension of the big, old house was another door. This one was closed, so Kelsey brought her attention back to the room in front of her.

It smelled clean, like it had been spit-polished recently, another thing that had fallen by the wayside for her the last few weeks. She'd packed up her apartment, sold all but the bare essentials, made a credit-card payment so her credit rating wouldn't tank while the bank and the police hashed things out, and lived a bare-bones existence for the last three weeks.

A thick bed, clean sheets and blankets, curtains and warmth . . . the room was a corner of heaven right here on earth.

"This is so nice, Mrs. Tompkins. I can't begin to thank you properly."

"No thanks needed. I'm glad you like it, but there'll be none of that Mr. and Mrs. Tompkins here. Call me Maggie. Everyone does, even the littlest ones. There's a bathroom right here." She pointed to the next door to the left. "With a shower and a bath. Take that one over as needed, we use the one downstairs, off our room."

"It's lovely."

"Well, it's old looking, but it suits the house, we think."

It did.

Avis climbed the stairs with the baby. "I left the car seat in the hall, and Jeb's bringing in the base. It's an easy detach system, Kelsey. They've made them simpler these days; it's a wonder for sure. Although our little friend did not like the idea of being tucked in that seat, not one bit. But I told her"—Avis leaned into the baby's face with a broad, shining smile—"it is for your very own good, missy, and that's all I'm going to say about that."

"Is that her name? Missy? How sweet!"

An awkward silence ensued, until Kelsey broke it. "She doesn't have a name."

"No name?"

It sounded stupid and wrong to admit she hadn't named her almost day-old baby. Kelsey shook her head and waited for a look of disgust or frank curiosity. She got neither.

Maggie simply patted her arm as if it were perfectly normal and said, "Well, that's lovely, dear. You've got time to rest and relax and think about what name suits. Now I know some folks have names all lined up these days, before they even have a family, but it seems extra smart to get to know your baby first. And it gives us something to talk about, doesn't it? Avis told me you've got two friends coming into town, and they're going to want to see you. And see this baby, too."

Kelsey was relieved that Avis had broached the subject. She nodded.

"I'm going to let you relax up here for now, unless you'd rather be downstairs," Maggie told her. "Whatever works for you, works for us. The nice thing about being this age is flexibility, and Jeb and I've got plenty of that.

"I've got one of those frozen lasagnas in the oven," she continued. "We got fresh bread while we were shopping, although usually we get it from Betty's Bakery across the way." She pointed toward Main Street. "She wasn't open this afternoon, with so much to get done for the big Christmas push. Christmas Eve is her busiest day of the year, you know. Well, that and Holy Saturday. Anyway, there's plenty of food, and your friends are welcome to join us. If they haven't eaten already."

What could Kelsey say? She hadn't seen the girls in a dozen years. They'd talked sporadically and had kept up on Facebook for a while, but they'd all backed off that a few years before. Other than Christmas cards they hadn't had real or even virtual contact in three years. "That's very kind, Maggie."

"Glad to do it. It feels good to be busy, Kelsey."

That was a feeling Kelsey understood well. She liked being busy and active, too. "I hear you."

Avis motioned her inside as Jeb brought her weathered suitcase up the stairs. "Let's get you settled because this little one is going to want to eat soon."

"You two do that while I go check on the food."

Maggie hustled away with quick, birdlike movements. When she was down the stairs, Kelsey turned to Avis. "She's so nice, Avis."

"She is. And I promise you, being here is as much a help to her as it is to you."

That couldn't be possible, but it was nice of Avis to say.

"Now I want you resting as much as you can when this baby rests. Let Maggie take care of you. My friend Susan is coming by for the night, just to make sure everything goes along all right, and I think it will. But let her and Maggie dote on you, okay? I'm going to stay for another hour or two. Maybe get a chance to meet those friends of yours. It's so special how they both were able to drop everything and come like this. At Christmastime, no less."

Kelsey stared out the window. The multicolored hues of the neighbors' holiday lights cast little rainbows through frosted panes. Tiny rainbows, just big enough for fairies.

She sighed and turned back to Avis. "I sent an SOS. That's why they're coming. Not because they know about the baby. They don't." Sadly, she touched the baby's tiny arm. "We were all foster kids together, back in Philadelphia. We made a pledge that we would never make the mistakes our parents made. We wouldn't do drugs, take life for granted, hurt others, or have kids without a husband on board. We vowed to get the schooling we needed to have careers so that we'd never have to depend on someone else's charity or lack thereof again."

"I see." Avis took a seat on the side of the bed and patted the space next to her.

Kelsey felt more like pacing, but she took the seat.

"What did you go to school for, pretty girl?"

"Education."

"Do tell." Avis smiled. "Big kids or little kids?"

"Elementary. I got my master's degree three years back, so I've been on the job hunt for a full-time position, but it hasn't happened yet."

"There's a lot of competition out there for teaching jobs right now."

There was, but she had no intention of giving up on her dream or her goals, even if she had to put them off for a little while. "That's part of why I set off for Pennsylvania. I liked what I saw about the adoption agency just outside of Harrisburg, and there are new openings coming up in their elementary schools. I've done three long-term substitute-teaching stints up in Canton and Potsdam, so now I've got experience added to my résumé. I was putting in applications up north when I met the baby's father. He was a sweet-talking man who swept me off my feet."

"Oh, I know that type, darlin'. We all do."

"I fell for it. All of it," she told Avis, and because she hadn't breathed a word of this to anyone the past nine months, she was almost relieved to say it out loud. "When I realized I was pregnant, I didn't panic because he'd already talked marriage. And then I realized it was just talk. And that he'd used my name and social security number to take out a credit card, one he used to get over eight thousand dollars in cash advances. When I went to the police, I found out he wasn't who I thought he was. He had a different name, a different life, and a wife down in South Carolina. He disappeared from her life much like he disappeared from mine."

"He used you."

He had, but she wasn't about to negate her responsibility. "Yes. But I'm not stupid, Avis. I may have acted stupid in that case, but I'm a smart woman. I let my head get turned. I didn't check the facts, and that was my own neediness and foolishness talking. He caught me at a time when I was hopeful for my new career and dreaming of the next stage in life. Something normal and nice. A life I'd never known." She shrugged. "A husband, the picket fence, kids."

"Wanting the dream isn't a bad thing."

"But changing up the order of events is," Kelsey told her firmly. "I made a promise. All three of us girls did. We were not going to be caught out like our parents. We would rise above."

"And you did."

Kelsey scoffed.

"You did," Avis insisted, "for over ten years. And then you made a mistake, yes. And here you are, making difficult decisions for your baby's well-being because you're an honorable person, Kelsey McCleary. So whatever you decide to do from this point forward, let's wipe that slate clean of past mistakes. We've got a holy day coming up, and a new year to follow. I say we greet that new year with the strength you've shown all along. And I know for a fact"—Avis stood up, picked up the baby from the little bassinet, and raised her to her shoulder—"loneliness is a harsh thing to deal with. If a body doesn't have faith to hold them up and that loneliness takes hold, it's a sorry state of affairs. You stop beating yourself up, you hear?"

Kelsey nodded, but this time it was Avis who made a skeptical face. "That was not one bit convincing, young lady. You rise above those bad feelings because you've come through this turn of events with great strength. I've delivered many a baby in my time, and if half my mothers had your courage and wisdom, my job would be almost unnecessary. Note that I said 'almost,'" she added, smiling. "I am putting you at the top of my prayer list, and I'm going to thank the good Lord for the circumstances that brought you here to our little town. Not the danger, mind you. But the chance for us to take care of you, because I'm willing to bet that not too many folks took care of you in your time."

"Truth."

Avis's smile deepened. She patted Kelsey's knee and motioned to the easy chair just inside the door. "That old, comfy recliner might be the best spot for nursing this baby, so why don't you settle yourself in there, feed this little one, and let us take care of you for a change."

It sounded good. So good. As if she could be accepted here for what she was. Above and beyond the mistakes. If she stayed here for a week or more, maybe she'd be able to find out something about her family. Unless Vonnie had fabricated the whole thing. She might have. Kelsey wouldn't put it past her. But to come up with a name like Wishing Bridge and talk about the town as if she knew it . . . maybe she had roots here, after all.

She wouldn't make trouble for anyone. That was never the goal. But if she knew more about who she was, where her mother came from, she might be able to make sense of where she was going.

As the baby latched, Kelsey settled into the recliner, with the footrest raised. And when Avis woke her nearly an hour later, it was to tell her that Thea and Jazz were downstairs.

Twelve years of keeping the faith, their pact, and now she had to face them and tell them she'd messed up. It wouldn't be easy. She didn't want to admit failure. But if anyone would understand her and stand by her, it was her two beloved high school friends. The Soul Sisterhood.

CHAPTER SEVEN

Avis tucked the baby into the bassinet while Kelsey checked out her reflection in the bathroom mirror. She looked tired and drawn, and her middle was rounded from her pregnancy, but Avis's words bolstered her.

Thea and Jazz might not understand her choice, but they'd love her through it, and that's why she'd sent the SOS. Because in the end, no matter what, the pledge meant something solid to each of them.

Stretching for courage she didn't quite feel, Kelsey walked downstairs.

Jazz spotted her. Kelsey paused, knowing this was the moment of truth. She took a breath and steeled herself against their reactions. She'd disappointed herself. Why wouldn't her two old friends feel the same way?

"Kelsey!" Jazz usually floated across a room or a runway, with long, rhythmic movements. She had graced the covers of glossy magazines, but she crossed the room quickly now and grabbed Kelsey in a hug. "I'm so glad you called."

"We both are."

Thea had approached from the other side. She spotted Kelsey's damp eyes right off and gave a warning. "No one cries alone in my presence, Kelse. You know this, so mop those eyes, my friend."

"I will." Someone thrust tissues into her hand. She wasn't sure who. "I'm just so happy to see you guys."

"Me, too." Jazz kept her arm around Kelsey's shoulders once Thea hugged her. "I can't believe we're all together again. It's been a long time, ladies."

"Are you gals hungry?" Maggie stepped right into their little circle. "There's some good food in that old kitchen."

"Starved," said Thea. "We were going to stop for food, but it was getting late and we didn't want to mess things up down here. This town is mighty cute, all lit up like a Christmas village with just enough snow falling to make it like a Christmas movie set, but . . ." She looked from Maggie to Jeb and smiled. "It's a little off the beaten path, in case you haven't noticed."

"Oh, we've noticed all right." Jeb seemed pleased to agree. "And we like it more for that very reason. We've got enough of what we need and don't much worry about the rest. Unless it's a tool or something important like that." His grin underscored the value of a good wrench or power sander. "Then Mother and I take a drive."

"Having the town all decked out for Christmas was better than any Manhattan storefront I've ever walked by, and there have been plenty of those over the years," said Jazz. "The whole thing is genuine, and we sensed that, driving in."

"It's all that." Maggie led the way into the kitchen and pointed at the old-style tile counter to her right. "Lasagna, garlic bread, salad, and dressings. You gals go ahead and fill your plates. I've got coffee going, but there's tea and eggnog, too. For a special treat."

"It all looks wonderful." Thea put salad and bread on her plate but passed on the lasagna.

Jazz moved to the counter smoothly, took small portions of each item, and found a spot at the table.

"You sit down, sweetie." Maggie slid out a chair for Kelsey. "I'll dish yours up. Rest while you can."

"Thank you, Maggie." Kelsey took a seat next to Jazz and across from Thea and got straight to the point. "I had a baby last night."

Thea didn't look surprised, but she was in medicine, so the still-rounded abdomen was probably a giveaway. Jazz set down her fork and sighed. "Oh, Kelse. A boy or a girl?"

"A little girl." She kept her eyes directed at the table. She didn't look up. Couldn't look up.

Maggie set a plate in front of her, then said, "Jeb and I are taking our plates into the living room. It's time for *Wheel*, and we never miss the opening because it's such a treat to see what Vanna's wearing. That girl is only eight years younger than me," Maggie gushed, "and doesn't she just look amazing?"

"She sure does," said Jazz.

"Amazing." Thea nodded.

"And such a nice personality," added Kelsey. "Remember how Mrs. Effel used to love that show?"

"I do." Jazz followed her lead. "And crossword puzzles on the porch, watching for us to come home."

"She died, you know." Thea set her fork down as Maggie and Jeb moved into the other room. "Mrs. Effel. About three years back. Cancer."

Another stab of guilt hit Kelsey. "How do you know?"

"I stayed in touch now and again. So she'd know how we were doing. She loved hearing about our schooling, our successes. She said she prayed for us."

"Every single day," Kelsey added.

"Yes, that's right." Thea sighed, toyed with the food, then sighed again. "I liked that she prayed for us. It meant something to me."

"I never contacted her." Jazz shifted her attention from Thea to Kelsey. "I should have."

"She told me she had posters of you all over the walls. And she found a picture online of Kelsey graduating and paid almost ten dollars to have a copy shipped to her. It went on the wall, too."

"She cared."

"About the only one who did for a long time."

"Thank you, Thea." Kelsey reached across the table and set her hand on Thea's. "For staying in touch. For saying thank you. I should have done the same."

"Me, too," Jazz echoed.

"She didn't care about that. Any of that." Thea took a bite of bread and smiled as if she were eating haute cuisine. "She cared about us. And the other girls that came through. We made her happy, and she said that's all that mattered."

"She wouldn't think so much of me now." Kelsey whispered the words around a full-sized lump in her throat.

"Of course she would." Thea set down her fork and spoke frankly. "Things happen, Kelse, and sometimes they happen for good reasons, and sometimes bad ones, but if you want to fully assess this situation, look how far you've come. That's what Joan Effel would tell you. You're a certified teacher with a master's degree. You're young."

Jazz made a face. "Comparatively. We're all turning thirty next year, in case you've forgotten. But that means we're still in our twenties for the moment, and I'm all right with that."

"You're not helping," Thea scolded, but she said it with a grin, and they all laughed. "My point is, this baby is a turning point. Not a dead end. And you've lived the downside of single parenting, so you know what not to do."

"What's her name?" asked Jazz. "The baby, I mean."

"I haven't named her yet. I was on my way to an adoption agency in Harrisburg so I could give her the chance to have a whole life. A mom and a dad who love her. Who could care for her. The storm came up, I had to get off the expressway, and then I hit a patch of ice. The car went airborne, I ended up in a ditch, and if Maggie hadn't seen the lights spin at just that moment, I might not be here now. We could have died out there. Me and the baby."

"You were in labor?"

"I wasn't when I left Potsdam. By the time they found me I was."

"Oh, honey. What a scare." Jazz clutched her hand gently. "I'm so glad it came out okay, Kelsey. Anything else pales in significance to that."

"Is the father in the picture?" Thea asked the question softly, and Kelsey shook her head.

"A con man. I fell for it, one hundred percent. I'm ashamed of myself for being susceptible, but that part's behind me now, except for the blight on my credit record when he took out cards in my name. I had to report him to get the charges off my account, and that wouldn't have looked good to the community. That's part of why I was relocating. The police were nice to me, but everybody dies famous in a small town. It wouldn't take much talk for people to figure out that the con job and the baby were all part of the same package. I needed to start fresh, and I love the hills of Pennsylvania. And that's how I ended up here."

Jazz muttered a word under her breath, then paused, one hand up. "Sorry about that. Far too much swearing goes on in New York, and I promised myself I wouldn't fall into that habit, but every once in a while I succumb." She toyed with the lasagna, raised a bite to her lips, then set it back down. "I'm sorry he duped you."

Kelsey nodded.

"But I'm glad you called us."

"I can't believe you were both available. That's like a miracle in itself."

"Well, the holidays." Jazz shrugged one gorgeous shoulder. "No one shoots over the holidays if they can help it. Unless it's a holiday shoot for next year."

"And I've got time off, too."

"Like it was meant to be."

Thea didn't look as convinced, and Jazz looked cautious. Cautious with the food and careful with her words. But then to keep a figure like Jacinda's, you had to be careful, Kelsey supposed. The front bell rang just then. A few moments later, footsteps came their way.

"Kelsey, I wanted you to meet Susan." Avis brought a middle-aged woman into the kitchen. "The baby is still sound asleep, and Susan will stay in the room alongside yours for the night, just in case there's a problem. After that I'm sure you'll do fine with Maggie and your friends on hand. And if you're all in town on Christmas, we've got the prettiest Christmas Eve service over at the Lutheran church on West Avenue. Maggie and Jeb are generally there, and please feel free to come if you've a mind. There's nothing like starting off the holiday with a beautiful service."

"It sounds nice." Thea smiled at her. "And I don't know how we can thank you for jumping in to help Kelsey, Mrs. Washington."

"Avis, honey. Just Avis. It just so happened I was in the right place at the right time when unexpected car trouble came my way, keeping me from my hospital shift in the city. We're both grateful for that, aren't we, pretty girl?"

"Indubitably." Kelsey smiled at Avis. "Thank you, Avis. And Susan, nice to meet you."

Susan waved. "I'm going to head upstairs and listen for the baby, but she's as peaceful as can be right now. Which means she probably won't be, come the middle of the night."

"And the cycle begins." Avis beamed a smile around the room. "I'll be by tomorrow. I'm going to drop off the breast pump I told you about, and Doctor Brandenburg will be here in the morning to check the baby."

Avis left, Susan went upstairs, and the three old friends sat quietly, looking at one another.

"What do I do?" Kelsey broke the silence in a soft voice, then gnawed her lip. "No job, no place to live, no money, and nothing to fall back on. I not only shouldn't keep this baby, I really have no right to keep her with absolutely no security to my name."

"Here's the thing." Thea took Kelsey's hand in hers. "You're kind of stuck here, aren't you? For the moment, anyway. In this cute little town, because your body needs some recovery time."

Exactly what Avis had told her earlier that day. "I told Avis I'd stay a week and reassess."

"That's a vital seven days after childbirth," Thea said. "So I propose we don't try to make major decisions before Christmas. Jazz and I have a room at the Woodsmoke Inn, and I think it would be good if we all take a few days to let the dust settle. If I had a patient in this situation, that's the advice I'd give, Kelsey. Not much can change in a few days' time, can it?"

Her thoughts sounded quite sensible. "Not really."

"You in, Jazz?"

"Absolutely." Jazz sounded so self-assured. Kelsey would like just a portion of her beautiful friend's natural confidence. "I've got nowhere else to be, so yes. I'm in."

"Then let the holiday reunion of the Sisterhood begin." Thea raised her glass of eggnog in a toast.

Jazz followed suit with her black coffee while Kelsey raised a glass of water. "To us. Sisters by fate, joined forever."

They used to say that all the time, back in the day. They clinked glasses, then Thea stood. "I hate to break up the party, but we promised the inn owner we'd be there by nine, and it's nearly eight thirty."

"Good point." Jazz slipped most of her food into the garbage can under the sink, then set the plate on the counter.

Thea didn't miss the maneuver. Neither did Kelsey. When Jazz turned, she read their faces. "No food after seven. Ever. But I felt rude saying no."

"Why didn't you say so in the car?" Thea asked. "I'd have stopped, Jazz. I didn't realize you were on an eating schedule. Or how strict it was."

"It's a competitive game," Jazz said. "I'll be more careful to eat early over the next few days."

"I'll make sure we do," Thea told her. "My schedule gets so crazy that I grab food whenever, so I don't think about the food or the clock."

"I'd love to live life like that." There was no mistaking the longing in Jazz's voice, followed by a face of regret. "Don't mind me. I'm just tired."

"Then this is the perfect little town to relax in." Maggie came into the kitchen and didn't fuss. She gave both women their coats and scarves. "Come back over in the morning so you can meet the baby, and I'll make my famous French toast bake for you. It's stuffed with pumpkin spice cream cheese for the holidays, and how can that be bad?"

Thea looked ridiculously happy. "I had something like that out west a few years back, in Nebraska. Oh my gosh, I loved it, Maggie."

Jazz aimed one of the most delightful and practiced smiles Kelsey had ever seen at their elderly hostess. "It sounds delightful, Maggie."

She didn't mean it. Kelsey knew that right off, and as Jazz slipped into a jacket not meant for the more rugged winter weather in Western New York, the sleeve of her ballet neckline sweater slipped off her shoulder.

Kelsey swallowed back a sound of concern.

Jazz wasn't just thin. She was bony. And as soon as that thought hit Kelsey, she squelched it.

Jazz was fine. No, she was more than fine, she was exceptional. She probably appeared overly thin because Kelsey felt fat. She felt huge, in fact, and had been feeling that way for several months. How wrong it would be to assess Jazz's choices by her skewed new normal.

"Miss Kelsey?" Susan called softly from the stairway. "Baby's up."

"Thank you." She hugged her friends goodbye, wishing they didn't have to go, then felt absolutely immature for thinking that.

"We'll be back first thing. And maybe Maggie has some jobs for us, to keep us busy." Thea smiled at Maggie and Jeb. "Anything you need. We're both workers, and we're not exactly used to relaxing."

"Well, that might be all the more reason to do it, don't you suppose?" Maggie chirped, smiling. "We'll see about it in the morning. Jeb's promised to build a fire in the fireplace, just like those fancy ski lodge places."

The kindness of strangers. Kelsey's heart stretched wider.

Maggie and Jeb didn't have to do all this. They didn't need to take in a stranger and a newborn baby. And then to open their house to her friends, to serve them food . . .

Who did things like this? Other than in this magically sweet little town?

She'd been focusing on the negative for so long, ever since she'd realized the truth about Chad, and yet here she was, a perfect stranger in a town that had opened its hearts and homes to her.

"See you in the morning, Kelse. And try to sleep when that baby sleeps," Thea reminded her. "Don't push it."

"I will, but sleeping on demand might be an acquired habit."

"Then let's acquire it sooner rather than later." Thea waved while Jazz held the door open, and then they disappeared into the snow-filled night.

For a few seconds she felt alone. So alone. Her two friends going off together, leaving her behind.

And then the baby bleated out a mournful cry, just loud enough to be heard downstairs.

Kelsey's chest squeezed tight.

Maggie gave her a sweet smile, tinged with something else. Longing, maybe? It seemed so. Kelsey started up the stairs. "I'll see to her."

"And rest well, Kelsey."

"I will. Thank you."

She didn't know if she would rest well, but she knew that in the past twenty-four hours she'd been treated with more love and care than she'd known in nearly thirty years, and that was reason enough to relax a little right there.

~

"This is it." Jazz pointed to their left. "The Woodsmoke Inn."

"It doesn't look like an inn." Thea leaned over the steering wheel once she'd parked the car in front of a neon sign that said "Office." At least it would have said it, but one of the F's wasn't working. "I'm pretty sure this might be the Bates Motel."

"Stop that. Do not be putting scary thoughts in my head at Christmas when all I want to think about is pretty music and sparkly trees."

"Have you ever in your life had a Christmas like that, Jazz? Because I haven't."

"Not one," Jazz agreed. "But Mrs. Effel tried to make them nice, didn't she?"

"On a shoestring budget and with bad plumbing."

"I wasn't as grateful as I should have been back then."

"Me, either," Thea acknowledged. "Then I grew up and realized getting sent to Hannah's was the best thing that could have happened to me because I met the two of you. And her. It saved me. It gave me hope when there was none. Faith and hope."

Jazz sighed, still studying the ragged-looking inn. "We were a mess, weren't we?"

"Yes, ma'am. And now." Thea stared at the inn, torn. "Is it as bad as it seems?"

"I'm not sure. I'm stacking it up against some solid hotels I get put up in on a regular basis. It's falling short."

"Ditto. Which means staying here will be an adventure. Don't you think?"

"Either that or a death sentence." Jazz followed Thea out of the car. They walked into the office and faced the gray-haired woman behind the counter.

"We've got a reservation," Thea told her. "Thea Anastas and Jacinda Monroe?"

"You almost missed check-in time." The woman's scolding voice made Jazz draw herself up taller, and Jazz was already tall. "We've got rules here to keep down the riffraff and the payroll. No checkouts before 5:30 a.m. and no check-ins after 9:00 p.m. We don't have to man the night shift that way."

"What if we have a problem during the night?" Thea asked.

"You mean something that can't wait until morning?" Disbelief tinged the woman's words. She drew her eyebrows together. "The emergency number is on your phone in the room. You just pick it up and dial and someone will come running. Not any too fast, mind you, but eventually. Now if you just sign here." She slid a notepad toward Thea. "And we need a card to charge. Just in case."

"Of course." Thea slid her card under the safety glass, briefly wondered if it was bulletproof for a reason, and instantly scolded herself silently. Just because a place was a little down on its luck didn't make it terrible. Necessarily.

"I need your signatures, too."

"For real?" Jazz didn't need to pretend surprise, it was flat-out genuine.

"We keep accurate records here. That way if something happens, we know who's who."

Thea refused to ask what might happen. Her imagination was rich enough to envision multiple scenarios. Lack of sleep and job worries added to the possibilities.

Jazz signed in using an indecipherable script, and as they walked back to the car, Thea spoke softly, "You did that on purpose."

"Yes, I did."

"Passive-aggressive people don't fare well in the long haul, young lady."

"You sound just like her." Jazz burst out laughing in the passenger seat. "How many times do you think Mrs. Effel used those words on me? On us?"

"Enough that we should all have an engraved plaque hanging on our walls," Thea admitted. "Now what if the desk clerk hunts us down during the night to get a proper spelling of your name?"

"That won't happen. She was tired, and if my nose is spot on, she's been nipping at some golden refreshment for an hour or more."

"She was drunk?" Thea hadn't noticed anything amiss.

"On her way to being drunk. Look, I know it's a little pricier and farther away, but they've got some decent places to sleep over in Geneseo. There's a college there, and when I did a Google search, they looked mighty nice by comparison."

"We could go there now." Thea paused and looked up at Jazz. "There's nothing in the rule books that says we have to stay here, Jazz. I can drive another thirty minutes."

"Except that we're paid here. Growing up poor taught me to be sensible with money. Throwing hard-earned money away doesn't sit well."

"Yes, but—"

"No, ma'am." Jazz got out of the car and started forward, leaving Thea no choice but to follow. "If there was a lesson I learned by being broke most of my life, it's that I never want to go back there again. Wasting money is not on the agenda. We're going to consider this an adventure of the highest magnitude, and besides"—she held the door open—"the room is kind of cute, isn't it?"

Thea looked inside and couldn't deny it. "It really is. I was expecting stained comforters and worn carpet. Not country-store-friendly quilts and braided rugs."

"It's crazy clean."

"Sparkling." Thea looked around, puzzled. "This doesn't add up."

"Doesn't matter. There's a solid bed and a tired body. That's enough inducement for me." Jazz set her small bag on one of the luggage racks alongside a closet. "And not a bedbug stain in sight," she added as she swept up the mattress underpinnings. "I've been in some pricey places that had bedbugs over the years. This wins out."

"Total bonus," agreed Thea as she drew her bag into the room and settled it on the second rack. "I'm still trying to figure out why the inside doesn't match the outside, though."

"That's why you took all those years of science classes, and I show off my God-given long legs." Jazz grinned. "You care about the whys of the world. And I'm okay with a more downscale, practical application."

Thea couldn't argue the common sense of the declaration. "Which means we make a good pair."

"We surely do." Jazz disappeared into the bathroom and came back out in record time. She'd tugged comfy, worn pajamas into place, then saw Thea's look of surprise. "Darlin', when you've had as many wedgies as I have been forced to endure for the last decade, loose clothing is my go-to fave. What were you expecting?"

"I love it." Thea sat on the edge of the bed and had to smile. "I've been watching you all these years, from a distance, and you looked so hard to reach, as if the Jazz I knew was gone and this supermodel superwoman had taken her place. But it's still you. Tucked inside. And I love that."

Jazz's face went blank. She didn't look at Thea, not directly. And then she lifted one shoulder as she slipped into the bed. "There are changes, Thea. In all three of us, I expect." Thea couldn't argue the point because it was true. "But I think the true person lingers within us. The

Soul Sisterhood is still linked by so much of the past. Our hopes. Our dreams."

"Did you find your dreams, Jazz? Because I know appearances can be deceiving." The shadowed sorrow in Jazz's eyes made Thea ask the question softly.

"Some." Jazz lifted her chin and met Thea's gaze. "Not all. I consider myself a work in progress."

"Aren't we all?"

"Well, you're a professional," Jazz said frankly. "You've got the education and skills to get a job anywhere. If I quit modeling, where would I go? Where does a long-legged, uneducated biracial woman fit into the normal scheme of things?"

"You're thinking of quitting?" Jazz was built for glamour. She'd pulled herself out of the despair of poverty to become a New York and international sensation. "Education isn't everything, Jazz. You know that. You own the fashion industry; it's like you were born to it."

"Just something I'm thinking about is all." Her face went still again, as if she'd drawn a veil. "But right now I'm too tired to be coherent. Let's get up early and get coffee somewhere before we have breakfast with Kelsey. We can talk then, when I'm awake."

"That's a great idea. And Jazz?"

"Hmm?"

"I'm glad we're here. Glad we're together."

Jazz turned toward her. Her drawn brow warred with her smile, combining to form a kind of wince. "Me, too. Getting away from the city, from my agent, from work." She breathed deep and curled up in the bed. "Saints above, I needed this more than I can say. More than I knew."

"Me, too."

Jazz tucked noise blockers into her ears while Thea got ready for bed. Within quick minutes she was tucked in and turned out the light.

The room felt fine. The bed was solid and clean. The odd woman was a concern, but Thea had double locked the door. Just in case.

She fell asleep, sound asleep, in full appreciation of a good mattress, and when a gut-clenching sound awakened her at 3:49 a.m., she almost shot out of bed.

Jazz didn't move. *The earplugs,* Thea realized.

She lifted her cell-phone flashlight and aimed it around the room. There was nothing wrong. Nothing moving, nothing out of place. Stillness surrounded her.

Then what had woken her?

She tiptoed across the room and edged the curtain back slightly. The parking lot lay quiet. No footprints marred the half inch of snow that had fallen in the last five hours.

She'd just crawled back under the covers, wondering what had shot her up out of bed, when the sound came again. Not close. But not all that far, either.

Howling.

Long, clear, plaintive, drawn-out howling. Howls that were answered by other creatures yipping and barking. But not the full, deep-throated barks of a big dog or the incessant and annoying yaps of a small dog.

These were in between.

Wolves?

The thought made her shudder. Were there wolves in these hills? She had no idea. The howl sounded once more, long and full, then nothing.

She huddled beneath the blankets, suddenly chilled, and it was a long time before she was able to relax enough to doze off again. She wished she could wear earplugs and trust that nothing would go wrong, but she couldn't. First, because the thought of not hearing approaching danger alarmed her. Her cautious nature didn't cede control easily.

Second, because she couldn't use earplugs when she was on call, so why get her body accustomed to something she could only use sporadically?

It made no sense, but when Jazz came out of the shower the next morning, looking beautiful and well rested, Thea decided she might have to rethink her position. A good night's sleep was a wonderful asset.

CHAPTER EIGHT

Temptation pushed Hale to tap the Facebook icon the next morning. He wasn't stalking his ex-wife. But if she'd posted Christmas pictures of Michael, he'd like to see them.

He'd looked last December and managed to break his own heart all over again when the Internet offered up pictures of a happy four-year-old. His perfectly beautiful little son, except he wasn't Hale's child by blood.

His finger shook slightly.

A surge of longing bit him, bit him so deep it made his stomach clench with just the thought of bringing up the page, but then his head overruled his heart.

He put the phone away and got ready for work.

Three hours into the early-morning shift, he met Garrett for coffee in Warsaw.

Hale strode in, saw Garrett flirting with the counter girl, and grabbed a table near the corner with full view of both entrances—total cop. Two women sat in the booth kitty-corner from him. They hadn't looked up when he came in, heads bent, deep in conversation. A conversation he could hear quite well, with the lack of background noise. He found the short reprieve from the usual endless loop of Christmas music refreshing, and the fact that he could hear their words so clearly a touch disconcerting. But it wasn't like he was hiding himself . . . or his uniform. He settled back in his seat to wait for Garrett and coffee.

"When did you hear it, Thea?" The taller woman with a mass of long, dark hair looked and sounded worried. "Are you sure it was a wolf?"

"Just before 4:00 a.m., and of course I'm not sure," the smaller woman answered. She made a face that almost made him laugh, a face that had "city slicker" written all over it. "It howled like a crazy banshee in one of those horror movies we weren't supposed to watch when we were kids."

"Well, this is the boonies, no lie."

Hale grinned because while Western New York was considered agriculturally friendly, Wishing Bridge was set about forty minutes from the suburbs of Rochester and Buffalo, so not exactly at the ends of the earth.

"What'd you do? And why didn't you wake me?"

"I decided to wait for the full-fledged attack before I went to those extremes," the smaller woman quipped, and her reply deepened Hale's smile. "You were sound asleep. Why should both of us be disturbed? Besides, we've got to be on top of our game if we're going to be any help to Kelsey, right?"

Kelsey. Right or wrong, his ears pricked up. Eyes down, he pulled out his phone and pretended to be doing something.

"Yes, ma'am. And smelling the breakfast here is putting me in mind of that French toast Maggie promised us."

These must be the friends Avis had mentioned. And yes, he listened closer now, because he was a cop first and when something seemed slightly off, it generally was. Or worse.

"Can you eat things like that, Jazz?"

The woman sitting on the far left from Hale shrugged.

"Do you have to watch everything you eat every day?"

The tall woman sighed, uncomfortable. Then she frowned. "Only if I want to keep my job, darlin'. But that's a whole other conversation."

"Job security a little shaky?"

"Yes, ma'am."

"Well, let's lay it all out on the table then." The smaller woman leaned closer. "Our medical practice got bought out by one of the Pittsburgh megamedicals, and my position was eliminated along with six others. Every doctor and nurse hired last year was let go four days ago. So after all those years of school and mac-and-cheese dinners and Little Debbie snack cakes, I got a pink slip from my first job as a big-city nurse practitioner."

"Thea, I had no idea." Genuine sympathy deepened the tall woman's features, features Hale recognized from . . . somewhere.

Garrett was bringing two coffees and two breakfast sandwiches down the aisle when the tall, gorgeous woman spoke. "Well, let's form a new branch of our sisterhood, Theadora, because if we're sharing truths here, I left the Castlebury Agency in mid-November to get a grip on my eating disorder. Again."

"Oh, Jazz." The smaller woman laid a hand on top of the other woman's. "I'm so sorry to hear that."

Jazz.

Hale swallowed hard because now he recognized the stately woman facing his direction.

Jazz Monroe had scored big in modeling. She'd been seen on the arm of some of baseball's biggest stars and a couple of high-level politicians, too. If he hadn't seen her on TV, hawking makeup and underwear and a totally out-of-character off-road SUV, she'd also graced the cover of almost every female-friendly magazine at the grocery store checkout.

And he was pretty sure she'd hit the famous swimsuit issue of one national magazine several times.

She was here, in the coffee shop, across from him, and he was listening in on her private conversation. Did that make him a total moron, or did it just add to the mystery surrounding the single mother who sounded and looked like his mother's old friend?

"I had them make your coffee extra hot, so give it a minute, okay?" Garrett slid into the seat flanking the other side of Hale's table. "If we get a call, it won't cool off instantly in the squad car."

Both women turned, as if just noticing him. The fact that Jazz Monroe hadn't noticed him was an instant smack to his ego, a well-deserved hit for listening in on private conversations.

"Thanks, Garrett. I appreciate it."

"Well, it's Christmas Eve and you said you were doing a double. I figured I'd treat you this morning. Merry Christmas."

The women stood to leave.

So did Hale.

When the shorter one turned, he held out his hand. "I'm Deputy Hale Jackson, and I couldn't help but overhear part of your conversation."

"Which means, of course, we need to kill you." Jazz deadpanned a look he'd seen her use in commercials, and he laughed.

"I'd prefer you didn't, but first, yes, I recognized you, Ms. Monroe. Welcome to Wishing Bridge." He didn't linger on her but turned quickly to the woman on his right. "And I'm pretty sure what you heard last night were coyote howls."

"There are coyotes here? In New York?"

He nodded. "They moved in a couple of decades back and seemed to like the area. They don't bother folks much, but when they get howling at night, or join up for a hunt, it can be disturbing. After a while you get used to them."

"I don't think I would, but then I thought that about police sirens, too, and I was wrong. I'm Thea Anastas. We're in town for Christmas because a friend of ours was in an accident."

No guile. No pretense. Hale marked both in the plus column for Kelsey McCleary. He'd found the old saying about birds of a feather flocking together to be generally true. Good folks found one another. So did bad ones. His gut told him there was nothing bad about these two, and that brought his concern for Maggie and Jeb down a few pegs. The thought of how Kelsey knew Jazz Monroe created a whole different circle of queries, but curious rather than worrisome.

"Hale's the one who rescued her."

Thea looked at Garrett when he spoke, then turned her attention straight back to Hale. "It was you? Seriously?"

Hale would never understand getting extra kudos for doing exactly what he'd been hired and trained to do. He hadn't understood it with football, and he didn't get it now with police work. "It's my job."

"Yes, but I heard the news reports on the drive here, they said the car had disappeared from sight. I can't even imagine how different this all might have turned out, Deputy Jackson. Thank you." She reached out and gripped his hands, surprising him. "You have no idea how grateful we are. Both of us."

A firm, light grip. An honest gaze. Seemingly nice and not crazy worried even though he had just heard her admit she was out of work. Any company feeling it necessary to excise people during the holidays meant Scrooge was alive and well in some corners of the marketplace.

"I'm just glad I found her. And she's in good hands at Maggie's place now."

"Exactly where we're headed." Jazz smiled at him.

Hale was six one. She met him eye to eye, and there was a substantial height difference between her and Thea Anastas. Kelsey fell somewhere in the middle, an interesting trio, making him wonder what had brought the women together. But then, he was a cop, and he tended to question everything. Possibly a habit he needed to break more often.

"Maggie's a great cook and has a heart of gold. I'm going to stop by there later myself. Enjoy your day, ladies. And your stay in Wishing Bridge."

He slipped back into his seat while Garrett stared after the women. "That was—"

Hale didn't let him finish. "Jazz Monroe. They're in town to help our accident victim. They're old friends."

"Well, Merry Christmas to me." Garrett leaned around the seat to gaze out the window as the women crossed to the small car.

"You're a moron."

"Agreed. But with a fine appreciation for God-given beauty. Who'd have predicted this turn of events?"

Not Hale, but Garrett's words annoyed him. *Why?* Because Garrett thought Jazz was hot or because businesses fired people at the holidays or because the women were ready to shower him with praise for simply doing his job? It was none of those. He knew that, but still anger built within him, as if injustices should be outlawed forevermore. "I just call it life. Full of surprises. All day, every day."

Garrett started to speak, then held his tongue and sipped his coffee. He glanced around the restaurant, as if there was something to see. There wasn't, but he avoided eye contact because he had heard the down note in Hale's voice.

Christmas.

Christmas did this to him. It made him bark and snarl when there was no cause. It made him think of what could have been if his wife hadn't cheated on him. It made him doubt. It made him doubt his self-worth and the integrity of the human race.

Maybe there was nothing odd about Kelsey McCleary and her plight. Maybe his holiday cynicism was wreaking havoc with his judgment.

The breakfast sandwich that had smelled so good five minutes ago now tasted like dust.

The coffee burned his upper lip and tongue.

He'd work as much as he could over the next seventy-two hours. It suited him, and it offered other deputies the chance to celebrate the holiday with their families.

And then he'd move on, again. Calving time loomed, keeping the first six weeks of the new year mind-numbingly busy.

And then spring would ease over the hills, into the valleys. The shadows would shorten. The days would grow longer. And he'd find it easier to breathe again.

"I'm heading out." He took the coffee and left the sandwich.

"Catch you later."

He didn't respond. Was he being a jerk?

Yeah.

But Garrett would forgive him. Garrett understood. If he got too bad, Garrett and Ben would give him a shot to the arm and tell him to wise up. Get over himself.

But they wouldn't do that at Christmas. Never at Christmas. Because they knew it wouldn't do one bit of good.

~

"Susan, who are all those people?" Kelsey settled the sleeping baby into her eyelet-trimmed basket and gestured outside. "It's just gotten light, and there's a crowd gathering. Do they do some sort of Christmas festival thing here?"

"No." Susan crossed the room, tipped back the curtain, then let it slide right back into place. "Reporters."

Kelsey couldn't have heard her right. "Reporters?"

"There are TV trucks and cameramen in every direction."

"Why? What's happened?"

"You, apparently."

"Me?" Kelsey definitely couldn't have heard right.

"Human interest, honey." Maggie came into the room and made a face of regret. "They've got the whole street blocked off, talking about what happened the other night, about how Hale saved you. It's on every local news channel, and I saw two of the big cable networks out there. And that guy who tracks down the weather storms all over . . . he's there, too."

"Oh my gosh." Kelsey sank onto the edge of the bed. Reporters. Television crews. Cable news. Her quiet, private plan had just exploded into a newsworthy event. "This can't be happening."

"People love a story with a happy ending, especially at Christmas," Maggie reminded her. "A snowstorm rescue. A baby delivered in a firehouse. All nestled in a snowy little town. Kelsey, this has Hallmark movie written all over it."

"But it can't." She stood and faced Maggie and Susan. "I wasn't supposed to be here." Emotions swirled up, choking her. "I was supposed to be in Harrisburg, have the baby there, and give her up for adoption. She has no father, and I promised myself I wouldn't repeat my mother's mistakes. My baby deserves the best life she can be given, but how do I do this now?" She waved a hand toward the window. "When everyone in the country will see me? See her? And if they can't, they'll find pictures online and use them, because there is no such thing as privacy anymore." She dropped her head into her hands, wishing she could think clearly.

"Kelsey."

She didn't look up, despite the warmth in Maggie's voice, but when the older woman shrugged an arm around her, it felt good. So good.

"Now listen to me, honey. I don't know the whys or the wherefores of this whole situation." Maggie's voice stayed quietly sensible. "And I appreciate what you were going to do, the sacrifice you were willing to make, maybe more than most, because my sister gave a baby up for adoption back in the day. Lord have mercy, it took some raw and wonderful courage for her to do that, so I know what you're saying. But then there's this."

Kelsey dropped her hands.

Maggie wasn't pointing to the reporters, thronging outside. She indicated the baby, tucked in the trimmed bassinet. "Sometimes our plans aren't his plans, Kelsey."

"His? Whose?"

"God's."

Shame bit deep because Mrs. Effel had made sure that each girl went to church on Sundays, and Wednesdays, too, if their church held services then. Kelsey went, not because she wanted to, and certainly not because she believed, but because Mrs. Effel would have been disappointed in her if she hadn't gone. "I don't—"

She started to explain how she wasn't a believer, but then she looked up, into Maggie's understanding eyes and Susan's sympathetic gaze. She swallowed back her words, unwilling to insult either of these women, but equally unwilling to jump on the bandwagon. Life was life, you did what you could, and then you died. If you were lucky, and maybe a good person, you left it a better place than it was when you entered. Although these days, with troubles running amok around the globe, Kelsey was pretty sure one person didn't make all that much difference.

"Timing isn't always of our choosing." Maggie laid a hand on her cheek, and this much they could agree upon. "Maybe this change in plans has happened for a reason, Kelsey."

"Maggie's right," Susan said. "Sometimes the best-laid plans get thwarted by circumstances we never thought to expect."

"But in the end I have to do right by the baby, don't I?" Kelsey faced them frankly. "Isn't that what motherhood is all about? Sacrificing and putting your child first? I'm a certified elementary-school teacher with a solid résumé and great references from Canton and Potsdam, but I don't have a full-time job. I have no medical coverage and no money. I don't even have an address right now, because I gave up my little apartment in Canton so I could slip away and not face gossip about being pregnant and alone and swindled by my boyfriend. Then Mother Nature went berserk, and you know the rest." She walked over to the bassinet and looked down. "She is so perfect. So sweet. And she has a chance at a beautiful and wonderful future. I don't want to be selfish and ruin that for her. I *can't*," she told the women. "I made a promise to myself that I wouldn't repeat my mother's mistakes, and yet, here I am. But having the world know about it, about me, well . . ." She grimaced as noises from below became audible on the second floor. "This puts me in a spotlight I never sought and surely do not want."

"Mother?" Jeb's voice called up the stairs.

"Yes, Jeb?"

"Kelsey's friends are here. They had to kind of sneak in the back way, but some of the reporters caught sight of them and grabbed a few pictures while looking for an interview. Pesky folk when they're at your front door, that's for certain."

"We'll be right down." Maggie had moved to the hallway railing so she wouldn't wake the baby. "Hello, girls."

Jazz and Thea.

The thought of her two friends, gathering with her in this small town, bolstered her. They'd figure this out together. They always had. And now that Maggie and Susan knew the backstory, they could all speak frankly.

"Is it Christmas Eve?" Kelsey asked, just realizing the date.

"It is. Jeb and I will be going to the service a little after six tonight. We go early to get a seat."

"It's the same at Holy Name," said Susan. "It's kind of nice to be crowded at church, isn't it? Brings back old times."

"You can stay here and rest, Kelsey," Maggie assured her. "No one's going to push you to go. Just think of it. Baby doll's first Christmas."

Her daughter's first Christmas.

No home. No money. No name. No gifts. No "Baby's First Christmas" ornament, the kind of thing loving parents bought for their child.

You're whining. And borrowing trouble. Stop it. You're not normally like this. What's gotten into you?

Hormones.

She'd read about it beforehand, in one of the many books she'd taken out of the library. "Knowledge is power," an adage she believed. But knowing she was going to experience hormone spikes and drops and being able to do something about it were two very different things.

Mentally shoving her emotions aside, she walked downstairs.

CHAPTER NINE

"Folks, I understand what you're trying to do, but you can't block the road and the sidewalk." Less than an hour after grabbing coffee together, Hale and Garrett faced a throng of reporters clogging Wyoming Hill Road. "It's Christmas Eve, and the people who live in these houses have things to do. Right now they're thwarted, because they can't get out of their driveways between the piled-up snow and the crowd of reporters."

"Deputy Jackson, can we get an interview with you?" an unfamiliar middle-aged woman called out. She used a pleasant tone of voice, and that got her a positive response.

"Move the vans, clear the road, and I'll answer any questions you have. Deal?" Hale flashed a smile at the middle-aged woman, and she grinned back.

"We can do that."

In five minutes most of the vans had pulled back, enough to give the locals room to navigate to shops or stores or wherever they might need to go on a busy preholiday morning.

"You should put the hat on," Garrett teased as the cameramen and reporters began to reconvene. "Give them a true glimpse of how you looked the night of the storm."

"And you should put a lid on it." Hale faced the crowd with a well-practiced look on his face. If nothing else, being an NFL quarterback had schooled him in the fine art of postgame press conferences. This wasn't much different. He leaned closer to Garrett and spoke softly. "I'd rather have them covering a story like this during the holidays than a host of other options. Right?"

"Amen."

The press began calling out questions to him, shouting over each other. He held up a hand.

They all got quiet.

He loved that. He loved how the uniform could have a positive effect, most of the time. "I've got ten minutes before I'm on to my next assignment. One at a time is going to get more done, agreed?"

They nodded.

"You." He pointed to the woman who'd approached him first. "You're first."

"What led you to go farther into the field that night? You've already said there were no visible tracks of a vehicle, nothing in the snow, no lights, no noise. A lot of people would have gotten back in their car and driven away. You didn't." She leaned her microphone closer. "Why?"

He could go the politically correct route and keep the grumpy county commissioner off his boss's neck. Or he could tell the truth. "I prayed."

Silence fell over the crowd.

"I know Maggie Tompkins, the woman who lives here." He indicated the house behind him. "Maggie's the woman who called it in. First, she likes me." He smiled, giving them a perfect photo op for still shots. "She'd never send me out into a wild storm for no good reason. But second, she wouldn't have called it in if she wasn't sure of what she'd seen. And knowing Maggie, if the car had been able to right itself, or turn around, she'd have seen that as well."

"Bad storm, low visibility. Only if there was a break in the action, correct? So the car could have righted itself and gone on its merry way, and no one might have been the wiser because of low visibility."

"I weighed that," he admitted. "And I almost got back into my car. It was a fierce night, and there was absolutely no reason for me to check further. There was no evidence of a car, tracks, spinout, or anything like that. But as I reached my door, I put the whole thing in heaven's hands. I had to, because if I turned my back on someone in trouble, and things went bad, I'd have to live with that. And as I asked for guidance, I looked back over my shoulder and saw a flash of pink. Just a flash, like when your eyes adjust, but it was enough to tell me God heard me. He sent a sign."

"You think God had something to do with that flash of pink light?" The reporter asking the question tried to mask the doubt in his voice, but he didn't quite succeed.

Hale raised his hands. "I learned the importance of timing in the NFL."

Most of the crowd nodded, familiar with his former career.

"And I try not to mess with God's timing. When I saw the flash, I knew it wasn't my eyes playing tricks on me. Something was out there in that field. Even though there was absolutely less than nothing to go on, and there was nothing to explain the color pink, it had to come from somewhere. Or someone."

"What did you do?"

He grinned and grimaced on purpose. "I closed my car door, pulled down the earflaps on my Yukon hat, and broke a path through the snow. And there it was, nearly a hundred yards out, tipped nose down into a ditch. And if Ms. McCleary hadn't turned on the engine right then, to warm her car for five minutes, I might have missed it again. But I didn't, she's safe, and that baby's safe."

"And all because you prayed." A different reporter's voice chimed in, soft but strong.

"I believe so, ma'am. Here in Wishing Bridge, we've got a powerful belief in wishes and prayers. How they're linked and how folks working together can make things come true."

"Do you miss your NFL career, Deputy Jackson?"

Folks always got around to asking that, as if having to leave football was the worst thing that could happen to a man.

It wasn't.

Giving up the child you loved outranked a change of career by a long shot. "I did at first." He'd been asked this question often, and his usual answer was pretty glib, but he didn't give that response today. Not on Christmas Eve.

"It seemed harsh to have it all taken away from me because of an injury, but once I got done feeling sorry for myself, I realized I'd been given a chance. Another chance," he corrected himself. "I had some money in the bank. Family here. Great land, wonderful people, and I'd always said if I didn't make it in football, I wanted to be a cop." He grinned, showing his wish had come true. "Because in the grand scheme of things, maybe, just maybe"—he played the crowd of cameras with his gaze—"this is how it was meant to be. If I was still in football, playing against the Ravens this weekend, I wouldn't have been here to find that car." Hale shrugged. "Things worked out, didn't they?" He raised his watch for the crowd to see. "And now we've got a—"

"A meeting inside the house," Jeb Tompkins interrupted from just behind him. "Mother's put out a request for you men to step inside while I dole out some of our best Wishing Bridge Christmas cookies to our new friends." Jeb moved into the crowd, carrying a large silver tray filled with cookies. All kinds of cookies, like you'd see at a huge party. "Here you all go. My wife is feeling bad that you're out here in the cold, but there's too many o' youse to ask the whole lot in." He grinned and started wandering through the crowd as folks thanked him for the cookies. "Hale and Garrett are needed inside, my wife's orders, and if the men in this crowd know anything about being married, if Mama ain't happy, ain't nobody happy."

Hale and Garrett took the opportunity to slip into the house through the door at the far end of the driveway. The old-fashioned side door entered on a small landing. To their right, stairs continued to the basement. On the left, a shorter flight led to the vintage kitchen.

Maggie greeted them from the kitchen. The back of their house overlooked part of the state forest preserve edging the upper reaches of the village, a perfect spot from which clandestine reporters could try and get candid shots of Kelsey and the baby. For some reason, that thought unnerved Hale when it really shouldn't have. They were just pictures, after all. Of regular people.

"What a morning!" Maggie flapped her apron as she came their way. "Come with me, you two. I know you've probably eaten already, but I made my French toast casserole, and there's enough for an army. If you boys wouldn't mind having coffee with us, we'd appreciate a little company from the outside. That crowd has us pretty well landlocked, as you can see."

"I'd love some coffee," Hale said.

He had intended to stop in at some point today to do his follow-up. The crowd of reporters had given him the perfect excuse. He kicked off his boots in the entry, hung his thick wool coat on a hook, and entered the kitchen, with Garrett following.

"We're in the dining room," Maggie told him, and that subtle change lightened his step. Maggie and Jeb hadn't had reason to celebrate for a while, and hosting people in the dining room was a move forward for the older couple. "It seemed fancier that way," Maggie said, "and Christmas should be a time for fancy, shouldn't it?"

"A time of rejoicing." He took Maggie's hand and held it when she paused. "You're amazing, Maggie Tompkins. And the cookies?" He thrust his chin toward the front yard. "A perfect touch."

"Folks are less inclined to write mean stuff when they're well fed. And I think every neighbor around the bend has dropped by with cookies and a huge tray from Betty at the bakery. Seemed like a good time to share."

"True words." Garrett gave her a half hug. "Can I take anything into the dining room for you?"

"Oh, you sweet thing, no. You boys go ahead, you've been working. Let me wait on you for a change."

She'd spent her life taking care of others, including Hale and Ben when their mother was caught at work, or if their father had taken off with the grocery money, leaving nothing but empty cupboards behind.

Maggie always had a bit put by . . . her saying, not Hale's. So when he crossed into the large dining room, the spread on the buffet did her proud. "This isn't brunch. It's a feast, Maggie."

He gave the room a general wave, then stopped.

Those eyes. Her eyes. Kelsey McCleary's eyes.

They grabbed him, just like they had two days before.

Her hair looked blonder now. Shiny clean and wavy, hanging just below her shoulders, with hints of honey streaking through.

She stared at him.

He stared back.

And if Avis hadn't broken the silence, he might have stood there staring forever, and wasn't that an odd turn of events?

"Kelsey, I don't know if you remember him, but this is Hale Jackson, honey. He's the deputy that braved the storm to find you."

"Um, I was there, too." Garrett raised one eyebrow. "But everyone seems to forget that little detail."

"A day late and a dollar short, I believe, Deputy." Avis poked at Garrett, and he laughed, which was good because it took the crowd's attention off Hale.

"It's good to see you looking so much better, Ms. McCleary," Garrett continued. "That was a rough night and an even rougher situation."

She stood. Then she rounded the table until she was standing right in front of Hale, facing him. He couldn't turn away if he wanted to, and he realized he didn't want to. Not in the least.

She seemed smaller than she had that night. Of course, delivering a baby might have been responsible for some of that, and he felt a little silly for even thinking it.

"I'm so glad you're here. I wanted to thank you in person. You saved my life that night. And my daughter's life. Thank you, Deputy Jackson."

And there it was again, the voice, so like Nora's. The eyes a spitting image, like his grandma used to say. "Hale."

She looked puzzled, maybe because it took him so long to say it or maybe because he was staring at her as if she had two heads. She didn't. She had one very pretty one, with a soft smile that seemed utterly sincere and eyes that held that same flash of fear or resignation he had sensed the other night. He pushed it aside.

"Just call me Hale. I figure if this story goes viral, and that would be my guess right now, judging from my mother's text that says"—he pulled out his phone, deadpanned a look to everyone at the table and read—"My phone is blowing up with likes and comments, the world is going crazy about you and that lovely girl and the baby. You're going viral." He slanted his gaze back to Kelsey. "I think that's indicative of a first-name basis, don't you? Since we've gone viral together?"

She flinched, as if the thought of going viral with him wasn't a whole lot of wonderful. For some reason, he wished it were, and wondered—for just a moment—if it could be.

"Kelsey, if you've got to go viral with someone, it might as well be a smokin' hot guy who wears a uniform so well," Jazz teased, and when Kelsey looked her way, the supermodel offered an encouraging smile.

Then Kelsey smiled back up at Hale, and his heart did that weird hop, skip, and jump thing again. For the fourth time. Which was ridiculous, wasn't it?

"Hale, here's a plate for you, and one for Garrett." Maggie handed them each a plate that was more like a monster-sized platter. "You boys eat up, and thank you for coming over and clearing the street. I don't know what would happen if there was an emergency, for real. How would equipment get through?"

"We'd guide them in and guide them out, same as always, Maggie." Garrett slung his arm around her shoulders. "Thanks for doing all this."

"I liked it." She sounded almost guilty to be enjoying her little breakfast party, as if relishing life after losing a loved one shouldn't be allowed.

Time helped. Time healed. Hale knew that. But it didn't let him forget the boy growing up in another man's house nearly three thousand miles away.

"Hale, take my seat. I've got a few calls to make before the doctor gets here, so I'm going to excuse myself and head to the front room. The signal's better there," Avis said, then she looked at Maggie. "These old homes are built like fortresses, aren't they? It's mighty hard to get a good cell signal anywhere on this side of the hill, but especially in the older homes." She moved to the living room across the entry hall, leaving the seat directly across from Kelsey open.

Hale finished filling his plate and sat down. He wouldn't insult Maggie by taking tiny bits of this and that, and when he took the first bite of her famous potato bake, hunger swept through him.

The women chatted, Garrett turned on the charm full force, and within two minutes, all the female attention had shifted toward his dark-haired, more amiable cousin. Not like that was a surprise or anything.

Hale raised his fork when Maggie brought a carafe of fresh coffee into the room. "You outdid yourself. This is all amazing."

"Consider it my way of saying thanks for all you do, Hale." She set the carafe down and took her seat at the head of the table to his left. "Did I hear you bought a property on Main Street, or is that a small-town rumor?"

Like any small town, Wishing Bridge had its share of talkers, and not all of them got the story straight. "Not a rumor this time. I bought the old Franklin building for a dry-goods store."

"For your mother." She put a hand on his left arm, approving.

"You know Mom. She's always wanted a storefront, and Max Reichert has been schooling me on how to do it affordably. And get a sizable tax write-off at the same time. I'm following his lead and putting a rental apartment upstairs. Mom will have the retail space below. A little sweat equity over the winter, and she should be able to get things started come spring."

"Perfect timing."

"What's a dry-goods store?" Kelsey joined their conversation and turned those wide, gray eyes his way. The combination of voice and appearance tweaked his cop instincts again. Common sense warned him to back off because she'd been through enough the past few days. He deliberately pushed his questions aside.

"It's an old-fashioned term my mother loves," he explained. "She's going to carry an eclectic mess of things. Vintage clothing—"

"All the rage right now, and some of it is absolutely beautiful," Kelsey said. "I love those old-time dresses with the fitted waists and the flared skirts."

He pictured her as she spoke. She'd be beautiful in one of those classic styles. She was beautiful here. Now. In jeans and a T-shirt. He quieted that thought and pulled himself back to the conversation. "She says there's a demand. How long that demand will last is anyone's guess."

"What else will she carry?"

"Sewing and needlework stuff. Whatever that means."

"Embroidery thread, yarns, patterns, and calicos. Plus notions," added Maggie. "And quirky things, too. Old style. It's been her dream for a long time to have a storefront in town. She built an online business before it was trendy, so this is a big step forward. And I think she's including an old-fashioned candy counter, so folks can buy some old favorites."

"Well, there you go." Hale smiled at her. "Maggie's got the scoop. I don't even know what half that stuff is."

"Folks will love it," Maggie declared. She faced Kelsey more directly. "Our town is coming back to life, Kelsey. It wasn't quite dead but close enough after the auto-parts factory shut its doors. We watched our kids grow up and leave. People retired and headed south. South Carolina, Florida, Arizona." She sighed. "For almost two decades we kept sliding downhill, and there didn't seem to be any way to stop it. Not once the jobs were gone. And then Max Reichert came to town, a big man with a quiet dream."

"He's helping?"

"He set the tone for the revival by buying old buildings and fixing them up, one by one," said Hale. "He rents the upper floors as apartments to cover the mortgage and utilities, and the bottom floors he rents for pennies on the dollar to help businesses get on their feet. When I came back to town, I saw what he was doing and realized the best way to rebuild a town was to jump on board and help him do it. Why invest elsewhere when Wishing Bridge is home?"

"And it's working," Maggie added. "Betty wouldn't be able to make money at the bakery if she had to pay a thousand dollars a month in rent."

"Along with eight other retail businesses that have come back to life."

"That's amazing." Kelsey leaned forward slightly. "Why is he doing this?"

"He's retired from law enforcement and loves fixing things. And he wanted a quiet, sweet town to live in and invest in. We're fortunate he chose Wishing Bridge."

"Either fortunate or the good Lord heard folks wishing and hoping for a chance to revitalize the town," said Maggie. "Once the factory was gone and jobs dried up, there wasn't much reason for the young and the smart to stay. You don't know how much one thing affects another until something goes wrong and things unravel. But Max's big heart is bringing hope back to the village."

The baby cried upstairs, interrupting brunch. Twin spots of moisture appeared on Kelsey's shirt. It wasn't like Hale was trying to notice, but it happened too quickly not to.

As Kelsey realized what had just happened, she looked positively mortified. She shot up, out of the chair, arms folded around her chest.

"It takes a bit to get this all in tune, doesn't it?" Maggie followed her upstairs, leaving the rest of them in an awkward quiet.

Avis returned from the living room as Jeb came through from the kitchen. "Jeb, do you and Maggie need a ride down to the church tonight?"

"We've taken to walking, and there's no ice or snow expected, but I appreciate the offer. If the weather changes, though, we'd like that. No sense clogging the parking lot with extra cars, small as it is."

"What time is the service?"

Hale didn't miss the surprise in Jazz Monroe's eyes as her friend Thea posed the question.

"It's at seven, but it's best to go early to get a seat," Avis advised.

"And they've got a living Nativity, too, set up just outside as you come into the church. When you go in, there's no baby. When you come out, there is."

"If only it were that easy in real life," quipped Thea. "I'm a nurse practitioner, so I know the reality behind birthing scenes, but I'd love to attend the service tonight. Jazz, you can either go with me or stay here with Kelsey. I'm okay going on my own."

"And Kelsey would be fine here on her own for a couple of hours. She can call me if there's a problem, and I can come right up the hill if necessary," added Avis.

"Or I can come by and check on things." Hale knew he shouldn't make the offer, but he did it anyway. She intrigued him. Not just her looks, or the innocence that seemed at odds with having a baby with no father in sight. But everything about her fascinated him, as if she was supposed to be here now and he was meant to find her that night. An absurd concept, and yet . . . it seemed right.

"You're working tonight, too?" Avis asked as Hale and Garrett pushed their chairs back.

"Giving the guys with families some holiday time off."

"You've got a good heart, Hale Jackson."

Sometimes, yes, but he took the doubles at Christmas for more selfish motives. So he wouldn't think about how alone he was while the world celebrated the birth of our Lord, and instead tried to escape the loss of his son.

"We've got to head out, break time is over, and while Christmas Eve is usually a quiet day—"

"And night."

Garrett was right, the holiday tended to be a blessedly quiet two or three days as long as no storms loomed.

"I figure the boss would like us to get back to work. Ladies, it was lovely to have brunch with you. And actually, I need to follow up on a few things with Kelsey about the accident, so I'll stop by later," he said as they moved toward the door. "Maybe the reporters will be home for Christmas Eve with their families by then."

"One can only hope," agreed Avis.

The doorbell rang. Jeb appeared a moment later with Dr. Brandenburg. "Avis, the doc's here to check on the baby like you asked."

"Ethan." Avis put out a hand. "Thanks for doing this. I know you're slammed right now. Any word on Doctor Wolinski?"

Ethan clapped Hale on the back, then took Avis's hand, looking stressed. "The prognosis isn't good."

Dr. Brandenburg had come to town as a fill-in doctor the previous summer. He'd taken the temporary job with Hillside Medical while waiting on an opening back in Chicago. A tragic accident had taken the lives of his sister and brother-in-law. As a result, he'd been named guardian of their two small children, and there was no way he could accept an intense critical-care fellowship in a busy urban setting and give his niece and nephew the time they needed and deserved. He'd brought them here for an interim assignment, hoping to go back to Chicago in early summer.

But when their local doctor had suffered a massive cardiac episode a few days ago, the temporary helper had become the man in charge, a position he hadn't wanted or counted on. Taking over a medical practice that was established over forty years before was a monumental task. Doc Wolinski had been taking care of people in their area for generations. Those were big shoes for a stand-in to fill.

Avis looked sad. "I am sorry to hear that. I knew it was bad, but . . ." her voice trailed off. "My expertise is limited, but if I can help in any way, call on me, Ethan. This is a tough spot to be in, and in the dead of winter, besides."

His expression echoed her words. Their town was small but spread out, and having a medical practice nearby had been a true lifesaver to the locals. Winter storms often precluded driving very far when Lake Erie kicked up her gale-force heels. To be down to one doctor was less than ideal.

"I could have brought Kelsey and the baby down to your office, but I didn't want to risk germs with flu going around, so thank you for doing this." Avis indicated the stairway. "She's feeding the baby. Her milk just came in, she's a primipara and understandably shaken by circumstance."

"A prima what?" Garrett asked, frowning.

"First time pregnancy or birthing," Thea explained.

"And that's my cue to go back to work." Garrett waved to the doctor as he headed for the back door. "Those of you I don't see later, have a Merry Christmas."

Hale followed him more quietly. They'd think he was weird for not saying Merry Christmas.

So be it.

He'd rather be odd than choke the words out of his mouth.

The clutch of reporters had thinned, but a few filmed them as they eased their squad cars down the road.

The town's streets were busy. Kids were outside building tiny families in the snow. It used to be you'd build one big snowman and be done with it.

Now folks would fill their yards with miniature snow people. Whole villages, destined to melt.

Get a grip. You're going off the deep end. Worse? You know it. Being sacrificial is great if you don't sit around whining to yourself about being sacrificial. I'm pretty sure Mark's Gospel spells it out plainly, doesn't it? Do it happily. Or don't bother doing it. You tried to make the best choice you could for Michael. You put him first. Take comfort in that.

Maybe working during the holiday wasn't the smartest thing since few calls came in over the holiday other than MVAs. And once folks got to their destination, those calls diminished. Maybe he'd be better off at the farm, checking cattle, spreading hay. But then his mother would expect him for dinner.

Nope.

Work was better.

CHAPTER TEN

He caught a three-hour nap between shifts, and when most people were snugged into Christmas Eve church services throughout the village, he pulled his squad car into the Tompkins' driveway. He'd just gotten out of the car when a voice called to him.

"Deputy Jackson?"

Northern Decembers were infamous for their long, dark nights, but Christmas lights brightened the neighborhood considerably. He turned as the female reporter he had spoken with that morning approached him on her own.

"Don't you folks go home for Christmas?"

She laughed softly. "Says the man in uniform who is also working Christmas. I didn't have a chance to introduce myself this morning, but I'm Glenna Nelson."

She'd looked familiar, because the coffee shop often had *Wake Up, America!* on the television when he stopped by to fill his travel mug.

"Our network wants an interview with you and Ms. McCleary. The human-interest side of this story goes beyond the rescue, as cool as that was, and straight to the baby. I'm here to ask Ms. McCleary if she'd be willing to do the interview. Ten minutes, that's all I need, and we have some big-name sponsors that would love to help out with baby costs."

"A bribe."

She shook her head and laughed at him. "A thank you. Why do cops always assume the worst?"

He hated that she was correct, and he was pretty sure he hadn't always been like that. "You want me to ask her?"

"If you would. My cameraman is in the car over there." She pointed across the road. "Here's my cell number. If she says yes, we'll come in while it's quiet, chat quickly, and everyone goes home for a merry holiday. Except for those who don't have that option."

Her words touched him because he understood the concept all too well. He moved to the stairs. "I'll ask, but it's up to Kelsey, of course."

"Of course. And thank you, Deputy."

Hale had called ahead, and Jeb had left the front door unlatched before they went to church. Hale let himself in and called Kelsey's name.

Jazz Monroe looked out from the kitchen. "Kelsey," she pretended to whisper over her shoulder, in a voice intentionally loud enough to be heard. "Hot cop alert!"

"Now?" Kelsey came through the kitchen door carrying a mug of hot cocoa topped with whipped cream. The smell of warm chocolate came right along with her. "Deputy, hi. I forgot you were coming back. I'm so sorry." She sounded actually upset that she'd forgotten his follow-up.

He began to answer, but Jazz lightened the moment as Kelsey set the mug of cocoa down. "Oh, direct ego hit, Kelsey. We never tell a man we forgot about him." Jazz winked in his direction. "Is it all right if I call you Hale?"

"Only if I can record you doing it so I can blow up my Facebook feed with a video of Jazz Monroe calling me by my first name."

She laughed, and it was such a nice, normal laugh that he wondered why her image always seemed untouchable. But that was a question for another time. He turned to Kelsey. "I've just got a few follow-up questions about the accident, but Glenna Nelson is outside."

"From *Wake Up, America!*?" Jazz lifted her brows. "She's a cool lady, and she's nice to everyone. We consider her a media rarity these days."

"That's such a nice show," added Kelsey. "She's really out there? Now?"

"She'd like an interview. She and her cameraman are both waiting outside."

Kelsey looked skeptical. "Who hangs out in the street looking for an exclusive on Christmas Eve?"

He splayed his hands. "Not everyone has family waiting for them at home."

His words hit a nerve. He saw it in the mix of understanding and reticence displayed on her face.

"Why do they want an interview?"

"Human interest. Christmas. Not so much about you and me but about a baby being born in tough circumstances and how the town jumped in to help."

"Did she mention sponsor donations?" Jazz asked. "It's real common for the big stations to bring sponsors on board when they want an exclusive."

"She did, actually. Nothing specific, but the suggestion was made."

"I don't know how I feel about the idea of being paid off to tell our story." Kelsey took a moment to consider the idea. "Doesn't that seem wrong?"

"It seems absolutely normal," Jazz insisted. "Honey, that's how it's done. They're going for ratings, advertisers love ratings, and donating some diapers or clothes is mighty cheap advertising these days. And sometimes they're just doing it to be nice."

"I don't know what I'd have done without you and this town," Kelsey admitted. "I kind of quake when I think about it."

"It *is* a great story," said Jazz. She took Kelsey's hands and spoke softly. "I know this didn't go according to your plan, Kelse, but I can't help but wonder how this all came about. It wasn't on your agenda, or mine or Thea's, but here we all are. I'm on hiatus, Thea's out of work, and you're here. And it's Christmas. There's something about that timing, my friend, something that says maybe your plans are about to change."

Kelsey hesitated, then frowned. "I look dreadful."

Hale disagreed instantly. "You look beautiful." Kelsey's eyes flew to his, and he should have been embarrassed, but he wasn't. She was beautiful. "It's up to you, Kelsey, and I'm not saying this to push you, but our town could use all the good press it can get. Recovery after a couple of decades of stagnation is a long, slow process. It would be nice for folks to see how far we've come the last few years."

That tipped the scales. She nodded. "Tell them to come in. Jazz, can you get the baby?"

"Absolutely, but darling, they're going to ask about a name."

She was right, so Hale looked at Kelsey for direction. She brought her brows together, then smoothed her features and said, "I've got it covered."

"Perfect."

He went back outside, motioned the news crew in, then waited to hold the door for them.

"Thank you, Deputy." Glenna paused, one hand on his arm, as she went through. "Thank you so much."

He pulled the thick inner door shut. "Kelsey loves your show, and she wants the town to know how grateful she is for all the help."

"And the cookies. Folks have sent them by the dozen." Kelsey moved forward to shake Glenna's hand. Her poise impressed Hale. She looked calm and composed. No trace of the worry he had sensed earlier darkened her expression.

They chatted for a few moments while the cameraman positioned himself and the furniture. When he was ready, Kelsey took her place on the couch, and Hale sat on the chair to her left.

"Hale, can you sit next to Kelsey, please? With one camera angle, we've got to be careful how we stage this to make the most of the setting and to make the film editor's job as easy as possible. We'll air this tomorrow morning and probably refer to it for the twenty-sixth and twenty-seventh, too. Folks will love it," she assured Kelsey. "Bravado, courage, the baby, the small town. The perfect elements of Christmas. And can we photograph the baby, Kelsey? Is that all right?"

"Yes."

~

Kelsey knew she shouldn't agree. She shouldn't say yes or let any of this happen, but the moment Hale talked about helping the town, Maggie's words from that morning came back to her.

Wishing Bridge had struggled. It had fallen apart, much like she had when Chad's lies had been revealed. But they were pulling themselves back together, and if she could help their cause after all the nice things that had been done for her, it was the least she could do. A polite, sincere thank you. End of story.

Wrong.

Three questions in and she found herself spilling the truth about the storm, about her intentions with the baby, and how she didn't dare name her, didn't dare get too close to her, but now it was too late. And Glenna kept the gentle questions coming while the camera kept right on rolling.

"And now what, Kelsey?" Glenna asked. Her voice soothed exactly the way you'd expect once you'd watched *Wake Up, America!* She looked and sounded as if she truly cared, and Kelsey had spent her life longing for people to care. "Do you have work? Do you have a home?"

The baby squirmed, burped, then settled back down. Kelsey shifted her slightly. "I'm currently out of work, but I'm a certified elementary education teacher with a master's degree and great recommendations.

Now that the baby is here, I can go back to subbing until I land a full-time position. You don't get rich doing that, but you get by, and getting rich wasn't why I went into teaching in the first place."

"You love kids," Glenna observed.

"I do. The thought of giving up my baby . . . my daughter . . . broke my heart, but I'd promised myself I'd break the cycle of being a single mom." She faced Glenna directly as if they were old friends, chatting over coffee. "Then the storm barreled through, I had to get off the expressway, and you know the rest. If it hadn't been for Deputy Jackson, we probably wouldn't be here today." She smiled at Hale, and when he smiled back, she felt safer. Stronger. "And I'm so grateful to Avis and Maggie and Jeb and all the kind people who've stopped by the house with cookies and eggnog and baby supplies." She faced the camera. "Thank you. This town has turned this from the most difficult Christmas imaginable to the most blessed, and I honestly can't ever repay you for the kindnesses you've shown me. Us," she corrected herself, smiling down at the baby.

"Does she have a name, Kelsey?"

Kelsey faced Glenna straight on and tipped the sleeping baby up slightly. "This is Hayley Margaret McCleary, named for the two people who saved our lives." Hale jerked back slightly, surprised, but Kelsey pressed on. "If Maggie hadn't made that call, and if Hale Jackson hadn't persevered, I can't imagine what the outcome would have been."

"So God answers prayers . . ." When Kelsey gave her a look of surprise, Glenna continued. "Hale told the reporters that the reason he found you was because he prayed. That he saw nothing out of the ordinary but couldn't leave until he asked for God's help. He did, and then he turned and spotted a flash of light."

He prayed?

She turned his way as a jumble of old thoughts mingled with new circumstances. She wasn't sure how it all fit together, but Mrs. Effel's promise and the snow and the roads and Hale's prayer formed a medley in her head. "Thank you for that."

"My pleasure. Although it wasn't all that pleasurable at the time." He shifted his gaze to the camera and Glenna. "The storm was at its height. Blinding snow, blizzard-force winds that fed into ongoing squalls off of Lake Erie. No traction—they'd called off the plows for the night . . ."

"They weren't going to plow the roads?" Surprise lifted Glenna's voice as Hale nodded.

"But when I saw the drifting snow, I knew we had a situation on Perchance Road and any other north-south road. We recalled the plows, and that's when I prayed because I've been out in a lot of storms, but for there to be no evidence of what Maggie had seen meant either she was wrong, and pretty much anyone in Wishing Bridge will tell you that Maggie Tompkins is rarely, if ever, wrong."

Glenna laughed. "I know a few people like that, and I'm pretty sure the world could use more of them."

"Agreed. So either Maggie was wrong or the storm had already obliterated any trace of a vehicle. And that meant I might be walking away from an accident victim, and how would I live with that?"

"How, indeed?" Looking pleased, Glenna smiled at him and Kelsey, then stood. "That's a wrap. We've got plenty to work with, and I'm so grateful to both of you for letting us interrupt your holiday. My cousin Bruce was a policeman, Deputy." She faced him while the cameraman stowed his things. "I lost him last year, in a shooting down south. He'd stopped someone to issue them a ticket for speeding, and they killed him. Our hearts broke that day. Kelsey, when I saw the story of Hale's faith and your stamina, I wanted the story for Christmas. I want people to see the person behind the blue uniform and the courage of a young mother to do the right thing. Whatever you decide, I'm praying for you. And thank you both." She glanced at her watch. "If we get on the road right now, we can be back in Manhattan by one and have this polished and ready to go for the eight o'clock hour. What do you think, Phil?" she asked the cameraman as he rearranged his equipment. "Are you too tired to drive?"

"I'm fine, and we can take turns. Miss McCleary"—the cameraman extended his hand—"don't get up, just relax with that baby, and I'd like to extend my congratulations. And those of *Wake Up, America!* This is a great story." He shook Hale's hand, then faced Jazz, who had deliberately stayed out of the picture. "Miss Monroe."

She acknowledged the recognition by dipping her chin and raising one brow.

"A pleasure to meet you in person, and let me just say that Dwight Akins was a fool for letting you go. Every red-blooded guy in the country thinks so."

Jazz laughed, and the cameraman grinned, then smiled harder when she hugged him. "I shall take those words as a Christmas gift. And just so you know?" She held his attention and his hand. "It wasn't something that would have ever worked out. Dwight did me a favor. It's all for the best."

"Gracious and gorgeous." Glenna had leaned down to peek at the baby. Now she faced Hale and Jazz. "You know, I might just come live in this town. I've been a big-city gal for a long time, maybe too long. This could be a game changer for me."

"Must love winter," Hale reminded her with a glance outdoors.

"I can do winter," she assured him. "I was brought up in northern Pennsylvania. Then I got my shot at New York and took it. But this"— she swept the house and the lighted street with a quick look and a smile—"this is the kind of place you can call home."

It was.

The warmth of Wishing Bridge wrapped around Kelsey like a hand-woven blanket. The town and the people—the ones she'd met so far— were open and genuine. Like family. But the fact that she might have family here meant she couldn't stay. She hadn't pulled off that road to start trouble, although she couldn't deny her curiosity.

The storm had left her little choice, but the storm was over now. And yet . . . she had absolutely no place to go at the moment, and no way to get there because her car was in the shop and would be for days.

Insurance would cover some of the damage, but the five-hundred-dollar deductible seemed like an impossible sum when her bank account held just shy of a thousand dollars with which to start a new life.

Hale shut the door and turned her way. "You did great . . . and you're worrying again."

"I see it, too." Jazz sat down next to Kelsey while Hale sat in Jeb's favorite chair. "I'm guessing the money situation has you in a tizzy."

"There's a lot to sort out." Kelsey couldn't spill all of her thoughts, not in front of Hale. She could share with Thea and Jazz later, but her mother's history in Wishing Bridge was best left unspoken. "I've got to figure out where to go, what to do, get myself put back on sub lists once I figure out where to stay . . ."

"You can't go back to Canton?" Jazz asked.

She shook her head. "It would be too awkward. I wasn't open about my reasons for leaving; I pretended I was simply moving away." She made a face of regret. "Of course they'll know the truth now, and I've already given up my apartment and sold everything that wouldn't fit in my car. I'm at a crossroads, and I just need a little time and maybe a blank piece of paper to sort things out."

"Paper?" Hale repeated, curious.

"I think better when I see things in black and white," she explained. "The visual helps. If it's all in my head, I tend to let ideas run away with me. Does that sound weird?"

"Not to me." He smiled as if he understood more than he cared to let on. "I laid out all my football plays on paper to commit them to memory. Once I saw them on paper, they jibed in my brain. When I needed to run a play, I just pictured the paper and what was on it, and it helped me keep the plays straight from week to week. All because that piece of paper was in my head."

"Yes. Exactly like that. You played football here?"

"Kelsey, please tell me you're kidding." Jazz looked from Kelsey to Hale and back.

"About . . . ?"

"I played for Warsaw, the town just south of us. That's where kids from Wishing Bridge go to high school once they're done with eighth grade."

"And then Alabama." Jazz ticked off her fingers.

Hale acknowledged that with a fist bump. "Roll Tide."

Jazz smiled at the reference to the famous University of Alabama slogan. "And on to the NFL."

Hale played in the NFL?

"Guilty on all counts." A crackle came through his radio, reminding them he was on duty. "You've done your homework."

"Not hardly." Jazz sipped her hot chocolate and sighed as if sipping cocoa in an old-fashioned living room were something special. Maybe, after years of glamour, it was kind of special. "Maggie was bragging on you this afternoon while Kelsey was napping," Jazz went on. "The whole town loves you. You could have taken your bankroll and the insurance payment for your injury and gone anywhere, and you didn't. A five-year NFL quarterback with a Super Bowl ring, who should have won the Heisman back in the day, according to Maggie."

"Now you see why I love her. And why I listen to her." He grinned.

"But you came back here, invested money, and became a cop. No one does that, Hale. Not these days. Do they?"

"Obviously some of us do." He left it at that and turned back to Kelsey. "You covered some of my questions about the accident during the interview, but I've got a few more. Are you up for it?"

"Yes."

"Were there any other cars involved?"

She shook her head. "No. Just me."

"Was your vision impaired by the storm?"

That was a no-brainer. "Yes."

"What was your rate of speed as you descended the hill on Perchance Road?"

"Slow until I hit the ice."

Hale paused.

"I couldn't see it on the downslope," she explained, "and I thought going slow would give me enough time to adjust if I needed to, but it happened so fast there was nothing I could do. Especially going downhill. I hit the ice, the car spun one way, then the other, and then it felt like it went airborne. I'm sure it didn't, but that's how it felt, and I just kept thinking, *this is it.*" She held the baby closer. Tighter. "That I was going to hit a tree and it would be all over."

"But you didn't."

"No, although I'm not sure how I missed them," she said frankly. "The edge of the road seemed to have a lot of them when we walked through the snow."

"There's a fair number along that swale and the curve. You didn't see snow drifts or piles?"

"No. I remember a flash of white, like I was in a cloud of snow; there was no visibility whatsoever, just whiteness. And then the car seemed to shoot forward on its own, into the ditch."

"And you tried to call 9-1-1?"

"Several times. My phone wasn't registering any bars, and the calls didn't seem to go through. I couldn't move the seat; I couldn't get leverage because I was trapped, hanging in the air, between the seat and the steering wheel."

"I remember." He closed his small notebook and stood. "That's all I need to finish the report. I had the middle and the end, but I was short on the beginning because one of us was busy giving birth."

"Thank you, Hale." Kelsey reached out and took his hand. She wouldn't cry. Not anymore. She wasn't a crier by nature, but the last few weeks had proven her wrong on that score. "You saved us. I'll always be grateful."

He didn't blow casual words at her. He held her hand, just for a moment, and then he smiled at her and the sleeping newborn. "You're welcome. I'll see myself out. I want to make sure there are no traffic tie-ups on Main Street when the church services let out."

"Merry Christmas," Jazz said, and she started to follow him, but he waved her down.

"Relax and enjoy your time. I've got this." As soon as the thick, heavy door closed behind him, Jazz turned Kelsey's way.

"I had no idea you didn't know who he was."

"I've been a trifle busy." She aimed a look at the baby and the surroundings. "An NFL player, huh?"

"Career-ending injury, hometown boy comes back to help make things better."

"That's a Hallmark story right there."

"I know, right? If one must get rescued in a blizzard, it might as well be by the tall, crazy-good-looking former athlete with a heart of gold. And no wedding ring."

Kelsey pretended she hadn't noticed, but of course she'd noticed. No. Wait. She'd not only noticed, she'd looked purposely. But that was silly schoolgirl stuff, because what famous, well-to-do guy would be interested in a down-on-her-luck single mother with no money and few prospects?

"He seems like such a nice man." Kelsey's gaze strayed to the door Hale had shut firmly behind him. "I'm sure he's got a significant other somewhere in town."

"Maybe." Jazz got up to get a fresh diaper, wipes, and a changing pad when the baby began to squirm. "I'll play assistant. You get the dirty-diaper honors."

"Practice makes perfect. Do you think it's weird that she doesn't smile at me? Like she doesn't know I'm her mother?" Kelsey asked as they arranged the pad and the baby on the sofa. "When you see babies on TV, they're always smiling."

Jazz made an exaggerated face of confusion. "Girl, I have not handled a baby ever, and I don't know why she doesn't smile at you because you're about the nicest thing there is, Kelsey. And when she's bigger, I'll tell her so. And we'll do silly things to make her smile. Do you think she's too little?" Jazz peered at the baby as if studying a biology lesson. "To smile, I mean. Are we born with emotions, or do they come later?"

Kelsey didn't know, but as she crooned little Hayley's name, one side of the new baby's face lifted slightly, as if she was happy. "Jazz. Did you see it?"

"I did, it was like the tiniest thing ever, but I think it counts as a smile or at least a half one, don't you?"

"I'm counting it," Kelsey declared. "She did it when I talked to her. When I said her name. Do you think she recognizes my voice?"

"Well, she has been hearing it for months from inside, so why wouldn't she?"

Kelsey studied the baby as she lay on the mat. "That's true. I hadn't thought of it that way, because I thought she wasn't going to be hearing me after she was born. And now she is, unless I go ahead with my original plans."

Jazz sank onto the floor next to her. "I don't have answers, Kelse. Only more questions. But the way things worked out, I think you need to give yourself that week or two to get stronger. Get over birthing and nursing and all the weird stuff that goes along with having kids . . . then figure it out. I think you were given time for a reason. Why not use it?"

Hale had prayed when he had been tempted to walk away. And then a glimmer of light had brought him back in her direction.

Only she hadn't hit the lights then. Or turned the car on. She'd sat there, scared of running out of gas, and waited the full interval before turning on the car's engine.

What had he seen?

She had no idea, but it didn't matter. He'd found her. He'd freed her. And he'd gotten her to help in time to save the baby. She owed him so much, more than she could ever repay, but after listening to him that night, Kelsey was pretty sure he wasn't looking for thanks. Or gifts. Or rewards.

He just wanted to do the right thing.

So did she. She just wasn't one hundred percent sure what that was right now.

CHAPTER ELEVEN

A baby's first Christmas should light up the sky, shouldn't it? Wasn't that your dream for this precious child?

Kelsey mentally pushed that thought aside as she, Jazz, and Thea spent Christmas Day with Maggie and Jeb.

No one mentioned the lack of decoration, the single Nativity scene gracing the mantel. They shared good food, played cards, and told stories between holding and walking the tiny girl in their midst.

There was no big celebration.

Maybe Maggie and Jeb didn't celebrate holidays. Or maybe older folks didn't worry about decking the halls and festive trees.

It made it easier, in a way. If Kelsey did give Hayley up to a barren couple, she'd have these sweet days to remember. But she wasn't stupid. With each passing day, making that decision would prove harder. Perhaps impossible.

Rochester was close. Only an hour away. She could contact someone from one of their agencies. She decided to pose that question to Jazz and Thea when they returned the following day. Hayley had been up half the night, still confusing her personal time-space continuum. By the time Kelsey woke back up, a chunk of morning had passed. She woke herself with a shower, got dressed in clothes Maggie had washed for her, then started down the stairs.

Boxes and mail pouches littered the hallway between the front door and the staircase. She whistled softly as Jeb came through with another armload of packages. "What's all this?"

"This is what happens when you're the featured Christmas story on *Wake Up, America!*, it seems."

She stared at Jeb, and when she realized his meaning, her jaw dropped open. "No."

"Oh, yes." Maggie came in behind him, carrying a smaller stack. "And there are gift cards. A ton of them. Folks got online and had them sent to the station, and they're sending them on to you. They were talking about it during the second hour of the morning. Come on over here, I bet they show it again."

They did.

The entire beautiful video that Glenna and Phil had put together came on at 8:45, just before the nine o'clock news, while Jeb moved stacks of packages into the living room.

"I'm so glad you did this." Maggie patted her on the leg. "It gives folks hope to see a true story like this come to life."

"But I didn't expect people to send me things. It sounds like I'm begging." Kelsey put her head in her hands and groaned. "I don't beg. I don't ask for handouts. I never did. I pay my own way, and all of a sudden I'm a stranded traveler with a newborn baby."

Maggie pointed to her single Christmas decoration, the beautiful Nativity over the red-and-charcoal-bricked fireplace. "Tale as old as time, dearie. Nothing like a goodwill story about a baby, especially at Christmas. Now how is nursing going?"

"That's my cue to leave," Jeb announced as he finished slicing the tape on the last box. "A man's got to know his limit, and that's mine."

"Says the man who worked a dairy farm for five years while he was going through school." Maggie shooed him off. "Go on with you, then, this is girl talk. And two pretties have arrived to add to the conversation."

Thea and Jazz had just come in through the back door, and Jazz hugged Maggie until the older woman offered protest. "Land sakes, what's that for? What's gotten into you?"

"Because you gave us the best Christmas I've had in a long time, Maggie Tompkins. The food was amazing, and listening to Jeb play the piano was positively inspirational."

Maggie cut that off with a pretend scolding. "If you tell him that, it will go straight to his head, and he'll play night and day. A body can only take so much of a good thing."

"Well, I loved it, too," Thea agreed. "It reminded me of my grandma when I was real little and how she'd play music for me. Before she passed away and my mother sold me to a band of traveling gypsies."

"She did not."

Thea made a face more at the girls than Maggie. "She kind of did, but that was a long time ago, and I need to see this wittle bitty sweetums." She bent over the edge of the Pack 'n Play, talking in the singsong voice everyone used around tiny babies. "Hey, precious, how adorable and cute are you this morning?"

"There! She did it! She did it again!" Kelsey had to keep herself from shouting as Hayley quirked one side of her little face up. "Did you see it?"

"The smile?" Thea asked.

"Yes!" Kelsey fist-punched the air. "I knew it was a smile. I was sure of it!"

"Oh, anyone who says babies don't smile hasn't been around very many babies. Either that or they're the sort of person no one would smile at, especially a baby," noted Maggie. "And why wouldn't she smile, such a happy girl?"

"Maybe because she's only a few days old, which is quite close to zero." Jazz made a skeptical face. "So that's really a smile, huh?"

"It sure was." Thea lifted the baby. "I know I shouldn't do this. I should let her get used to lying there, amusing herself. That's what the books say, but books are stupid. Why wouldn't anyone want to hold a sweet, itty-bitty schnookums like this?"

"Did she just say . . ." Jazz looked positively pained as she indicated Thea.

"Oh, she did," breathed Kelsey. "Who knew?"

Thea raked them with a scathing glance. "Who knew that tough old Thea had a soft spot for precious little babies? For how sweet and perfect and amazing they are? Is that the question, Miss Hayley McCleary?" She leaned in as if to whisper. "Well, they don't know so much, do they?"

"I need a video of this," Jazz teased.

"Reason enough to go back on Facebook," added Kelsey. "Although that might blast Thea's tough, professional image out of the water."

"You can be a strong professional and a tender person," Thea told them. Then she smiled. "But not necessarily at the same time. What is all this stuff, Maggie? Are you a closet binge shopper?"

"Folks sending gifts for Kelsey and the baby."

"No." Thea's mouth dropped open. "Are you serious?"

"But the show just aired yesterday," added Jazz. "On Christmas. No one goes shopping on Christmas, even in New York. Everything is closed."

"Online shopping, overnight delivery," explained Maggie. "One of the gals from the show called here and told me what to expect, but who'd have thought it, this early? And yet, here it is."

"I'm beyond amazed and going straight to shocked." Thea walked around the massive pile of gifts. "I never thought of this as an outcome."

"And it adds a bit of weight to the decision, doesn't it?" Kelsey asked softly. "If I get too comfortable, how can I possibly be strong enough to walk away from this baby?"

Maggie ticked off her fingers. "You said you needed a place to live, a car, and a job, correct?"

That's what she'd told the reporter, so Kelsey nodded.

"Well, you have a place to stay right here," Maggie declared. "We don't need rent, we're not hard-pressed for money, and there are a bunch of school districts that need subs, so we can get you put on their lists once school reopens and you're able to work. Your car is in Webster's Collision, and once he's done looking at it, he'll submit the claim to your insurance. If you need a loan for the deductible, I'll cough that up out of my bingo money. I put aside anything I win at bingo." She lowered her voice as if her bingo stash were a state secret. "There's nearly seven hundred and fifty dollars in the envelope, just for things like this. That way I don't have to touch the old-age accounts."

Not one of the young women acted surprised that the older woman didn't want to touch her old-age accounts, but they didn't dare make eye contact, either.

"Maggie, I've already imposed on you for too long."

"It's not an imposition. It's a blessing, having you here. More than you know." Maggie patted Kelsey's knee, then stood and headed for the kitchen. "I'm going to make us a pot of coffee, unless Theadora would prefer tea this morning? That's such a pretty name, don't you think?" She didn't pause to let them answer. "There are fresh muffins from the Galliotti family up the road. They're so excited to have you here, and Gina Galliotti makes the best pumpkin muffins I've ever had. Even the big bakeries don't do them as good!" She puttered around the kitchen while the three younger women exchanged looks.

"You could do what she says." Thea spoke softly. "Stay here. What would be the harm in that, Kelsey? A new beginning in such a beautiful town?"

Staying here could do more harm than they could possibly imagine, so Kelsey motioned them closer. "My mother."

Jazz pulled back, frowning. "Say what?"

"My mother," Kelsey repeated softly. "This was her hometown . . . if she was telling the truth way back then. So it might be, or it might not be. Which means my father could be here. And her story about my conception complicates matters, but I never knew what to believe and what to ignore, so that hikes the level of difficulty. I might have family here, I might have brothers and sisters, I might be related to the next person who walks through that door." She jutted her chin toward the big, solid-wood entry. "If people find out, I could ruin someone's life. Or put myself and the baby in danger if my father is a criminal. No one wants to be brought to justice thirty years after the fact."

"True, but how does one go about finding this stuff out discreetly?" Jazz whispered.

"That's the big question, isn't it?" Kelsey had no idea. "I don't want to cause trouble. This whole thing is such a mess."

"Or an amazing opportunity," argued Thea.

"That's some spin you're talking." Kelsey didn't try to mask her doubt as Thea leaned closer.

"You've always wanted to find family, Kelse, although in my experience, they're grossly overrated." Thea said the words lightly, but Kelsey knew the rugged circumstances of Thea's youth. Her mother had traded her twelve-year-old daughter to a drug ring for a year's supply of heroin, then died two months into the deal. Thea had escaped, but only because of the kindness of one man. Four wretchedly incompatible foster homes later, she'd ended up at Hannah's Hope.

"But not this way." Kelsey grimaced, still whispering. "I thought I'd find out who they were, or who I thought they might be, from the Internet, but now I'm right here. And who knows if she was telling the truth anyway? She lied about so much. Why not this?"

"But you're here. With the door wide open," noted Jazz.

"Which means leaving is senseless," Thea added. "At least until you know."

Staying here. On her own. Knowing she might have family nearby. Or not. Fear and temptation did a tug-of-war inside her.

She knew her mother had changed her name, or rather, used the surname McCleary. Vonnie wasn't big on legalities or proprieties of any kind.

But that's about all Kelsey knew, except for the occasional mention of Wishing Bridge when she was little. She'd thought her mother had made the name up. Who lived in a town called Wishing Bridge?

No one. It was the stuff of fairytales, another one of Vonnie McCleary's lies.

But Kelsey had looked it up as a teen on a school computer, and there it was, tucked in the rolling, forested hills of Western New York. A little town, a blip on a Google map, but if the town was real, then maybe she did have roots someplace. Maybe here, in the sweet town now offering her comfort and healing. "I'll think about it for the next few days. I don't know." She kept her voice low as she faced her old friends. "There's a lot to consider, from both sides."

"There is. And there is a season for everything, Kelse. Just like they say in church. I believe that. I see it in medicine, all the time," Thea told her.

"Which makes you and me being out of work somewhat ironical," mused Jazz.

"Or providential," Thea suggested.

"That could be a stretch, my friend." Jazz looked unconvinced. "That's a lot of coincidences strung together."

"Well, you never see it beforehand," Thea told her as she got up to walk the baby around the shadowed room. "But it's always clear in retrospect. And Kelsey could be right, maybe all of this is a God thing. The right people in the right place at the right time."

"Most things are clear in retrospect, which is why I'm a great Monday-morning quarterback," Jazz noted. She stood and stretched. "But I'll have to get back to you on the whole Providence angle. That might be a tough argument on your end, but lately . . ." She hesitated as if weighing possibilities. "Who knows?"

Maggie called them to the kitchen just then, and Jazz led the way. "Something smells marvelous, and I've been doing too much sitting these past few days. I wonder if there's a gym nearby?"

Her question brought a look of surprise to Maggie's face. "Hereabouts most folks just go walking."

"Like outside?"

"Those hills." Maggie pointed to the kitchen window overlooking the forest reserve.

Jazz nodded.

"We've got trails that go every which way in the reserve. All marked out."

"Covered in snow, I expect."

"The day or two after a bad storm, yes. But we love those trails, and folks in town take their plows and snowblowers and whatever they can get their hands on and clear them out. Look. See?" She drew the sheer curtain back, and sure enough, they could see a trail snaking through the trees. "They're wide enough for four people, easy, because they use them for those four-wheeled thingies in the summer. We've trained two top runners here on these hills, dearie. I think there's enough gumption in Wishing Bridge to keep you in shape."

Jeb came in from the side driveway in time to hear the last little bit. "And if you don't have proper winter clothes, we've got—"

"No."

Maggie's harsh tone brought the entire room to a halt.

Everyone stood silent and still, waiting for Jeb's response, or maybe waiting for Maggie to laugh and say she was sorry for alarming them.

She did no such thing.

She pinned Jeb with a tight, dour face, hands braced against the table.

Jeb faced her, hurt, then rolled his shoulders back as if they pained him, or maybe it was her who pained him. He tugged his hat back into place and went back down the stairs and outside.

"Maggie, are you all right?" Thea moved forward, always the healer. "Can I help you with something?"

"I'm fine." It was hard to watch the kindhearted old woman struggle to regain her composure. She was not fine, but her attempts to pretend made the situation worse. "I'm going to go sit by the baby for a few minutes is all. If that's okay?"

She faced Kelsey. A sheen of tears brightened her eyes.

"Baby therapy is the best," Kelsey told her.

Maggie crossed to the sitting room. She took a seat near the portable crib and sat there, chin down, looking desperately sad. In her wake, three women exchanged expressions of concern because the last thing they wanted to do was cause Maggie and Jeb angst. And yet, somehow, they just had.

CHAPTER TWELVE

"What just happened?" Jazz looked around, uncomfortable. "Did I mess up, saying I wanted to work out?"

"No. I think it touched a nerve. Or Jeb touched a nerve, and Maggie reacted. But it was strange to see her bark like that."

"And did you see his expression?" Kelsey had been facing Jeb. "He looked so sad. So spent."

"He looked hurt, sure enough." Jazz eyed the spread of muffins and coffee fixings. "I vote we pretend all is well and eat the muffins."

"Least said, soonest mended," Thea agreed. "Moving on . . ." She poured three coffees before picking up a chocolate-chip muffin. "I've said it before and I'll say it again. Short women should always be born with an aversion to carbs. Unfortunately, that's not the case here." She broke off a piece of the muffin and tasted it. "I am officially declaring this Gallini woman—"

"Galliotti," said Jazz.

"I stand corrected. Whoever she is, she is now my BFF because I've never had a better muffin than this. All consternation has been wiped from my brain at first bite."

"Amazing." Jazz had broken a blueberry muffin in half, clearly pleased with the taste herself. "If I were a cook, I'd want this recipe. And that one." She pointed to the chocolate-chip muffin on Thea's plate. "Perhaps all of them, because why wouldn't we want a buffet of muffins?"

"Muffin buffet works for me," agreed Kelsey, "and I like the idea of hiking through the woods. It's so pretty and peaceful out there. I can picture myself walking Hayley along the paths in a stroller. How pretty that would be. When she's bigger, of course."

"But not a place to be caught in a storm." Maggie rejoined them as if nothing had happened. "It's easy to lose your bearings. And we've got black bears here, but they don't generally bother folks. And then there are the coyotes, rimming the farmlands."

"Manhattan suddenly seems tame by comparison." Jazz sent her a teasing look and, to everyone's relief, Maggie smiled.

"Well, there's city and there's country, and it's different for sure. I don't mind visiting grand places, but I'm more at peace when I come home."

"You don't like big cities." Jazz made the observation quietly, and Maggie shook her head as she took the seat next to the high-fashion model.

"I love cities. I worked in Baltimore when I was fresh out of school, doing fancy stitching for a clothier there. Then I moved to office work, and that's how I met Jeb. He's an accountant, and every business, every town, for that matter, needs a numbers guy. His parents were from here, and when we fell in love, we decided to leave the city and raise a family here. And it was a good choice," she assured them. "No place is perfect, but Wishing Bridge comes mighty close."

"Do you have kids, Maggie?"

Maggie studied her coffee intently. "One of our own. Bonnie. Bonnie Jean. Such a joyous child. Always wanting to please. She made it all seem so easy, you know?" She crossed over to a picture on the wall and lifted it down. A young girl offered an over-the-shoulder smile at the camera. "Then there were two we adopted." She didn't look up and didn't sound happy. "It didn't end up well with them. They were older and hated being here. Now they're grown, and we don't have much to say, either way. They got their way and moved on and never looked back. Just as well." She stared at the photo as if heartsick, then returned it to the wall. "It's Jeb and me here now. Like it was way back when. Nothing I bring myself to talk about at the moment, though."

The three younger women exchanged a quiet look before Thea changed the subject.

"Jazz, you did a shoot in Italy last year."

Jazz took the hint. "The Mediterranean and then the hill country. Neither one was as warm as they pretended, and we froze. But it gave me a nice chunk to put in my pension fund, because we all know that supermodel careers are generally limited by the clock, and if there's anything I don't ever want to be again, it's poor."

Thea took another piece of her muffin, as if breaking it into small pieces made it healthier. "Me, either. And I remember how pretty that background was, Jazz. Gorgeous."

"But none prettier than the here and the now," Jazz told Maggie. She laid her hand over the older woman's smaller, paler version. "And I do think I'm going to try some of your hiking. Fresh air is nothing to be taken for granted. Believe me." She stood and put her plate into the sink. "I know."

"Laundromat first. I saw one listed in Warsaw," began Thea, but Maggie waved her off quickly.

"We've got a washer and dryer downstairs, and nice ones, too. One of them front loaders, and I love it, once I got used to how things worked," she admitted. "Bring your stuff in and save yourselves some money. Laundry isn't cheap over there."

"We couldn't, Maggie." Jazz shook her head.

"Of course you can. Jeb and me, we like helping out. It makes us happy." She didn't add anything about why she'd been so unhappy a half hour earlier, but she looked and sounded sincere. "The wash can be going while we take a peek into those boxes and bags. And unless I miss my guess, that car engine means there's more coming." She hurried to the door so whoever it was wouldn't ring the bell and wake the baby, but it wasn't a package delivery.

It was a woman, not too short, not too tall, with light-brown hair that matched her eyes. She was carrying a wrapped box.

When Maggie had taken the woman's coat, she called them in from the kitchen. "Kelsey? Girls? Jill Jackson's here, she's Hale's mom. She came by to meet you."

Hale's mother stood next to Maggie, a little taller and considerably younger.

Hale looked nothing like her. With a different head shape and body type, she had almost nothing in common with her hulking, football-loving son.

Jill Jackson smiled at all three of them but moved toward Kelsey. Before she handed her the box, she paused and held Kelsey's gaze. Her eyes narrowed slightly, but then they widened again. "I am so very glad I raised the kind of man who doesn't give up easily and so happy he found you. Welcome to Wishing Bridge, Kelsey."

She handed Kelsey the beautifully wrapped box. She'd used classic paper, covered in scattered roses, and an ash-pink bow on top.

"It's almost too pretty to unwrap."

Jill Jackson's smile grew. "I love a pretty presentation. It's one of those little amenities that seem to be going by the wayside, but it makes me happy."

"Jill, are you hungry?" Maggie asked.

Hale's mother shook her head. "I'm not, but if you have coffee, Maggie, I could go for a cup. I just mailed out post-Christmas orders, and it's amazing how many people actually take time to shop online on Christmas Day."

"We've experienced the truth in that." Maggie indicated the pile of packages in the living room. "We were just going to get to these while Hayley sleeps. Or eats."

"I saw the interview when you announced her name." Jill waited until Kelsey took a seat, then sat down across from her. "And I saw my son's reaction. You made his day, Kelsey."

"He saved us." Kelsey didn't have to elaborate. "And it's a beautiful name. I should probably thank you for not naming him something preposterous because that might have tipped the scales differently."

Jill laughed. "I was in a very English Lit phase back then. Hale and Bennett bore the brunt, I'm afraid, but they're good, strong names."

"Here's your coffee, Jill, and if Kelsey's all right with this, maybe we could start opening these packages?"

"Lots of help on hand." Thea reached for a box. "I vote yes, mostly because I can't wait to see what's inside."

"I'll make a list for thank-you notes." Jazz tapped into a page on her phone. "We'll make it like a baby shower right here."

"Coffee, tea, muffins, and gifts. Perfect!" Maggie beamed as she chose a seat next to Jill.

Kelsey unwound the dusky-rose ribbon from Jill's package and slipped the paper off carefully. "Remember how Mrs. Effel lined our dressers with wrapping paper, to make them pretty?"

Jazz had been typing. She paused. "I'd forgotten that."

"One of those little kindnesses that meant so much," added Thea.

The housemother had been a woman of few means, sharing everything she had. She'd tried to make things nice for them, as much as she could. In retrospect, those little things meant a great deal now. Kelsey opened the box and sighed. "Oh, this quilt is lovely. Too lovely for words. Did you make this, Mrs. Jackson?"

"Call me Jill, please, and I only wish I were that clever." She laughed. "I have an Amish woman who supplies my online store with handmade clothes and quilts. They'll be featured in my new shop. She and her daughters and nieces have been working on inventory for the past year. I stopped by there on Christmas Eve and told her I needed one for a little girl, and she had this one complete. But I did embroider Hayley's name in the corner."

Kelsey checked the corner: *Hayley Margaret . . . Welcome home.*

"Oh, that's charming. And such pretty script." She passed a hand over the threaded letters and sighed softly. "Thank you."

"You're most welcome. Ladies, do you want help?"

"Sure." Thea slipped the baby into Jill Jackson's arms. "If you wouldn't mind holding your son's namesake while Kelsey opens these, that would be lovely."

Jill's eyes lit up. "Mind?" She snuggled the baby into a more comfortable position and looked positively delighted. "What an absolute pleasure."

Onesies. Dresses, of all sizes. Outfits to grow into. Blankets. Bottles. Cups. More clothes than any one baby could possibly wear even if Kelsey changed her outfit a dozen times a day. And gift cards to department stores, grocery stores, and baby specialty stores.

The doorbell rang as they were finishing up. Nearly ready for food again, Hayley began to stir. The doorbell made the baby wince, then yawn, and then two little eyes peeked up at Hale's mother. Jill studied the baby, then Kelsey. "She's got your eyes."

"You think so?" Kelsey asked as Maggie accompanied a tall, older man into the room.

"Not the color yet, but the shape. And color changes as they grow. I think she favors you a lot, and if her eyes lighten up, she might be your mini-me. Do you resemble your mother?" Jill asked easily.

Kelsey shook her head. "I don't, no. You really wouldn't have thought we were related, to see us together."

"It happens like that, sometimes." Jill adjusted the baby to her shoulder as Maggie introduced the man.

"Kelsey, this is Brian Cunningham, he's the current head of our school board. He'd like to talk to you for a moment."

The head of the school board had come to see her? She started to stand. "Of course."

"Don't get up." He waved her down. "I didn't come to disturb you. I'm sure you need your rest. My wife and I have three kids, and I remember long days and longer nights when they were babies. Although I've got a high schooler who's given me a few long nights this fall."

Commiserative looks all around said the women understood that.

"I wanted to extend a personal invitation to you." He spoke directly to Kelsey. "Several of us saw your interview, and we'd like you to submit an application to the district. We use the standard New York State form, and I expect your references are up-to-date?"

This couldn't really be happening. Could it? She nodded as she answered his question. "The administrators in Canton and Potsdam were very forthcoming, so everything is current."

"Excellent. Of course I can't make any promises because I'm sure we'll have several applications, but we've just discovered we're going to have a class opening in second grade. One of our staff is unexpectedly moving out of state, and we'd like you to have a shot at the position if you choose to stay local. It will have to go through the normal channels, of course . . ."

"Of course," she agreed, but inside her heart was doing a crazy dance.

How had she gone from jobless, pregnant, and fairly desperate a few days ago to awash in gifts, with a healthy baby, a cozy home, and now a possible job offer?

Things like this don't really happen. Do they?

"Mrs. DiSchino at the elementary school will be watching for your application. I didn't want to senselessly tighten the schedule by waiting until school resumes next week. Would you be physically able to return to work the first week of February?"

For a full-time position? With benefits? Kelsey didn't dare think about possible fallout from relatives, especially relatives who might not even exist. She nodded quickly. "I'm sure I would."

"Then we'll look forward to seeing things in print. Maggie, I'll see myself out, and Ms. McCleary, congratulations on the birth of your daughter. We're all happy to see you and this baby doing so well."

He strode out the door as if he hadn't just offered her the chance of a lifetime. True, she still had to win the job, but personally extending an invitation to apply meant a great deal.

"Add that to the unbelievable factor," muttered Jazz.

"I just did. Whoa, girl." Thea bumped knuckles with Kelsey. "I guess it pays to go public with your wish list, darling."

"Well, you are in a town that specializes in wishes." Jill brought the baby to Kelsey. "I suspect it's feeding time?"

"It is." Kelsey stood. "Maggie, I'll take her upstairs, and then we should organize the gifts. I can't possibly use all of those clothes, can I?"

Jill and Maggie both shook their heads.

"Would you be willing to help me, then? Help me figure out what I need and what I can donate? I'm sure there are lots of young mothers out there who are down on their luck. I'd be thrilled if this outpouring of generosity could help some of them."

"Do you have time, Jill?" Maggie asked.

"I do."

"And we can get that laundry business taken care of, too," Maggie went on. "Girls, if you bring it inside, I can show you how the machines work downstairs. No sense feeding a Laundromat your hard-earned money when I've got everything right here."

"Thank you, Maggie."

Thea and Jazz went outside to grab their laundry from Thea's car while Jill and Maggie began sorting clothing into sizes and colors.

And Kelsey took the baby upstairs to the comfy recliner.

She'd stated her needs on national television, not because she wanted pity but because she knew folks would understand that sometimes things just went wrong.

And here she was, fewer than two days later, with an amazing number of things going right.

Prayers? Blessings? Wishes?

She didn't know where one left off and another began, but she settled into the recliner with a more grateful heart than she'd had in a very long time.

~

The next morning, Hale was coming out of the barn when his mother pulled into the driveway. "Hey, nice unexpected visit." He wrapped an arm around her shoulders and kissed her cheek. "Checking up on me?"

"No, actually. I wanted to talk to you."

"When women want to talk, that's my hint to cue the scary music."

"Got time, inside?" She pulled her coat tighter. "That wind is sharp."

"Time and coffee. I'm not on until two today."

She hooked her coat on the entry wall and waited until he'd brewed her coffee. She puffed air across the top to cool the surface and waited while he made his. "We like our coffee the same way."

He made a funny face. "That's not news."

"And we look nothing alike," she went on. "Bennett looks like me. You look like my dad, the spitting image, like he used to say. The other day you mentioned that genetics were a funny thing."

He nodded and laid both hands around the hot mug to warm them.

"I took a gift to Kelsey yesterday."

"Ah."

She breathed out a sigh. "And you're right. She's the image of Nora when she was young."

"Voice, too, right?"

"That sweet, husky, musical voice. Yes. I used to love June Allyson— she's an actress from long ago. Your grandma used to watch her movies, in black and white, and we used to say that Nora got June Allyson's voice. So did Kelsey."

"But like you said, stuff happens with genetics."

Jill hesitated, then grimaced. "Except that this time I think it happened for a reason. Nora had a sister. Yvonne. She took off after a big family fight, and no one ever heard from her again. She'd been in and out of trouble, she'd broken all kinds of laws, man-made and God centered, and when she left, there were a bunch of folks who breathed a sigh of relief, I expect. Not Nora, of course. She loved her. But she told me often enough that she had never understood her. Why she was always so empty. So unhappy. I'm kind of wondering if somewhere along the way she had a child. A daughter. And if Kelsey might be that daughter."

"Man, that's a stretch, isn't it? Of all the gin joints in all the world she'd end up in Wishing Bridge?" He paraphrased one of Jill's favorite movies. "I mean, what's the likelihood of that?"

"I don't know, but I'm going to call Nora and chat. She might know something. Or she might know nothing. But I felt as you did when I talked to Kelsey. It was like Nora was talking to me, even the hand gestures. If she turns out to be Nora's niece, then it's explained. But that means she's still got family here, Hale. Family that doesn't know she exists."

"Cousins. And a grandfather."

Jill nodded. "I'll let you know what Nora says. I hate stirring up old waters, but on the other hand, it would be wrong not to. The school board has asked her to put in an application for an elementary-school position."

"So she might be staying?" The thought appealed to him, and yet it shouldn't. *Should it?*

"She sounded confident about her résumé and recommendations. I think she captured hearts with that interview."

She had, Hale knew. He hadn't been able to get her soft words out of his mind for three days. "She handled it well."

"She's handled all of this the same way," Jill agreed. "She's got a servant's heart. Like you."

Did he? Or did he like being big and strong and having people look up to him? Depend on him? "You hungry, Mom? I can throw on some eggs."

She shook her head. "No, I'm on my way to the post office for today's packages, and I'm meeting Max to go over some ideas for display space. He said he was going to advise you on a couple of things with the renovation?"

"That's his nice way of saying he'll show me what to do and then let me do it. At least some of it. Now there's a guy with a servant's heart."

His mother agreed as she tugged her coat back into place. "We owe him a lot, not that he'd let folks repay him. Or give him credit."

"Humility is a wonderful and scarce thing these days."

"I'll see you later." She hugged him but didn't prolong the hug. She knew the holidays were rough, and, in typical Jill Jackson fashion, she expected him to move on. Christmas was over, a new day dawned. "Are you doing anything on New Year's Day?"

"I'm off that day, so I'll be here, feeding cattle and watching for signs of labor. We brought the heifers into the near field so Ben and I can keep a close eye on them."

"AccuWeather is predicting lake effect again on the weekend. You're smart to have them close by." She gave the rolling acres behind his simple house a look of approval. "This is beautiful, Hale, with such sweet purpose. In all four seasons."

And a time to every purpose under the heaven.

Her words brought the verse from Ecclesiastes to mind.

A time for everything. A purpose for everything. Until human error and sin blew it all out of the water.

"Anyway, I'm doing a crown roast of pork on New Year's, with stuffing and homemade applesauce."

"My favorites." He'd take pork and applesauce any day of the week, but he wasn't opposed to a flame-broiled steak, either.

She smiled because of course they were his favorites.

"I'll be there," he promised. She was doing this because he avoided Christmas. She was wise enough to let that go, and then recreated a holiday dinner for him. Through all the crazy ups and downs of their lives, he and Ben had been blessed with an amazing mother, and he didn't take that lightly. "Thanks, Mom."

"See you Sunday."

She hurried to her car, head ducked, a woman with a big heart and a purpose, qualities she'd passed on to both her sons.

CHAPTER THIRTEEN

Max Reichert texted him late afternoon. Talked with mom, have some ideas about her shop, where are you having supper?

Hale didn't generally eat a full meal on the job, unless it was something amazing like Maggie's brunch a few days before.

Full caricature, he texted back. Coffee and doughnut, six-thirty, Doughnut Shack.

Max sent back a head-scratching emoji, then See you there.

He was on his way into the coffee shop when Ethan Brandenburg pulled into the spot next to him.

"Hey, Doc. Hi, kids." He smiled at Ethan's niece and nephew, the pair of orphans who'd faced way too much tragedy in such young lives. "How are you guys doing?"

"You might get more of an answer than you bargained for," Ethan answered. "We'll talk inside. Keegan needs to take the quickest route to the nearest bathroom. Hey." He had Mara by the hand and Keegan in his arms. "Would you mind keeping an eye on Mara while we're in the men's room?"

"Glad to." Little girls and men's rooms weren't a good mix, and the local doughnut shop didn't have a "family" restroom. "Can I order something for you?"

"Will it look bad if the town doctor is buying his kids doughnuts for supper?"

"My lips are sealed."

Ethan laughed. "I'll order once I'm back out."

He turned right, and Hale guided the little girl to the left. Head down, she didn't make eye contact with him, but when he looked away, she peeked up, studying his profile with a pensive expression.

He didn't see Max, and there wasn't a line, so he placed his order, then paid it forward by having the clerk add Ethan's and Max's orders to his card.

He'd just set his coffee and doughnut on a corner table when Max walked in from one direction, while Ethan and Keegan approached from the opposite side.

Mara looked up. She didn't smile. Didn't react. She stayed quiet, as if she carried the weight of the world on seven-year-old shoulders. After suffering a brutal loss like she had, maybe that's how it felt.

Keegan peeked at Hale over Ethan's shoulder and waved. Just that, a tiny wave, but enough to pinch his heart.

"Hale, thanks." Ethan turned from the counter when he realized Hale had paid his bill. "I owe you."

"You don't, that's the beauty of it." Hale offered the doctor a coffee salute. "You've had some tough times at your medical practice these past two weeks."

"A rough go. And more crazy to come." He guided the kids to the booth next to Hale's, then set juices in front of the kids with straws and cream-filled doughnuts. "I'm pretending the juice is half healthy."

"I won't judge. The kids look pretty good to me, Doc. And since I'm doing the same thing, I'm giving you a firm thumbs-up."

Ethan acknowledged that with a grateful expression as the kids got settled. Once straws were in place and the kids were seated, Ethan stepped closer to Hale's booth. "This wasn't exactly how I envisioned this job going when I signed on last summer. With Paul gone, I'm not sure what to do, and there's so little time that I can't get to the proper channels to figure things out. It's a mess."

The loss of an invested part of their community would be hard. Paul Wolinski had been a cornerstone in their little town, an old-school practitioner with a gruff manner and a heart of gold. He would be missed in many ways.

"It would be different if you had bought into the practice," Hale noted. "Then you'd have a say in what happens, right?"

"Except that wasn't the goal. And still isn't. But I don't feel right letting things fall apart, either. I'm fairly new here, I don't know the people and their backgrounds the way Paul did, and there's no way a single doctor can handle all of this. I know there are itinerant practitioners who go from place to place, but they generally come north in the summer to help cover vacations. Not in the middle of winter. I can't imagine there are too many people willing to drop everything and move here this time of year, and who has time to interview them? Not me."

Max approached from the other way as Ethan spoke. Hale and Ethan acknowledged him as he slid into the booth, but then a thought occurred, and Hale turned back to Ethan. "Thea Anastas."

"Who?"

"You know about Kelsey McCleary, the accident victim."

"Yes, of course, I checked out the baby on Christmas Eve, and she's supposed to bring her in for a one-week check on Friday."

"I overheard her friend talking, the shorter one."

"You mean the one who wasn't a supermodel in every major international city known to man?"

"Okay, good point. Anyway, Thea's a nurse practitioner. She was with a family practice in Pittsburgh but when a major health group bought them out, everyone who was a new hire was let go right before Christmas. She's here, and she doesn't have a job."

"You're sure about this?"

"I'm sure about what I heard, but not about her response," Hale answered. "If she's open to the idea and already in town, maybe it would work as an interim solution at least? Some folks will be crushed at losing Doctor Wolinski, and some will be glad to welcome a newcomer, and a woman at that. Worth checking out, right? If for no other reason than it would be nice to get home to these kids at night."

Ethan's guilty expression said Hale's words had hit a sore spot. "We've got school vacation this week. Mrs. Harper usually has these guys, but it's Christmas week and she's got holiday company at her place. And I was so busy in December, then with Paul's collapse, I never thought of making other arrangements. I'm so far beyond swamped I can't even put it in words."

"You need someone to watch the kids this week?" Hale asked.

Ethan nodded.

"My cousin Charlotte is home from grad school. Garrett's younger sister. She'd love to earn some extra money, and she's great with kids. I can see if she's available. She goes back to school after New Year's, but they'll be back with Mrs. Harper then, won't they?"

"Yes."

Hale sent the text while Max faced Ethan. "We need to get you and your practice moved into something more substantial, Doc."

"Permanent site for a transient doctor?" Ethan shook his head. "Can't happen. I'm an add-on, remember? But I agree. The office needs a substantial upgrade from where we are now." Thirty years back, tucking a medical office into a strip mall probably seemed like a good idea, but with the other businesses around it fading, the strip mall had fallen into disrepair.

"Paul wasn't the type to notice his surroundings, which is only good up to a point," Hale said. "Some folks might not take to the peeling paint and leaky gutter décor."

"Whether or not you decide to leave, the practice still needs a serious upgrade. I've got an idea I'd like to run by you."

Max Reichert was a big, burly, former state trooper with a keen eye for renovation, a skill he practiced on buildings and people alike.

"I'm only here on a twelve-month contract," Ethan reminded him. "Why give folks the wrong idea?"

Max wasn't afraid to argue his side. "If you decide to leave next summer, I think folks will understand. They'll miss you—you've been real good for this town, Ethan—but they'll understand. But when the practice goes on the market as a presentable practice package for an incoming physician, two storefronts in a failing strip mall aren't exactly inspirational. Becky's been after Paul to change things for a few years, but they don't come more stubborn—"

"Or tightfisted," Hale interjected, not to be mean but because it was true. Becky Wolinski had always been a practical voice of reason when the aged doctor took a hard stance over anything.

"That, too," agreed Max. "I've got a site I want you to look at. I just bought it, and I think we could turn the first floor into a really nice medical practice for the community. I'd have space for a two-bedroom apartment upstairs. I know moving would be disruptive, but think about it," he added as Hale sent a second text. "Presentation is key when you're selling anything, and getting that medical practice out of the strip mall will make it more appealing. And might be a help to Paul's wife when the time comes. I can run this by Becky, too. When the timing's right."

When he moved back to town, Hale had quickly become a fan of Max's restoration efforts. "If anyone knows his way around making things look better, it's Max," he told Ethan. A tone signaled an incoming text on Hale's phone, followed by another one. "Ethan, Charlotte says she'd love to help out. I'm texting you her phone number so you guys can talk directly, and . . ." He smiled as he read the next text. "Kelsey says that the thought of big-city Thea in small-town Wishing Bridge makes her laugh, but that Thea would be interested in talking interim status." He rolled his eyes at the formal language. "Is eight thirty tomorrow morning good for you?"

"I'm pretty sure someone just threw me a possible double lifeline, so yes, eight thirty is perfect. If Charlotte can take over first thing in the morning, I can meet . . . Thea?" he raised a brow, questioning the name.

"Thea. Yes."

"I can meet her at the practice at eight thirty."

"I'll come by then, too. With the ideas," Max told him. "If I don't grab you then, you'll never make time for this, and this town deserves a solid medical practice. We're the perfect center crossroads for a lot of folks."

Hale watched Ethan surrender, mostly because he didn't have much choice once Max got an idea in his head.

"All right. Meet me there, same time. We might as well have this gal in on the option. And I know you're technically right. A well-laid-out, clean practice will be a lot more attractive than the current situation. I just never thought I'd be in on the decision-making process because it's not my practice. Come by and show me what you've got in mind."

"Will do. Which brings me back to your mother's shop." Max turned toward Hale as Ethan helped Keegan manage the cream-filled center of his doughnut. He laid out a frame-in design on a scrap of paper—typical Max. "Here's what I'm thinking." By the time Hale had finished his doughnut and coffee, Max had presented the apartment setup above the store and the fun, country look his mother wanted downstairs. "I salvaged a bunch of wood from an old barn that fell down last year. It's a crying shame to see that happen, but I was able to bring a trailer load back to my barn. I've got enough to do two accent walls and a joined beam system to show how the old beams fit together, which can also be used to suspend racks or displays."

"Mom will love it."

"She'll like it well enough, although she's got opinions of her own," Max admitted as Ethan got the kids ready to go home at the next table. "Putting her thoughts into action isn't what I'd call a piece of cake."

"I want her happy."

"I know that, which is why I didn't argue with any of it. I figure if I guide you through the basics, I can step in and do the plumbing and the electric."

"No fancy stuff," Hale warned. "I'm all right with a nail gun and a saw, but don't put me on fine carpentry. We'll all be sorely disappointed with the outcome, guaranteed."

"I won't." Max grinned in understanding. "I uncovered old hardwood floors both upstairs and downstairs today, so that pleased your mother and saved a boatload of money. We'll get them refinished and have solid flooring for a fraction of what replacement would be. And all because the old owners kept a solid roof in place. A good roof makes all the difference in buying, selling, and fixing."

Max respected a solid roof and wasn't afraid to tell anyone who might listen. "I'll order what we need to have on hand once the demolition is complete." He pulled out his phone, and they settled on a day to tear down the old walls and fixtures. "A clean slate, except for the floors," Max told him.

The thought of taking a sledgehammer to walls appealed to Hale. "I'll make sure Ben's available to oversee the farm so we can work."

"Perfect. Thanks for the coffee."

Hale followed Max out the door and heard a call come over his radio. He jogged to his cruiser as the fire siren went off and his radio barked in his ear. The wind picked that moment to gust, adding speed to his actions.

He turned out of the doughnut shop lot and headed north, but he wasn't going back to Wishing Bridge. He made a sharp right onto Old Woodsmoke Road and swung his car crosswise to prevent through traffic.

Two fire trucks had beaten him there. Approaching sirens said more were on their way. He'd left enough room for their rigs to pass his cruiser, and within minutes the air was filled with shouts, radio crackle, and flashing lights. When the new arrivals set up the big ground flood-lights, Hale got the full impact of the raging fire behind him.

The Woodsmoke Inn was engulfed in flames.

Black smoke poured from the semiattached units as if burning equally throughout.

He wasn't a fire investigator—he'd leave that up to the Warsaw fire chief—but Hale knew enough about fire and wind direction to draw a pretty quick conclusion. This fire wouldn't start at opposite ends of a spread-out property and burn equally unless someone had set it to do just that.

Jack Hilbert.

He'd bought the place in a contentious sale a few years back, not long after Hale had returned to town. He'd had good intentions, but some rough family circumstances had pushed back many of his sched-uled improvements. An irate neighbor, who had tried to buy the inn but lost the deal to Jack, had petitioned the town in mid-December to close it down, citing lack of speed at addressing problems. In truth, he was probably hoping to buy the property at a bargain.

And now this.

Jack wasn't a bad person. He'd put forth honest effort, but Hale saw the writing on the wall. An insurance claim was better than a "No Occupancy" notice stapled to the doors, and that's what Jack would most likely be facing once the town board reconvened in January.

Maybe Hale was wrong.

Maybe the wind had fed the fire, and Hale just happened to be here as the whole building went up, end to end.

His phone buzzed a text. He pulled it out as two other sheriff's cars arrived to help steer traffic around the emergency.

Is the Woodsmoke Inn really on fire? Maggie's name appeared above the question.

Yes.

And then she wrote something else, something that made him realize she wasn't being the typical nosy small-town neighbor from her house on the hill: Thea and Jazz were staying there. All their stuff is in Unit Nine. Except the laundry. Oh my.

He cringed and typed quickly. So sorry. Looks like total loss. Be safe. Praying.

She would, too, but what were the odds that the nurse practitioner would stay once she realized someone might have intentionally burned the motel and all of her belongings?

The wind picked up. Snow started falling, not heavy, but not exactly light, either, and the wind pumped both the snow and the fire.

A third fire team arrived, followed by a fourth, and as the trucks drenched the wooden structure with jets of water, the rank smell of wet, burned wood filled the air.

Not many would lament the loss of the inn, not in its current state of disrepair, but if Jack was responsible for this fire, the repercussions would be far-reaching. Hale couldn't think about that now.

Folks were arriving to watch the show. A summertime fire brought out a lot of onlookers. Winter—not so much.

But this time and this fire brought out a lot of folks, well bundled. Someone brought a tray of coffees from The Doughnut Shack. Someone else brought a tray of leftover doughnuts in a big box. The ladies auxiliary came through the blockade and set up a coffee and hot chocolate tent for the firefighters behind two big rigs.

And through it all, the brave men and women of the local fire departments fought a hopeless battle against old wood, established fire, and strong wind. If Jack had lit the torch to burn his ill-fated investment to the ground . . . he'd picked the perfect night to do it.

~

"Maggie." Thea clutched the older woman's arms. Jazz was in the living room and Kelsey had gone to bed once the baby fell asleep. "You can't be serious. Are you? Is the inn really on fire?"

"Fully engulfed. Hale's mother just called to tell me. We haven't had news on, but I guess there are local reporters there right now. And multiple fire companies, trying to take care of things."

A fire.

A sharp pain grabbed her, temple to temple, the kind of pain she got when she studied too hard or worked too long.

The mental image of their room burning . . . the strange job offer . . . the pretty town and the howling coyotes . . .

Thea hadn't allowed herself to live by chance since she had escaped the drug bosses as a girl. She scripted her life, her goals, her days, her nights.

Everything.

She'd aced exams, pulled all-nighters, and lived by a clock that kept absolute time, buoyed by the pretty verse from Ecclesiastes: "To everything there is a season."

That's how she saw things, that's how she did things, and now, in the space of a week, everything she had done and planned had been turned inside out and upside down, and none of it was in her control.

This couldn't be happening. Could it? Thea studied Maggie's face as Jazz came up alongside her. "What's going on?"

"You don't want to know." Thea crossed to the window overlooking the festive neighborhood surrounding Maggie's home and leaned her head against the cool glass. "How did this happen?" She wasn't asking anyone in particular, because she was pretty sure no one had the answer, but when Maggie filled Jazz in, it was all Thea could do to keep from banging her head against the golden oak window frame.

Alternative universe?

The thought almost made her brighten up, but did anyone really want to get caught up in string theory and mirror-image physics?

She'd hated physics, so the answer was no.

"The inn is burning?" Jazz's perfectly sculpted brows arched. "Is everyone all right? Was anyone there? What about the funny old woman, the one who liked whiskey?"

"No one was there. Half the units were being kept empty so Jack Hilbert could fix them up, and there were only two guests staying there."

"Us." Thea turned as common sense attempted to take hold. "This could have been a lot worse."

"It could," Maggie agreed. "No one's been hurt, and the ladies auxiliary has set up a food and coffee tent for the firefighters."

"I will be relegated to staying inside for a while, though." Jazz made the announcement in a firm tone.

"Because . . . ?"

"I left my makeup in the room. No one's seen Jazz Monroe's face without proper preparation in a long, long time."

"I've got mascara and eyeliner upstairs," Maggie reassured her. "I don't use it much, and sometimes I have to add water to the mascara and jiggle that brush thing back and forth real good to mix it in, but it's better than nothing. Although," she continued, studying Jazz, "I think you're absolutely beautiful just the way the good Lord made you, so if you don't borrow my makeup, that's all right, too."

"And I'm telling myself that at least we had the laundry over here."

"Something to wear is always a good thing. Especially when you have a job interview first thing in the morning," said Jazz.

Job, fire, small town . . . Thea fought down a sense of impending panic. She wasn't a small-town person. She had never been a small-town person. She loved the hustle and bustle and lights and action of cities, and she'd always seen herself in a big, burgeoning medical practice, doing her best for scores of patients. Here, the nearest hospital was forty minutes away . . . unthinkable by modern standards. "I'm not calling it an interview."

"No?"

"No?" Maggie perked up, too.

"More like a professional agreement meeting. I can see how this poor doctor needs help on hand. And other than getting my roommate to replace me in our outrageously priced apartment, I have nothing holding me to Pittsburgh. So why not stay for a little while and help if I'm needed?"

"The fact that we're in the direct path of Mother Nature, Lake Erie, and lake-effect snow doesn't dissuade you?" Jazz asked. "Philly and New York have their share of rough weather, but if we're talking degrees, this small town has them both beat, hands down."

The weather wasn't a concern, not after the vagaries of Pennsylvania throughout her life. But the quiet streets, empty after seven o'clock? The utter silence, broken by wolf-like howls? That was another matter entirely. Thea shook her head. "Weather's weather. Always something to deal with or complain about, right?"

"They do their share of complaining in the city, that's for sure," agreed Jazz. "It seems like folks don't know what to do these days if there isn't something to complain about."

"So being in a clean, small town, with Kelsey and the baby here . . . maybe this was meant to be." Maggie's bright smile made easy sense of the situation.

Jazz's dubious expression said she wasn't quite buying it, and Thea couldn't blame her, but for the moment she'd deal with the unlikely circumstances that had combined to bring them to this place. This time. "Mrs. Effel used to school us about turning lemons into lemonade."

"I don't like to think of our sweet town as a lemon." Maggie aimed a pretend frown at Thea. "But I understand the analogy and agree whole-heartedly. If you stay awhile, maybe it would be good on both sides of the fence. Good for Wishing Bridge. And good for the two of you. We've got an extra room upstairs. If you gals wanted to stay here until you're on your feet, or find a place, Wishing Bridge is a real nice place to hang your shingle."

Thea wasn't going to be there long enough to hang a shingle, but she'd never hurt Maggie's feelings by voicing that thought.

"Only one of us has a shingle." Concern deepened the doubt on Jazz's face. "One of us has no marketable skills and needs to keep busy or go crazy."

"Do you have money in the bank, Jazz? I know how pricey New York is. Housing and living are a constant money drain."

"I've been careful with money, so yes. I can get by for a while."

"Then it's more keeping busy than financial need?" Maggie asked.

"Yes. Although I'm not like Kelsey and Thea. I didn't go to school. I've got no fancy list of letters or alphas and omegas after my name. It's just me. Jazz Monroe. At your service."

"There's always something to do," Maggie supposed. "And when you're young and beautiful, more folks are inclined to let you do it. You don't want to go back to New York and modeling?" She drew her brows together. "Did you quit?"

A fine knife could have split the silence in the room. And then, quietly, Jazz spoke. "It was killing me, so yes. I did. In November."

"The food thing." Maggie spoke as if she understood Jazz's problem, but she couldn't have, because Jazz had kept it under wraps for a long time. "It's a terrible cross to bear when folks don't let you just eat and behave like a normal person because they have abnormal expectations." When Jazz looked surprised, Maggie went on. "I know about these things. Too much, I'll tell you, and it's nothing I take lightly." Worry creased her face, her brow, and for just a moment she looked downright scared. But then she drew in a deep breath and tucked Jazz's arm more firmly in hers. "You quit modeling because you wanted to get better?"

"I want the chance to run my own life again." Jazz kept her voice low. "I don't want to have to think about bikinis or dresses with plunging necklines glued to my chest."

The thought of gluing material to skin made Thea cringe.

"I'm tired of wedgies, of cold beaches wearing next to nothing while cameramen wearing quilted coats jack the wind machines up for effect. I want to be me again. Just me. But"—she unclenched her hands—"I'm not sure how to do that anymore."

"Then maybe here is the best place," Maggie kept her words soft, too. "Maybe it *is* meant to be. Somehow. Some way."

"Well, my makeup did go up in smoke," Jazz noted. "And I can opt out of my New York digs—there's always someone in line for those apartments. I'm sure the real estate agent can sublet it quickly."

"You'd stay?" Thea faced her. "I'm no expert on eating disorders, but I know it's important to stay away from triggers. And your job had to be full of triggers."

"Every moment of every day." Jazz turned toward Maggie. "You sure you wouldn't mind us being here? Until we can find an apartment?"

Maggie didn't just look kindly and helpful. She looked determined. "I'd consider it an honor, Jacinda. Such a pretty name, isn't it?"

"My grandma called me Cinda."

"Now that's a fairy-tale name," declared Maggie. "Pretty, like its owner."

"It's worth a try. Isn't it?" Jazz turned back to Thea. "I've tried everything else, and nothing's worked. Maybe stepping completely away from Manhattan is what I need to do."

"And if Kelsey doesn't get a full-time job, she can substitute teach in the local districts." Maggie kept Jazz's arm tucked firmly in hers. "I'll be on hand here to watch the baby, if she'd like. What a blessing that is, right there, to have a baby in the house again."

Maggie's open heart, offering space. Jazz's predicament, nothing to be taken lightly. Her job in Pittsburgh gone, and a possible one opening up here. Maybe it would be all right, for a time. Time to rekindle her friendships, and earn a living, helping others. The fact that it all made sense surprised Thea.

"I'm in." Jazz put her long, slim hand over Maggie's. "Because one way or another, I've got to break this cycle. Before it breaks me," she added.

"I'm in, too." Thea laid her hand over theirs. "And I'll try to make a difference here until something else comes along."

Maggie unlinked her arm from Jazz's and crossed to the small cherry table on the far side of the entry. "Let's write them down."

"What?" Jazz lifted her gorgeous brows as Maggie returned with paper and a pencil.

"Kelsey said she likes to see things on paper." Maggie held up the lined white sheet as an example. "Around here a lot of us like to write down our hopes and wishes. It makes them more real to see them in black and white, don't you think?"

"And then do you take them to the bridge and ceremoniously toss them over the side? Because that might be considered weird," Thea told her, and Maggie laughed.

"We don't do anything of the kind, although I know folks go up there to pray from time to time. A long time back, a Catholic family put a little grotto on the edge of their land, just south of the bridge, and it's sweet. There's a holy family statue there, Mary and Joseph and that sweet baby, all tucked back in the rock ledge." Her expression became more thoughtful. "It helps some folks when they think about that little family's trials and tribulations so long ago. Can you imagine having a baby in some kind of place meant for animals? Having shepherds come by, angels singing, and kings traveling far and wide to follow a star? Escaping to a foreign land because your government wants to kill your child?"

"I've never quite thought of it like that," Jazz admitted.

"A time of trials in a time of trials," Maggie noted. "So it's nice for folks to see that statue tucked by while they're dealing with their own issues. To think of Mary, taking that journey with her son, from the stable to the cross. Folks find that to be a pretty good example of cour-age and faith."

Trouble had dogged mankind for a long time. Thea knew that. It was part of the reason she kept strict control on all variables. Once she'd gained control of her life, she'd clung to that control. She wasn't a bob-and-weaver. She walked a straight line with her goals firmly in sight. Until now, when she had been left with little choice in the matter.

"I can't disagree." She took a deep breath. "Let's get that clean laun-dry out of the car and figure out what I'm going to wear tomorrow morning because most of what I washed were blue jeans and T-shirts. Unless Kelsey's got some prepregnancy things tucked away."

"She's got two bags in the trunk of her car. Jeb told her he'd ride to the collision shop and get them," Maggie said, "but if Ethan Brandenburg's in over his head like I think he is, he's not going to care what you're wearing. It's cold and flu season in Western New York, and when that snow starts falling, folks like to find their doctors close to home. One man, especially one with Ethan's responsibilities, is going to need help. And fast."

CHAPTER FOURTEEN

"Are you feeling this whole déjà vu thing?" Kelsey poured her friends' coffee the next morning as Thea readjusted the collar of her pullover for the fifth time, and that was just since Kelsey had walked into the room. "The three of us together again and a sweet voice of wisdom guiding the way?"

"Does that count as forward progress or regression? Wait, don't answer that." Thea sipped the coffee and did a quick intake of breath.

"It's hot."

"Yeah, got that. Do I look as ridiculous as I feel?" Thea faced Kelsey, and her concern was apparent, as if the simple shirt and pants made a difference.

"You look fine, but that's not the question," Kelsey reasoned. "The question is, do you have the self-confidence to let your education, degrees, work experience, and long list of credentials talk for you? Or are you going to worry about casual clothing?"

"Clothing. Absolutely. The unprofessionalism of the moment is messing with my carefully scripted equilibrium. My structure's been disrupted."

"You've always been good at maintaining structure. I learned that from you," Kelsey told her. "But like anything else, rigidity can be carried to extremes. Go." She pointed to the door as Thea pulled her navy peacoat into place. "Meet the doctor. He seemed like a nice guy when he was here, and if you end up staying here for a while, I'm going to consider this the best slumber party ever."

"Certainly the longest." Thea squared her shoulders, as if drawing up her courage. "See you later."

"Call us, okay?"

"Will do." She went out the side door as Jazz came in from the living room. "She's on her way?"

"Yes. And unnerved. But while she's doing that, do you want to help me write those thank-you notes?"

"Happily. Any word on the inn, Maggie?"

Maggie had been on the phone. She came into the kitchen as Jazz asked the question. "The inn is a total loss. They'll do an investigation into the fire once the area cools down."

"Is that normal?"

"Yes." But she stretched the syllable out as if that might not be completely true.

"Do you think the fire was set on purpose?" Jazz had crossed to the coffee pot but paused when Maggie hesitated.

"I'm adopting a wait-and-see attitude, but others have taken an alternative route."

"At eight o'clock in the morning? The fire's only been out for a few hours."

"That's a small-town thing." Kelsey popped bread into the toaster. "I was between Canton and Potsdam, but I was in both often enough to realize that each town has its own informational network."

"A bane and a blessing," declared Maggie. "In some instances, it brings instant help. For others, it's like a destruction zone. And this one is fueled on nothing but speculation, but that hasn't stopped folks in the past, and isn't likely to curtail them now. We're not exactly high crime here, so the thought of someone burning a building is big news."

"I'm just glad no one was hurt," Jazz told her. "And my grandma was always the first in line to help others, so while I was raised in cities all my life, I know what that informational network is like. Ours was in our neighborhood, and G. G. Joan was either working, baking, fixing, sewing, or cleaning. When folks had something mean to say, she spun out a list of proverbs to cut it short. And it worked, at least as long as she was in the room."

"She sounds like a wonderful woman, Jazz."

"She was," said Jazz. "I was fourteen years old when she got sick, and the first thing she worried about wasn't herself. It was me. She worried so much about what would happen to me that I felt guilty because she should have been focusing on herself right then. On how to get better. I think back now and again, wondering how she was the only one in my family who cared what happened to me—but when I met Kelsey and Thea I realized how lucky I was to have that one person who had cared enough to put me first. It helped put things in perspective."

"Life's like that," said Maggie. "Kelsey, are you up to company today?"

"I am if you give me time to shower. Please say it's not reporters."

"You've done your part with them, so no." Maggie flashed a quick smile. "A local farmer's wife was going to stop in with some supplies. If that's okay?"

The generosity of the little town was almost disconcerting. "Everyone's already done so much, Maggie."

"Well, it's not every day that we get national news coverage, and if I know Donna, she'll err on the side of practical, not whimsy. She's on three church committees over at Wishing Bridge Community. Have you heard that old adage, 'Ask the busy person to do one thing more'?"

Jazz shook her head, but Kelsey nodded. "Very popular in schools, too."

"That's Donna. I've always thought she might like being in charge a little too much, but that's neither here nor there. She and her committees do a lot of good. I suppose that's what matters in the end."

"It sounds right to me. I'll go feed Hayley and shower quickly. Maggie, if there's anything I can do to help—"

"Oh, darlin'." Maggie had been fluffing a pillow. She paused to look at Kelsey, and there was no mistaking the quiet joy in her expression. "You're already doing it. Just by being here."

~

Thea approached the older man standing inside the doorway of a storefront doctor's office. It took a lot of effort not to compare this strip-mall setting to the state-of-the-art practice she'd called home for the past eighteen months, but she'd done a stint of medical mission work in Haiti, and this was a step up from that. Though not a big step.

"Hi. Are you on staff here? I'm Thea Anastas, here to meet with Dr. Brandenburg."

The man shook his head. "Max Reichert. I'm here to consult on a few office matters. Ethan should be right out."

Three women entered the room from a back office. Two were crying. The third was fighting tears, and as they moved toward a single desk and a box of generic tissues, the worn-looking doctor followed.

"Here's Ethan." The man motioned her ahead, a thorough gentleman.

Dr. Brandenburg moved their way. "Max, thanks for coming. Ms. Anastas"—he stretched out a hand to her, too—"I'm Ethan Brandenburg. I met your friend Kelsey the other day, but we were never introduced. Sorry to keep you waiting."

"It's fine, Ethan. Some things take time." Sympathy laced the older man's tone as he noted the staff with a glance.

"It's good to meet you." Thea said the words, but she wasn't sure of their veracity. The weathered strip-mall office wasn't what she had expected. It smacked of want and need. She saw it in the staff, in the building, and in the doctor's gaze.

She didn't want to be needed. Not here. Useful, yes. She could do useful.

But needed was something else. Needed meant a commitment, a commitment that could upstage her carefully constructed plans.

"Let's go in the back and we can discuss things. Sheila." He paused by the front desk. "We're going to meet for a few minutes, and I won't have a lot of extra time today, so you'll need to do phone triage. Hold some for tomorrow if you can, and send some to the quick-care center in Mount Morris as needed."

He was going to have them refuse patients because he was short-handed? That didn't sit well with Thea. "What if you're not on your own?"

"It's probably best to go slow, don't you think?" He seemed hesitant. Because she wasn't an MD? Because she was a woman?

"Go slow?" Thea had never had such a thought in her life. "Of course not. You've got patients who need care, we're both available, and I'm licensed to practice here. The practical side of my nature says why wait?"

"Because we haven't discussed compensation or hours or anything."

Leave it to a man to need i's dotted and t's crossed. "Are there extra scrubs around?"

One of the women got the gist and came her way quickly. "In the back. Kate and I always keep extras."

"Grab me some? Or a lab coat?"

"Yes." The woman returned within seconds. "I'm Laura. This is Kate. Sheila runs the front end."

"Thea Anastas, nurse practitioner with a specialty in family practice."

"How did you find out about the opening?" Where Laura seemed overjoyed, Kate looked suspicious. "We only just found out that Dr. Wolinski won't be coming back. There's no way you could have known unless Dr. Brandenburg sent for you."

"Hale sent me a message."

That information seemed to lessen Kate's frown.

"I'm in town for a little while and available for the moment. Hale said you guys could use some help."

"We sure can." Sheila had dried her eyes. Now she stretched out a hand to Thea. "Welcome aboard. Should we call you doctor? Or nurse? Or—"

"How about Thea?"

"Just that?"

"Works for me."

Ethan motioned her to a small office behind the nurses' station.

"I'll be back. Thanks for the lab coat. And can we do up a quick nametag, like you guys have? I had a couple, but my suitcase was at the Woodsmoke Inn."

"Oh, no. You were staying there?" Laura looked surprised and sympathetic.

"Yes. I had some clothes in my car, and my medical bag was there, too, but no scrubs or anything like that. It will take a couple of days to have them sent in. I'm staying with Maggie and Jeb Tompkins until I can find an apartment. I'll be right back." She followed Ethan and Max into the room.

Ethan shut the door and folded his arms. "You're a take-charge person."

She'd taken charge at a young age, so there was no denying that. "Yes."

"And you didn't think it prudent to talk with me about hours or expectations or responsibilities before you jumped in on the job? What if I don't offer you the position?"

The older man—Max—whistled lightly between his teeth.

She looked at him, then Ethan. "Like you've got other options?"

He didn't, she could tell that from his expression, and the last thing she wanted to do was step on this guy's toes or ego or whatever fragile male entity she might be trouncing. "You need help, correct?"

"Yes."

"I'm available right now. Also correct?"

"But—"

"Doctor." She nailed him with a look that gave him pause and possibly made him angry. At the moment she didn't much care. "I might not have the degree you do, I might not have your years of experience, but what I do have is a high regard for patients and good health. Since we appear to be mutually dependent for the moment—you need medical staff who can prescribe, and I need a job—why can't we just shake hands and get on with it?"

"I like her." Max grinned her way and shoulder-nudged the doctor. "That's my kind of woman."

The doctor rubbed a hand across his face. His tired face, she realized. Maybe she should cut him some slack.

"Max, maybe we shouldn't discuss your plans now." The doctor looked exhausted already, as if going toe-to-toe with Thea and the women on staff had already drained significant energy from his day.

"I'm here, you're here." The older man laid out a legal pad of paper alongside a cell phone. "Here's what I'm thinking."

Thea spotted the picture of the gracious old home on his phone and sighed. "That Queen Anne colonial is stunning."

"Nice, right?" Max grinned at her. "Six rooms on the first floor, the perfect setup. I see four exam rooms, a waiting room, and a double office here behind a blood draw/tech area."

"You mean this could be a new medical office?" Thea looked from him to the doctor and back again. "How perfectly inviting."

"That's my goal." He pointed out the rough sketch. "I know we don't have room for high tech, but if we need high tech we could consider a mobile unit at some point. For now, this would clean things up well. It would be a nice place to visit." He didn't say that the current setup wasn't nice, but then he didn't really have to.

"There's plenty of parking in the municipal lot here." He pointed just east of the building. "And eight spaces on the street. I can make the front handicapped accessible by creating a ramp off the south side of the porch."

"Is this your place?" she asked Ethan and couldn't bite back a hint of excitement because she could see the new practice, just the way the man described.

He shook his head. "His. Thea Anastas, Max Reichert." He waved back and forth between them. "And Max, this is Thea."

"You can do all this?" she asked Max.

He nodded.

"Sweet." She studied the house and his quick sketch once more. "If this is affordable, it would be a great asset."

"For whom?"

The doctor's question surprised her. "The town, of course. And the staff. But mostly the patients. There's nothing wrong with a clean, neat environment inviting people in."

"This practice might not be fancy like the one you were with in Pittsburgh."

She bit her lip to keep from saying something she shouldn't.

"But it's still solid medicine. Just a little worn around the edges."

"Exactly why I was thinking this would work for Hillside Medical, Ethan." Max tugged a copy of his rough sketch out of the legal pad and handed it to the doctor. "But it's up to you. I can set up another business here; it just seemed ideal for you and Paul. Of course things are different now. And of course we'd need Becky in on the decision. She'll be the actual investor when Paul's gone, and she might not want to take all that on, understandably. Unless someone buys the practice before then."

And just that quick, another medical practice was changed completely.

"Thanks for thinking of this, Max." Ethan indicated the paper with a glance. "I can see the improvements. I'm just not sure I'm the man to make them."

"It's all right." Max closed up the plans, then paused. "But remember, even if you're not slated to be here forever, the folks in this town mostly will be. What you do now with Becky's approval could affect the future here. That's something to think about. Pray about, I guess. I'll see you later. Thea"—he flashed a quick smile her way—"nice to meet you. And welcome to Wishing Bridge."

"Thanks."

He left, and she turned to Ethan. "Here's how I see this."

His phone chimed incoming messages. He checked them quickly, then set it down. "Go on."

"My being here allows you and your staff to help more people and gives you time to interview for this position. It's a stopgap, no more, no less, but I think it's convenient for both of us. But this is, of course, your practice."

He hesitated before he drew his eyes back to hers. "It's not."

She frowned, confused.

"It's not my practice, my town, or my life, and I won't be interviewing anyone for the position because it will cease to exist in a few months. The practice will be sold or dissolved, and Wishing Bridge will deal with the fallout. I will go back to a highly regarded cardiology program in Chicago, which I was supposed to be in this year. Fate had other ideas. What happens then is anyone's guess."

"Do you think someone will buy it?" She didn't mean to sound rude, but didn't he understand the simple logistics of selling? First you pretty up the item, then you list it. There was nothing attractive about the current location.

"They will or they won't, and that might be left up to Paul's estate or Becky to figure out. I'm here until June. Then I'm gone."

Cool. Decisive. Maybe judgmental, but possibly just plain, old-fashioned wiped out. He was leaving. She was leaving. And that could leave the people of Wishing Bridge in a bind, but that wasn't her fault.

"Then let's make this a successful winter as far as patients are concerned," she proposed. "You take care of your future plans. I'll take care of mine. And in the meantime, we help the people of this town the way they've helped my friend."

He named a salary that would allow her to pay her student loans and car payment, and keep an apartment nearby, but wouldn't stretch for a lot of extras. That was all right for the moment. These folks needed medical care to ease this unexpected transition, and she had the time to offer. "Deal."

She stuck out her hand as his phone chimed again.

He grasped her hand but didn't reach for the phone. Not yet. He took her hand in a firm, confident grip and met her gaze. "You all right with long hours?"

If she'd been expecting a "welcome aboard" speech, she'd have been disappointed, but she'd figured out something in the past few minutes.

He didn't want to be there.

This wasn't his dream any more than it was hers, but here he was, running a practice that didn't belong to him, and dealing with change he hadn't engineered.

Welcome to my world, bud. She kept his grip and gave him a crisp nod. "Long days, short nights, say hello to medicine."

She'd hoped for a smile.

She got a grunt instead, and when she released his hand and moved toward the door, she was pretty sure that Ethan Brandenburg was another one of those egocentric doctors she usually avoided at all costs. Hard to do in close quarters, but the rooms had doors, and she knew how to use them.

"Thea."

She paused when he said her name. Glanced back.

He yawned, then scrubbed his face with his hand, before he reached for a cup of coffee. A cup that Max the builder had left there. "Welcome aboard."

He didn't mean it, but he said it, and Thea had learned that lesson a long time ago. Every new beginning began at a crossroads.

This was hers.

CHAPTER FIFTEEN

"Ah, Kelsey. There you are." Maggie smiled up at her as Kelsey came down the stairs. "Come on over here, there's someone I'd like you to meet. This is Donna Voss." The woman stood to meet Kelsey. "She and her husband have a farm outside of town and three beautiful kids."

"All grown now, of course. Our youngest is a senior at Cornell."

She tossed off the name of the Ivy League university as if it were nothing, but there was no mistaking the distinct note of pride in her voice. She'd been sitting with Maggie. A mug of tea lifted steam into the air next to her seat, and Maggie had fixed coffee for Kelsey.

Donna took Kelsey's hand and offered her a thin smile, the kind of insincere smile that made hairs rise on the back of your neck. "It's so nice to meet our media star."

Snatch your hand back, turn, and run.

Kelsey fought the mental warning but paid attention to her gut reaction. She might be naïve, but she wasn't stupid, and growing up on the wrong side of the tracks had sharpened her intuition. When something felt wrong, it was generally for a solid reason.

"Inadvertent media star," Maggie corrected with a broad smile. "We're just so glad things went the way they did, aren't we, dear?"

"Yes." Kelsey pulled back, but the woman didn't release her hand. She locked eyes with Kelsey, a tight, hard gaze. Then she deliberately softened it. She let go of Kelsey's hand and offered her a greeting card.

"Our ladies' guild purchased a few gift cards for you and the baby. If you decide to keep her," she added as if it was all right for strangers to offer advice on her situation.

It wasn't all right at all.

"We saw the interview and realize that you've been placed in an awkward position. I hate it when my plans are thwarted, and the first thing I do is plot how I can get myself back on the track I set for myself."

Another warning knell hit Kelsey. Few people mentioned her original plan to give Hayley up for adoption, and now, after caring for her precious daughter for days, wrapped in the generosity of the town, she could envision keeping Hayley with her, raising her to be a fine, strong young woman.

Kelsey sat near Maggie and kept her hands lightly in her lap, but it took effort. "I'm not sure what my current plans are, but I'm grateful that Hayley and I ended up in Wishing Bridge." Maggie flashed her an encouraging smile, and Kelsey returned it. "I can't imagine what would have happened if I hadn't turned off the interstate when I did."

"An interesting choice, because there is literally nothing at that exit, is there? Except a random sign for the town. No convenience stores. No gas stations. Not exactly the ideal spot to exit in a storm."

Kelsey's pulse had accelerated when the woman hadn't released her hand right away. Now it went higher. Why was she questioning Kelsey's choices? What business was it of hers? Was she one of those busybody church ladies who did good with their hands while they slashed with their words? Except Maggie wouldn't be friends with someone like that. Would she?

"In a bad storm, you take whatever exit you can get to, I expect." Maggie reached over and patted Kelsey's knee. "I'm just so glad I saw her lights. What if I hadn't? But there, I won't even think about that anymore, because I did, and it's all worked out for the best. And if Kelsey gets a job hereabouts, or takes a subbing job, we might be able to convince her to stay."

Kelsey laughed softly. "The warmth of this town is a big inducement."

The dark-haired woman zeroed in on one word. "Job?" Her attention darted from Maggie to Kelsey.

Maggie grinned. "The school board has asked Kelsey to submit her application. She had it ready, so she sent it over this morning. Jeb dropped off the hard copy, and Kelsey submitted all the online stuff. It's amazing how they can get all that worked out these days, isn't it?"

"You might work here?" Donna Voss didn't look surprised. She looked shell-shocked. She shifted her attention from Kelsey to Maggie. "In Wishing Bridge schools?"

"Could be in the same hall as your Kristen," Maggie went on, delighted by just how well this might all turn out. She hadn't caught Donna's dark expression. She turned toward Kelsey. "Donna's daughter teaches fourth grade, and the second-grade classroom is right next door. Odd numbers on one side, evens on the other. Wouldn't that be lovely?"

There was no resisting Maggie's optimism. "It would." She shared a smile with Maggie as Donna stood. Then she sat again, and there was no missing the look of disbelief.

"You're staying?" Donna couldn't quite hide the shock in her question.

Maggie hadn't caught Donna's initial vibes. Now she did because the woman's abrupt tone unmasked them. She shifted toward Donna and sat taller and squarer in her seat. "Life isn't easy for a young mother on her own, and Jeb and I are happy to help. And what better town to raise a child in? I don't believe for one minute that Kelsey stumbled into our town by accident." She beamed a happy smile Kelsey's way. "I figure the whole thing was the good Lord's doing."

"Not an accident." Donna gave Kelsey a long, slow, studied look, then stood again. "I expect you're right, Maggie."

A chill danced up Kelsey's spine, not from Donna's words but her expression. Cool. Hard. Knowing.

Baby peeps came through the infant monitor. "There's my signal." Kelsey stood and moved toward the stairs. "Thank you so much for thinking of us, Mrs. Voss. We appreciate your generosity and that of the ladies from the church."

Hayley squawked louder, allowing Kelsey to hurry up the stairs. She didn't want to hear the other woman saying goodbye. Or feel her long, searching look.

Donna Voss didn't trust her. Maybe she had a suspicious nature . . . or maybe she just suspected something about Kelsey. Was it possible that people in town had already known of her existence? Did the name McCleary mean something to some of them?

She hadn't thought of that because she'd never seen her mother have any contact outside of the trashy friends she had hung with in South Philly. She'd said she took the name because she liked the sound of it. Kelsey had no way of knowing the truth of that. Her Internet search years ago hadn't turned up any McClearys in Wishing Bridge or Wyoming County. Maybe the search had given her a false sense of security.

Hayley had writhed her way out of her cozy blanket. She kicked her thin legs and drew her face into a massive frown, ready to wail.

"Hey, darlin'," Kelsey crooned as she lifted the baby from the bassinet. "Hey, hey. Mama's here. Mama's here for you."

Her words soothed the baby's distress. She slipped into the comfy recliner and loosened her top to feed the baby, and when Hayley latched on, a deep, sweet wave of maternal feeling flooded Kelsey.

She hadn't expected this instant attachment, but there it was.

As the baby nursed, her tiny fists began to relax. And when she was sated, her whole body oozed contentment. Looking down, Kelsey realized she could do this. Really do this.

A job. A good town. The kindness of strangers. Best friends on board.

It was almost as if all the variables had been brought together like the pieces of a puzzle. Things didn't happen that way purposely. Kelsey knew that. The accidents of timing were strictly that.

But as Hayley flickered a tiny half smile of utter contentment, Kelsey wasn't quite so sure.

I'll pray for you every day. Mrs. Effel's encouraging words came back to her.

Hale had been ready to climb in his cruiser and head back to town.

Maggie had wondered if she should bother anyone with what she thought she saw.

Avis had been in town that night because her brand-new car had refused to start, and the storm had taken hold by the time she'd found an alternative ride to the hospital, so she stayed put.

Kelsey had taken that turn toward Wishing Bridge, not because she wanted to, but because she needed to find shelter from the storm. She wasn't on a fact-finding mission. So if her presence here became an issue . . . if she found family or they found her . . . was that fate or faith deciding?

She didn't know, but as she held her daughter in the cozy upstairs room of the solid old house, a part of her didn't care. She'd come this far on her own. She'd navigate the rest of her journey the same way, most likely. But as her eyes drifted shut with the baby snugged in the curve of her arm, the thought of staying in Wishing Bridge seemed too sweet to shrug off.

~

"Here's our doctor gal!" Maggie's voice was exactly the welcome Thea needed after nine hours of cold and flu season in the cramped, chilly offices. "How did it go? I can't believe you jumped right in like that, but I'm so proud of you, honey. Seeing a need and stepping in."

Maggie had cited the very thing Thea was determined to avoid.

"It felt good to be working," she admitted. "And who'd have thought there were so many sick and ailing people in this town?"

"They come up from below, too," Jeb explained. "Down Warsaw way and across the county. There's other good docs around, but Doc Wolinski took care of nearly two generations hereabouts, plus more, and there are some that won't go anywhere else."

"And others that will. Like me." Where Jeb sounded accepting, Maggie seemed defiant. "Medicine has changed a lot in fifty years. Seems to me that doctors need to change along with it."

"To keep up on new things, I agree. And that's the perfect blend, isn't it?" Thea asked as she hung her coat on the kitchen hooks near the side-door entry. "Wisdom of experience coupled with staying abreast of new findings. Best kind of medicine there is."

"Paul didn't hold much with learning new things."

Thea knew the landscape of medicine was changing with the growing success of immunotherapy and DNA-targeted treatments for diseases. At the same time, doctors had scaled back antibiotic prescriptions, realizing the body's best defense often lay within itself. "And new things are happening almost daily in medicine. I've always wanted to be that kind of family practitioner," she told them as she accepted a mug of coffee from Maggie. "Wise from experience and cautious enough to stay book smart."

"That's a good attitude, Thea."

The scents of something simmering made Thea's stomach gurgle. She couldn't remember the last time she'd finished a day and came home to food waiting. It had been years, literally, unless she was on any one of many bad dates.

"Something smells amazing, Maggie."

"Pot roast. With potatoes and carrots and sweet potatoes, all done up in the broth."

"I've never had food smell so good." Jazz came into the kitchen. She was wearing warm-ups over running gear, and Thea raised a brow.

"I don't remember those being in the laundry."

"Jeb and I went down to Warsaw, and I stocked up on some essentials. And Maggie was right about those hills. Anyone running through these forest paths will stay in shape forever. At least that long. I'm going to grab a shower," she added as she moved toward the hall stairway. "Your day went all right?"

"It was good. Busy, but good."

"I thrive on busy. When I'm not starving myself to death," Jazz went on, mocking herself.

Jazz didn't see Maggie's pained expression because she was already heading up the stairs.

Thea couldn't miss it. Pain and longing darkened the circles around the gentle woman's eyes and deepened the creases by her mouth.

"We've got to make sure she does okay, Jeb."

Concern shadowed Jeb's face, too. "It ain't always that easy, Mother."

"Don't I know it? But she's here, and we've got Thea and Kelsey here, too. I don't want to see that pretty thing hurting herself over something as simple and good as food." She sounded hurt and worried as her voice implored Jeb's agreement.

Jeb stared out the back window, into the thick, dark woods beyond. "If it was just food it would be easy, Maggie. You know that."

"Jeb's right."

He turned toward Thea, but Maggie kept her hands busy at the far counter, chin down.

"The mental-health aspects of eating disorders are tough to figure out and hard to address," Thea went on. "Jazz knows this. And it's good that she's being open about it and is willing to fight back before it takes too much of a toll on her body. Things like a lack of self-esteem, a longing or lust for control, and type A personalities that run amok can manifest in an eating disorder. Once it's turned on, it's tough to turn off. I did a clinical session at an eating-disorder center in Pittsburgh," she explained. "I wanted to be able to relate to all the aspects of family medicine, and that meant deepening my understanding of what makes people tick."

"That's some smart doctoring, right there." Jeb said the words but looked more sad than happy.

Kelsey brought the baby into the kitchen just then. "You were surrounded by a lot of dysfunctional teen girls at Hannah's Hope. That offered you some solid life experience."

"Maybe the best I had." Thea gripped the mug with both hands, letting the heat seep into her still-chilled fingers. "Not the girls so much, but how Mrs. Effel handled us. She saw the good in us and helped us to see it, too."

"Helping us to help ourselves."

"Exactly. That's what I try to do with medicine. Using the whole body, heart, and soul. Not just treating symptoms but teaching the patient and the body how to heal itself. Not all patients are open to that idea. The thought of a quick fix is ingrained these days. Most want you to prescribe a pill and get them on their way."

"I expect you saw some of that today." Jeb sank into a chair, looking tired. "The folks that loved Doc Wolinski aren't going to switch allegiance quickly. A good share don't want a thing to do with Ethan, and that's a darn shame because he's a good man. A smart man."

"Smart men don't go to work with chips on their shoulders," Maggie reminded him. "There's more to doctoring than brains, but it's no wonder he's worried with all that's rained down on him. He's caught like we were, trying to help those who don't want his help. It makes for a long, tough day all around." She brought over a basket of fresh, warm rolls and a plate of seasoned oil. "I learned to do this at that fancy restaurant over in Mount Morris when Jeb and I went out for our forty-fifth a few years back. It was a lovely meal, and cost a sweet penny, but fancy enough to be special."

She'd changed the subject, leaving Thea no chance to inquire about Dr. Brandenburg's struggles. Maggie's reference meant Thea wasn't imagining it, and the guy's chronically worried expression wasn't exactly fun to be around, but that was his problem. Not hers.

As she reached for one of Maggie's melt-in-your-mouth rolls, a different picture came to her. The older man that morning . . . Max Reichert, showing Ethan plans, not pressing. But she hadn't missed the concern in his eyes or how he'd brought Ethan coffee.

A simple act of kindness.

Random acts of understanding.

Picturing Max's face, she realized she needed to work more on her own understanding. She judged too quickly sometimes. Sure it was important for a medical practitioner to make swift assessments, but this was different.

The older man had treated Ethan gently. And the staff seemed divided over their allegiance to him. He wasn't staying, he'd made that clear, and those three women needed jobs.

No practice, no jobs.

"It's tough to get young medical folks in the country these days."

Jeb must have been reading her mind because she'd never considered working rural medicine. She wanted fast-paced, big, beautiful hospital-on-hand type medicine. Didn't she?

"Course we need 'em as much as anyone, but when a town's failing, it don't hold much of an invite for the young to stick around. Unless they're teachin' and such," he added with a smile toward Kelsey.

"Then we give it time, old man." Maggie didn't speak harshly, and she put a gentle hand on Jeb's right shoulder. "We turn to God and let him do the heavy lifting."

She said the words but didn't look like she necessarily believed them.

"You're right, Mother." He reached up and patted her hand with such an understanding touch it made Thea blink back tears. "If that baby needs holdin', I'm on the job, Miss Kelsey. And I washed my hands just in case you wandered this way with her."

"You must have seen me eyeing that coffee pot." Kelsey handed the baby over to him, and then surprised Jeb and the other women by kissing his forehead. "I don't know what I'd do without you guys, and I can't begin to thank you. You're the best."

She moved to the coffee pot and missed Jeb's smile.

Maggie didn't miss it, Thea noted. She saw him beam as he lifted Hayley onto his shoulder.

She sighed softly, then clasped her hands in front of her striped apron, as if praying—but not quite.

"Maggie, what time are the services this weekend?"

"New Year's holiday is the same as last week. Christmas on a weekend crowds things, doesn't it?" Maggie broke off a piece of a roll and swiped it into the herbed oil. "And then back to normal, nine and eleven on Sundays. Of course we've got five churches, all a little different, and all fine. One way or another, good ways to set with the Lord."

"Which service do you and Jeb prefer? And would you mind if I go with you?" asked Thea.

Maggie didn't hesitate. "I'd love it," she declared. "Generally we go to the nine o'clock so's I can get things done on Sunday. And football, too."

"Playoffs," said Jeb, as if the single word painted enough of a picture. "You a Steelers fan, coming from Pittsburgh? Or the Eagles, maybe, since you grew up around Philly?"

"Green Bay. Any fan base willing to wear cheeseheads like they do in Wisconsin had to win my heart."

"My kind of girl." Jeb stood with the baby. "We're going to have a walkabout and peek out the windows at the pretty lights. Don't know quite what she can see yet, but folks'll be taking them down before too

long, and our little gal needs to have a glimpse of her first Christmas."
He moved toward the living room.

Maggie shifted slightly. She watched him go with a look of sadness
Thea sensed but didn't understand.

Kelsey brought her mug to the table and sat down. "Maggie, have
I mentioned how grateful we are to be here?"

The sadness lifted as quickly as it came. "Only a few times a day.
Not nearly enough."

Kelsey laughed. "I hope you know what a blessing you are to all
three of us. I'd forgotten how to laugh this year. How to hope. How to
sing." She smiled toward the front room. "Having Hayley here with all
of you has brought that back into my life. It's like a dream come true."

"It works both ways." Maggie bent to lift the roaster from the oven
and paused too long.

Thea was by her side instantly. "I'll get this. You sit."

"I'm fine, just a touch winded."

"Go." Thea took the hot pads from her hands and waited until
Maggie sat down before she lifted the heavy roasting pan to the stovetop.
"Stubborn women need help, too. And it makes us feel like we're earn-
ing our keep around here. Of course if you let us pay for the room . . ."
she added with a pointed expression.

"Kindness doesn't need payment, but if you throw a little extra into
the missions, there's some little ones in Haiti we've been sponsoring. Jeb
and I don't need money."

"Then we'll do that, gladly. How long have you been losing your
breath like that?"

Maggie waved off her concern as if it were nothing. "A little head
rush is all. Nothing major. I had the doc look into it a few years back,
and it's more than likely a neck problem, he said. Common enough
among older folks."

Thea wasn't so sure. "When did you have your last physical?"

"Healthy folks don't have to run to the doctor to be checked for this and that and the other thing, do they?"

"Did he put you on any medication?" She'd never seen Maggie take more than a baby aspirin, and Maggie confirmed that.

"He didn't suggest it, and I didn't want it, so's we were equal on that. I think most older folks get a little dizzy now and again, don't they?"

"They do, sure, and it's generally because there's a reason, Maggie." Thea squatted down between Maggie and Kelsey. "Come see me. Friend to friend. It doesn't have to be official. Humor me, okay? Because I'd hate to think of Wishing Bridge losing one of its sweetest residents too soon."

Maggie refused to look Thea in the eye or agree, but when Thea stayed right there by her side, she finally huffed a breath. "I'll think on it."

"You just show up, no formal appointment. We'll keep it off the books? Just you and me."

"Like I'm just stopping by to bring you lunch?"

"Perfect subterfuge. I get food, and you relieve my worries."

Maggie eyed Thea, then the roaster. She pressed her lips together. "Salad or sandwich?"

"I am sick to death of salads, so a turkey sandwich would be lovely. If we still have some left over? With mayo?"

"I'll bring the sandwich. The rest? We'll see."

Thea knew better than to press. "Sounds good to me. I'm going to put the food on the platters you set out, all right?"

"Fine."

She and Kelsey double-teamed the process, and when Jeb brought the baby back to the kitchen, he drew a deep breath of appreciation. "Smells good, Mother."

Maggie stood quickly, as if sitting might raise his suspicions. "Girls, when you marry, make sure it's a man who loves a good meal. And if he can step in and cook now and again, all the better."

She moved around the kitchen quickly. To show Thea she was fine, perhaps? Or to keep Jeb from worrying?

Both, Thea decided, and one way or another she'd like to find out why.

~

"We've got company, Hale." Max pointed toward the front of what would, in a few weeks' time, be a customer-friendly rustic-looking shop. Right now, it was a mess of demolition dust and destruction.

"Mrs. Voss." Hale pulled off his dust mask as he moved forward. "It's kind of nasty in here. Did you need something?"

Donna Voss waved to Max before she drew close to Hale. "That girl you saved." She kept her voice soft. Real soft. And questioning.

That wasn't what raised his ire. It was the fact that she called Kelsey "that girl," as if she didn't quite measure up. He went on the defensive instantly and wondered why. Because she was questioning him in that tone of voice? Or because of how she referred to Kelsey? He wasn't sure of the reason, but he was certain of the quick reaction.

"Kelsey."

"I don't like it, Hale."

Hale kept his face neutral. "Don't like what?"

"She's hiding something."

He'd had an inkling of the same thought, but Donna's prying didn't strike him well. "Like?"

She frowned and looked truly concerned, which made him feel bad for his reaction, because hadn't he felt the same way?

"I don't know, not exactly." She made a face of worry. "There's just something. I can sense it. What do we know about her? I heard from Maggie that the school board might offer her a job in our schools. With our children." Her eyebrows lifted higher, as if hiring a teacher equated to swinging from high-voltage lines. "Why would they do something like that for a total stranger?"

"Except she won't be a stranger once they go through her application process and the recommendations and references. It's a pretty lofty bar they use before they hire on, even for long-term subs. You know that, Donna, because Kristen works at the elementary school. They don't take just anyone, even if they feel sympathy for the person."

She leaned even closer. "Brian Cunningham is up for reelection to the school board this spring, and if you know the Cunninghams, you know they love to see their name in lights. Hitching his wagon to the feel-good story of the year would be just like him."

Hale scrubbed a hand to his neck because this wasn't making a whole lot of sense, although it triggered questions he'd had all along. "It's a volunteer position, so—"

"With power attached," she interrupted. "And there are those among us who thrive on power. You know that, Hale."

He raised his hands in defeat. "I'm not sure what you expect me to do. If Kelsey *does* get a job here, I would say it's because she earned it."

"The naiveté of that remark is amazing."

Hale hadn't felt naïve until the bossy woman had called him out.

"I don't like to interfere—"

Sure, she did. With anyone and everything, which meant he couldn't take her concerns too seriously, and yet . . . his mother had picked up vibes and had promised to call Nora to check things out, but Nora was on an overseas cruise with her husband—a gift from their two sons. That made her unavailable for at least two weeks.

"What was it exactly that bothered you, Donna? Because I think Kelsey's delightful."

She sized him up with a narrow look and pursed lips. "I see."

"Nothing to see, but maybe a chance to help someone down on their luck."

"You think it's luck that brought her here?" Donna's eyes narrowed further, but then she paused and took a step back. "Never mind. You're obviously smitten . . ."

"I don't even know what that means."

Although he did. Kind of. But he wasn't smitten with Kelsey or that beautiful baby she had named after him, and the fact that he'd been dropping by to see them daily wasn't a big deal. It was just another chance to check on things. How the baby was doing. And how the baby's mother was getting on.

"Forget I stopped by." She moved to the door, clearly displeased. "If it's not worrying our sworn protectors, why should the concerns of a simple farmer's wife be taken with any degree of seriousness?" She moved through the door. A burst of wind and snow swirled in her wake, a whirlwind effect.

"You've riled something there." Max had stayed quiet during the back-and-forth, but Hale knew he'd been listening. Once a cop, always a cop.

Hale turned around. "But what? And why?"

"No idea, but I went toe-to-toe with a few facial expressions like that during my trooper years. Not one of them came to much good."

Hale glanced back at the door. Donna's headlights veered quickly away from the parking spot and onto the street. "She's ticked."

"Yeah." Max leaned on his sledgehammer. "But why? What is it about that young woman and newborn baby that threatens her?"

"Threatens her?" Hale moved back to the wall he'd been dismantling. "Don't you think that's a little extreme?"

"Not after that." He jutted his chin toward the door, then turned back to his side of the room. "Something to gnaw on."

It was. More so now that Max had chimed in. The retired trooper had a strong sense of right and wrong and a heart for helping others.

Donna Voss had neither. She was married to one of the nicest guys around, but she liked things done her way, in her time, and she wasn't afraid to push her agendas. He'd seen that growing up, how she always had a ruling hand in everything her kids did, right through high school.

He'd been little more than a kid himself back then, so maybe he was off base, but coming home to Wishing Bridge had shown him the same thing. Donna liked to stir multiple pots, and she and her little group of friends weren't opposed to inciting trouble now and again through their loose talk. He'd never thought too much about it until now, and that was because Kelsey was involved. And that baby.

"There's a proverb about that." Max had gone back to work, but he paused. "Of course, there's a proverb about most anything, but these days we just forget to look back and pay attention. It says how the righteous are concerned for the rights of those down on their luck, the ones that are lonely and forgotten. And the wicked don't understand such concern. Maybe because they're too busy worrying about themselves."

Hale wasn't all that righteous. He understood the dark anger that lingered inside, how it clouded his joy and sometimes his vision. He changed the subject. "I hear you're coming to dinner on New Year's. Football and food."

"And one of the nicest women I've ever met, even with those strong views." Max glanced around the major project they'd undertaken, then turned back to the work at hand. "You boys get your kind hearts from her, I expect."

"I expect we do." Hale didn't have to mention the obvious, that his father was low account. Everyone in town knew that. Of three Jackson men, two were shadier than a sugar maple in June.

And then there was Garrett's father, the only decent man of that generation.

"You and Ben understand how hard it is to be a single mom. I don't expect Donna's got a lot of sympathy for any part of that equation." Max put his goggles back into place. "She's too busy polishing her crown to notice the regular folks walking up and down the street."

"A high-and-mighty farmer's wife? I'm not sure I can handle the irony."

"It's not about what you do for a living." Max took a strong swing at a section of stained drywall. "It's about ego and self-importance, and that"—he slanted a look of resignation back at Hale—"can be far more dangerous, my friend."

~

"I know Christmas was kind of quiet." Maggie set a square laundry basket filled with Hayley's clothing on the couch the next day. Eyes down, she began folding tiny garments. Onesies. Sleepers. Soft flannel receiving blankets. Kelsey joined her while the baby slept nearby, her eyes shut tight. "In its own way."

"It was lovely, Maggie. You spoil us." Jazz shook out prefolded flannel diapers to use as burp cloths. "And I don't think housing three women and a newborn baby can ever be construed as quiet."

"Maybe dim is a better word." Maggie smoothed an aged hand across the stack of pink clothing and didn't look up.

Jazz and Kelsey exchanged looks. "Are you all right, Maggie?" Kelsey crossed the short distance between them. "Is there something you want to talk about? To tell us?"

"Just enjoy this baby." Eyes down, she passed her hand over the pile of tiny garments. "Just enjoy every single minute you can."

"I will. And did you mean what you said about watching her while I work? Because I can't imagine leaving her with anyone else."

"It would be the best thing I can think of, is all." Maggie looked up then. Her eyes glistened with moisture, or maybe it was a trick of the dull afternoon light. "There is nothing like a child to make the sun shine on a cloudy day."

"They've e-mailed me an interview schedule for next week."

"You up to that so soon?"

Kelsey nodded. "They're on a tight timeline. And I was thinking we could use a couple of those gift cards to stock up on bottles for you to use when I do go back to work."

"If I moo like a cow, will you be offended?" asked Jazz.

"Of course not, Jazz-ma-Sass. I'll simply murder you in your sleep."

"No one's called me that in twelve years."

"Too long, then. I'm going to go out for a walk while Hayley's sleeping, if you two are okay here. I need to get outside. Stretch my legs."

"I think that's a marvelous idea. It's sharp today. Bundle up."

Maggie's words held a mother's tenderness, the maternal mind-set that had skipped Vonnie McCleary completely. "You know that little library down on Main Street?"

Maggie looked up. "Friends Free Library."

"Does it have Internet?"

Maggie nodded brightly. "And two computers!" she exclaimed. "When Horst Grueber the fourth passed on, he left funds so the library would be kept up-to-date. Whenever something new is on the scene, the library orders it in. Horst was a good man. Horst the first had a pottery factory, one of those frontier businesses back when they built the Erie Canal in the 1800s. That first Horst was right there, creating all kinds of pretty things that his family started shipping back east."

"They made a killing and kept growing." Jeb had come into the room as Kelsey tugged her coat into place. "Four generations of Gruebers ran that business. When it finally got sold, the fourth Horst Grueber invested a bankroll of money into technology stuff."

"He died rich but sad."

Kelsey had been looking back and forth between them during their crisscross conversation. She waited, sure that one or the other would fill in the blank. Jeb did the honors. "He lost his wife in a tragic accident.

And one of his boys went afoul of the law and ended up in jail. But he had his Sally here, and that made a difference. Not all. But some."

"Sally's his daughter?" Kelsey supposed.

"His dog," Jeb explained, and Kelsey refused to laugh because the kindly man looked far too serious. "Janet's his daughter. She's got Sally now, they're both on in years, and Janet got the bulk of his estate. She's nice enough, but a little hoity if you get my meaning. But Sally, she's a golden retriever, one of them darker ones. She's a good old girl."

"You've got gloves?" Maggie asked.

The couple couldn't have been cuter or more genuine if they tried. Kelsey held her gloves up. "There are two bottles in the fridge. I've got my phone if you guys need me. And I won't be long."

"We've got this." Jazz offered an encouraging smile. "Take your time and breathe some of that fresh air. I forgot air could smell so good. So sweet."

Maggie agreed. "It's different here, isn't it? Like it's really special?"

"Exactly like that." Jazz stretched her legs. "If I'm not careful I'm going to end up getting too comfortable and never leave."

"Wishing Bridge is a settling kind of town," said Jeb.

"But not too much in the way of employment opportunities," said Jazz with a laugh. "And I'm going to need to do something before too long. That's the New York side of me showing. Everything quick, in a New York minute. Or faster."

"We do like to breathe now and again up here," Jeb admitted. "But stuff gets done quick; we're not much on lollygaggin'. Just not as quick as in the city."

Kelsey slipped through the front door. They'd set up a Pack 'n Play in the dining room that morning so Hayley could nap there. Kelsey was pretty sure the baby would never stay asleep on the first floor, but Hayley surprised her. Nothing had bothered her, not the sound of nearby voices or the vacuum cleaner in the next room.

She found that pretty amazing.

She turned right on Main Street and realized she should have turned left, toward the firehouse. She made a quick reverse and almost ran into a sheriff's car that hadn't been there ten seconds before.

"We've got rules about jaywalking, ma'am." Hale Jackson eased out of the driver's door, looking good. Real good. Too good. "You weren't thinking of crossing Main Street outside the marked lines, were you?"

"Not anymore."

And then she couldn't help it because he was just too cute, too nice, and right there. She smiled at him. Not flirting, but yes, flirting. Because it seemed like the most natural thing in the world to flirt with the man who had saved her life. In a fairy-tale world, that would be fine, but Kelsey was dealing with more of a reality-TV scenario.

"Are you patrolling the town to keep us safe from desperados, Deputy?"

"Exactly that, ma'am." He grinned.

So did she.

"And you're going . . . ?" He glanced around.

She pointed, feeling almost guilty, but how was she supposed to find out anything if she didn't do some quiet research? "Library. Hayley's sleeping, and Jazz and Maggie seemed excited about watching her."

"I'll walk you."

"Oh, no, I—"

"Civic duty, ma'am." He'd come around the front of the marked SUV and tipped his hat. "Being new in town, you could get lost."

"Except there's only one main road and we're on it."

"There are a few cross streets." He trained his gaze forward but kept right on smiling. "Might make a wrong turn and end up in the woods. Go through the whole search-and-rescue scenario a second time." He stayed quiet for six or seven steps before adding, "I'd do it again, though."

His words made her heart skip a beat. "Would you?" She stopped walking and looked up, speaking softly.

"Well, it got the sheriff's office a whole lot of good press, and that's important these days because otherwise the county commissioner would have given me a public dress down for calling out the plows when he told folks to stay off the roads. And then there's Betty." He pointed out the bakery as they walked past. "She was so proud that she gave me a little cake. No charge." He stressed the last part and winked. "So, yes." He'd been ticking off his fingers like he was making a list, but then he dropped his hand and met her look. "Yes, I would. Anytime."

You're not who he thinks you are. You could be related to him, and wouldn't the school board love that? Use your head and figure this out before you go any further.

"That's good to know if I ever get lost in the woods," she told him. She stopped flirting and teasing and kept her voice normal. Not because she wanted to, but the common sense of the situation said she needed to. "I expect the woods around here are beautiful in the fall." She kept her voice easy. "I was in the flatlands around Philly, and then just outside the Adirondacks in Canton, but every now and again I'd take a drive into the hills. It always seemed easier to figure things out in the hills. I don't know why."

"You might be around to see the leaves change next fall. Then you can see for yourself. I'd be okay with that."

In a perfect world, so would she, but she kept it casual. "It's a big step from applying for a position to landing one. There's a lot of competition for teaching jobs in New York."

"True enough. But it would be nice to have you here. It's a good place to raise a family."

"Do you have kids, Hale?" He wasn't wearing a ring, but she knew better than most that marriage wasn't required to have a family. She bit back a sigh of self-recrimination.

He didn't answer right away, then shook his head, but the hesitation was odd. It wasn't a hard question. You either had kids or you didn't. "No."

His voice flattened. The smile faded. And as they came to the corner to cross the road, he gazed out over the quaint village, but Kelsey was pretty sure he wasn't seeing old-fashioned colonials and twinkle-lit facades. "Is the baby doing all right?"

She rolled with the change of subject. "She seems marvelous. She goes to see Dr. Brandenburg tomorrow. Or Thea, I guess. One of them. And hey." She nudged him as they crossed the street. "Thanks for thinking of Thea when the doctor needed help. She loves to stay busy, and losing her job was an unexpected blow."

"Glad it worked out. Ethan's a great guy. It's hard when life dishes out more than our fair share, and he can sure use the help."

Kelsey had lived the truth of that her entire childhood. "It is. But if we take that bad and use it to become stronger, maybe it's all right."

"Is that what you did, Kelsey?" He looked down at her this time.

She gazed up into gorgeous eyes, green and gold with hints of caramel, bright and questioning. With thick, long lashes, the kind every girl longed for and rarely got. Square jawed, rugged features, and a firmness about him that appealed.

If life was fair or even a little bit normal, she might have enjoyed the attraction, but she was here under pretense, and he didn't know that. Her presence . . . her possible family relationships . . . might mess things up in this close-knit hamlet, and that wasn't her goal. She made a skeptical face. "That's one of those long stories best told over pots of coffee. And several years," she added. "Thanks for walking me, Hale."

He didn't delve further. "My pleasure," he said, tipping his sheriff's hat in one of those sweet gestures that seemed to fit perfectly in Wishing Bridge. "My pleasure. I was planning to stop over later today. Just to check on you and Hayley."

"And now there's no need." She kept her face neutral with effort. "We're both doing well. But thank you."

"Doesn't mean I won't stop by, Kelsey." He'd stepped back, but not far enough that she could miss the teasing in his tone. "Just means I get to see you twice today."

Oh, her heart.

Her silly, tempted heart.

She pulled open the library door and crossed to the computer carrel, then realized she needed a card to set up a password. A few minutes later she was set and took her place in front of one of the two computers.

How to search?

She stared at the screen, then noticed a basketball flyer from a local school posted on the bulletin board.

High school.

If her mother was really from Wishing Bridge, there would be high school pictures, wouldn't there? But would they have the old yearbooks online?

She found the school district, then a tab marked "Our Alumni." She clicked on it.

There were no yearbook photos, but notable Wishing Bridge alumni were listed in chronological order. Hale was there, one of the most recent lauded graduates, and when she scanned the information on him, her cheeks flushed.

What was a wealthy, former pro-football player doing as a deputy sheriff?

It seemed wrong and yet somehow right, as if that was exactly the kind of thing a good man would do. Except it made no sense to risk your life for others if you had enough money to make it unnecessary. Or was she being cynical?

All County. All State. Sectional championships. Scholarship to Alabama, and then a quarterback in the SEC before being drafted into the NFL.

Thirty-three years old.

He'd had it all. Done it all. So why was he here, in uniform, rescuing damsels in distress?

She plugged in his name, and the career-ending injury came up toward the top of the Google search.

He could have gone anywhere. New York, LA, sports networks, ESPN . . .

But he'd come back to Wishing Bridge. To snow and wind and dangerous conditions. Why?

She had no idea, but a glance at the computer clock said she was wasting valuable time.

After eighth grade, kids were sent to either Warsaw High School or the Catholic high school in Batavia.

She brought up the Warsaw School District page. Along the side was a different alumni link, which took her to a yearbook link.

She barely breathed then hit the button for the 1980s editions. Page by page she scanned, looking for a Vonnie or Yvonne.

She knew what her mother looked like as a drug abuser/party girl, but what would she have looked like as a high school girl? Was she in a club? Did she play a sport? Or a musical instrument?

She had no idea what her mother might have been like, or might have enjoyed, so she studied picture after picture.

Nothing. She knew her mother's age, but maybe that wasn't truthful, either. People forged driver's licenses all the time. Could Vonnie McCleary have done that?

Absolutely. She'd managed to get one with a name that wasn't hers, so maybe the dates on the license were someone else's dates to match the social security number her mother used.

She sighed.

It was getting late. She needed to close the page and head back to the Tompkins'. Hayley would be awake. She'd want food. She'd want—

You left them bottles. Let them feed her. She's going to need to take a bottle when you're working. If you keep her.

If—

Day by day that "if" grew more distant. Yes, she'd been offered marvelous opportunities in Wishing Bridge, but once people discovered the truth, she couldn't possibly stay. Could she?

She turned a page, then another, and then—

> Nora Colleen Hannon. Regents diploma, Honors, Band 1,2,3,4, violin, All County Wind Ensemble 2,3,4, Humanities Award, Civics Award, Alfred University

The young woman's picture was like looking in a dated mirror. Her hair was darker than Kelsey's, and her chin more pointed, but there was no mistaking the resemblance.

Nora Colleen Hannon.

Kelsey glanced at the clock, then typed "Yvonne Hannon Wishing Bridge" into the search bar.

The Internet pulled up two scraps of information.

Yvonne Hannon had been arrested for possession of a controlled substance.

Kelsey cringed because that wasn't a big surprise, but there was no picture to go along with the report. Quickly she clicked through to the other site.

This one featured a nursing-home picture, and there she was. A young Yvonne Hannon next to an aged woman with a bright smile. Yvonne wore an outfit that looked like that of an old-time nurse's aide, and her smile seemed bright and sincere. The date on the picture indicated her mother would have been about eighteen then, and yet there was no record of Yvonne Hannon in that year's graduating class.

A soft phone chime indicated that Kelsey needed to get going. She sent the three pages to the printer and closed down her searches.

Once she slipped on her coat and drew the scarf around her neck, she retrieved her printed pages and started for the door.

An older woman was standing beside the desk. She held up a hand.

Kelsey paused. "Yes?"

"Did you find everything you needed, Miss McCleary?"

The way she said it . . . the way she pronounced Kelsey's name, as if stressing it, sent tiny hairs rising along Kelsey's neck. "I did, thank you. And you are?"

"A friend of the library. We like to support the goal of higher education and accessibility for all."

"Hence the name."

The woman frowned, and Kelsey pointed to the sign over the desk. "Friends Free Library."

"That's different." She didn't sound impressed. "I'm not one of those friends. We're a group who works to support the library."

"So you're not a Quaker?"

She looked startled that Kelsey understood the "friends" reference. "No."

"But how nice that they began and supported so many schools and libraries in New York and Pennsylvania. Much to be grateful for."

"I expect that's so."

Kelsey kept moving.

She wasn't sure why the woman had stopped her, but intuition told her to keep on walking, so she did.

She got outside and let the cold air bathe her face.

Nora Hannon.

Was Nora Yvonne's sister? Cousin? It certainly wasn't a coincidence that the girls shared the same last name and that Kelsey so strongly resembled Nora.

Nora . . .

Would she have the answers? Would she talk to Kelsey? Or would finding her dredge up a wretched past best left forgotten?

She didn't know, but when a now-familiar pins-and-needles sensation tingled through her chest, feeding time became more important than finding family.

She crossed the street and walked toward Wyoming Hill Road. Porch lights and holiday lights came on as the late-day shadows deepened. She'd noticed a couple of people taking them down that day as she'd walked Hayley around Maggie and Jeb's living room.

Another Christmas gone by, but with a difference this time. A monumental difference.

She was a mother now, and would be forevermore. That made figuring out this family stuff even more important, because it wasn't just her who would be affected by staying in Wishing Bridge.

It would be Hayley, and Kelsey wasn't about to let scandal mar her daughter's life. She might not have a father, and she might have had a precipitous birth, but she was a beloved child, and Kelsey had every intention of making sure old disgrace would have no effect on her life. She owed her that much.

As she approached the corner, the town's quaint gaslights flickered to life, lining the main road with a vintage flare. The floodlights around the town Nativity winked on. Three beams shone on the little family, strangers in need in a long-ago land. A cow and two lambs lay on a bed of straw, while the young mother bent toward her baby in a classic pose.

Shepherds stood in awe on one side while three kings of foreign lands knelt and stood opposite them.

Helped by strangers, just like she had been.

A child born in a small town, much like Hayley.

"O little town of Bethlehem . . ."

She didn't know the song, but she'd heard it a thousand times on Christmas-music loops.

Born in a manger.

Visited by angels.

Gifts coming from afar.

She gazed at the young family through different eyes now. Any other time she'd have passed by with barely a glance, but at this moment—here—she wanted to give the stranded travelers a second look.

One light faded, brightened, then faded again.

She bent and tightened the bulb, just enough.

It glowed solidly now and she stepped away, feeling like she'd done something good and right.

It was silly to feel that way about a light bulb, but maybe not so silly when she figured it was *their* light bulb. A light to show the way.

Maggie's porch light came on just then, and Kelsey hurried toward the house. Leave it to Maggie and Jeb to make sure a light shone through the darkness to guide her home. Of course it wasn't really home, but it was the first place that felt like it could be home, and that made all the difference.

CHAPTER SIXTEEN

"Roast pork, homemade applesauce, mashed potatoes, and football. It doesn't get any better than this, Mom." Hale lifted a mug. "And perfect coffee alongside. Thank you. And Happy New Year."

She smiled at him from the kitchen while Ben loaded the dishwasher. "Glad you enjoyed it. It doesn't feel like New Year's if we don't do a big dinner. My mom always did a fresh ham on New Year's, probably because it was a fairly inexpensive way to feed a crowd. The Hannons would come, and my aunt and uncle and their three kids. A busy house and a fun day."

"Have you heard from Nora?"

"I did, but it wasn't much help." She covered dishes as she spoke. "We didn't have much time because she was in port for just a short while. She said anything was possible with her sister, but she hadn't heard from Yvonne since the day she left. How sad is that?" she asked, not expecting an answer. "She mentioned DNA testing, but I don't exactly know how you walk up to a stranger and ask them to do one of those. Awkward, at best. I think we go on like we've been doing and treat it as a coincidence. Max, are you ready for pie? Or should we give it a rest?"

Max started to stand. "A rest, and I don't mind helping with dishes. I like being useful."

She waved him off. "Ben's got it covered, but thank you. You're doing enough with the demolition at my store. I can't believe how much you two got done in just a couple of days. That goes so far beyond 'useful' that giving you a little time off for good behavior seems prudent. I don't want to be a pest."

"We consider demo to be fun." Max sipped his coffee, but his gaze stayed on Jill. "And I don't think you could ever be a pest, Jill."

"Well." She smiled, looking down. He returned the smile from the living room, and Hale couldn't remember his mother ever smiling like that before. She'd been single for over fifteen years, never dating, leading her own life. Until now, perhaps?

"Demo is fun," Hale agreed. "Because you get to wreck stuff on purpose, without getting into trouble."

"It doesn't look fun or easy, but I'm glad you two think so. I can't pretend I'm not excited about having a storefront on Main and Franklin." She carried her coffee into the living room while Ben started the dishwasher. "I'm already planning next year's holiday displays for the front windows. It's eleven months away, but that's not stopping me. I've been able to shop all of the postholiday sales, and I'm going to have the time of my life."

"I've been thinking about those windows, and I've got an idea to run by you." Max picked up his ever-present pad and pencil. "I'd like to create a box effect beneath the windows so you have display areas built high enough for people to see as they walk by. That way you don't have to maneuver the height each time you want to change the season or the sale, and you could use the inside of the window seat for products to sell, and the top for window displays." He did a quick sketch to illustrate his thoughts.

"You can do that, Max?"

"It's kind of simple, really. No big deal."

"It's simple in Max's hands," Hale said. "The cabinet crafter comes alive."

"That would save me a lot of time and effort," said Jill. "I'd love it."

"Good. I was thinking I'd use a distressed wood to go with the barn wood. If there's not enough of that, I'll rough up some milled lumber to keep the look."

Ben took a seat on the recliner opposite Hale. "Did you happen to see Mrs. Pritchard at church this morning?"

Gail Pritchard worked as a volunteer at the church and the local library. Hale shook his head. "I got a call three-quarters of the way through the service. Why?"

"She's got a bee in her bonnet about your friend Kelsey."

His friend Kelsey . . .

He started to frown, but Ben stared him down. "You've stopped by to see her every day this week."

He had done exactly that, but he didn't think Ben had noticed. Clearly he was mistaken.

"So the term 'friend' applies. At the very least," Ben added. He hunched forward, hands folded. "Mrs. Pritchard made it clear that an unwed mother might not be fit for teaching our young."

Hale had been reaching for his coffee. He stopped, amazed to hear this kind of backlash for the second time this week. "You're kidding."

"I wish I were. Now, she's not a person of influence, and her complaints will probably be ignored by the board in favor of the best person to do the job, but she said 'we' when she spoke to me, and we all know what that means."

Max frowned. "I don't."

"That's because you keep yourself out of the fray, Max. You're too busy to be in the know," Jill told him. "It means that once gossip takes hold within a certain group, it's liable to become fact, even when based on fiction. Sharp tongues can cut just as deep as any blade. But why would she say that? Do this? It's not as if Kelsey would be the only single parent in the school system."

Ben raised his hands. "No clue. Why do folks do anything? Greed. Jealousy. Anger. Self-protection."

"That makes quite a list right there, but it's probably simple," noted Max. "Someone else is in line for the job, and if they smear Kelsey's name, she's less likely to get it. Could it be that easy?"

"It could." Jill frowned. "Except I'm familiar with the group of ladies in that circle. I can't imagine any of them have someone vying for an elementary-school position."

"Kelsey needs a job." Hale's collar seemed tight all of a sudden. "If she's going to stay, she needs to support herself. And the baby. She's been upfront about that all along."

Ben and his mother exchanged a look.

"Stop," Hale told them, because it wasn't hard to read their expressions. "Don't make a big deal out of this. I just want things to go smoothly for them. I thought that's what we're supposed to do. Help those in need. So forgive me if I'm more than a little annoyed that churchgoers are talking smack about a nice woman and an innocent baby."

"No big deal here." Ben sat back in the recliner and motioned to the big-screen TV. "I'm one hundred percent football from this moment on. But I thought you should know, because when it comes to some folks, where there's smoke, there's fire, and I don't think your friend Kelsey"—he stressed the word "friend," eyes on the second-half kick-off—"deserves the smackdown."

She didn't, and Hale couldn't imagine what had instigated the loose talk, but one way or another he intended to find out. And then put a stop to it.

~

"I didn't mean to hold you up, Doctor." Sara Hilbert looked worried as she slipped her four-year-old son's arms into his thick jacket while Thea wrote a prescription for an antibiotic the following week. In Pittsburgh she'd have messaged the scrip to the pharmacy of choice. In Wishing Bridge she had a preprinted paper pad, old-school but also effective. "I knew he should be looking better by now, and when he wasn't, I wanted him seen. I hope that's all right."

"It's fine."

"We don't have insurance," Sara said softly. "We had to stop making the premiums a while back. They were crazy high, and when everything got messed up for Jack, we took a chance. We had to."

Talk of money had put the look of apprehension in the young mother's eyes. Thea shrugged it off. "I'll send you a bill. No worries."

"Doc Wolinski generally had us pay at time of visit. He didn't like to waste time and money with bills."

"Luckily there are exceptions to everything, including billing," Thea told her. "I'll make a note that we don't expect payment until March. Will that help?"

Sara lifted her brows, surprised. "Our tax refund will be here by then, so yes. That would be wonderful."

"And if you need anyone seen before things get better, don't hesitate, all right? And here." She took a brochure from a three-shelf organizer and handed it over. "This gives you all the information you need about enrolling the kids in Child Health Plus. It's easier for me to remember to hand them out if I keep them here on my desk," Thea added. Child Health Plus was a New York State insurance plan for dependent children whose parents fell into a certain financial range. Handing out the information in the privacy of her office saved patients the embarrassment of asking at the front desk.

"I'll read this over, but Jack's been against it. He's always paid his own way, and he went out on a limb when he bought that inn, and now—" She made a face of regret. "I was embarrassed coming here because I knew you lost your things in the fire. And with all the rumors going around . . ."

Rumors that accused her husband of burning down the inn because he was the most obvious culprit, the one who stood to gain the most. But Thea had been raised around thugs and thieves all her young life, and she knew one thing for sure. The most obvious answer was often incorrect.

"I don't listen to rumors," Thea said kindly. "I'm a facts-only kind of gal, and it's a tough business climate for lots of people these days."

She didn't add that her availability was due to that same roughed-up business model. Cost cutting in medicine had become a problem across the country.

"Thank you," said Sara. The little fellow laid a tired head against his mother's shoulder as she lifted him into her arms. "I appreciate your understanding, Doctor."

"Thea," she told her. "Just Thea will do."

"And I'm Sara."

Thea noted the billing request in the file and slipped it onto the front desk to deal with in the morning. She'd sent the rest of the staff home at their regular time, and by the time she'd closed things up and moved to the front door, what she saw surprised her.

More snow.

Thea eyed the broad drifts and her short boots.

It looked like it had been snowing all day—lake effect, Sheila called it. Whatever that was. And now that the office had closed, the plow guy had shoved snow into the corner where she parked her car. She'd chosen the spot so patients could park closer to the door. It was the right thing to do, but something to regret at the moment because the lightweight shovels inside the back door to the office were no match for the thick, packed snow preventing her from moving the car forward. She went back inside and grabbed one of the shovels. She refused to think of Maggie's warm house and a hot meal, the simple delight at the end of each day. She went back outside and stabbed at the deep snow.

The shovel bounced back. She choked down a sigh and tried again as approaching car lights hit her square in the face.

"Thea?"

She shaded her eyes when she heard Ethan's voice. "It's me, all right."

"What are you doing?" He climbed out of his car and came her way. "They packed your car in like this?"

He sounded heated. Insulted, even, like the plowman's foolishness was a direct affront, and for a brief moment, she almost thought he might be nice. "Why did you park over here?"

Nope.

"I've been parking here since the first day. You haven't noticed?"

"This is the plow corner, where he's supposed to push all the snow." She raked the long stretch of empty parking lot border a slow look. "He's got over a hundred and fifty feet there. He could have possibly picked a different part of this side, I think, with endless opportunities like that."

"Town code." Ethan frowned and glanced at his running car as if in some all-fired big hurry, and if he took off and left her here, she'd—

He didn't. He turned back to her and explained. "The town insists that the major piles be put here because the prevailing west wind and drainage won't mess things up for the lot next door. It's a weird thing, but they're right. If they push the snow over there and we get a sudden melt, the convenience store floods."

"Except no one managed to tell me that, and I parked here because patients should be able to park near the office. Don't you think?"

He glanced at the car again, and it took all of Thea's resolve to avoid insulting him. "Listen, this is my bad, and you're in a hurry. Go home. I should be able to have this shoveled out by morning."

"Maybe." He almost smiled, and she almost kicked him. "Let me tuck the kids in the office. We can have you out of this mess pretty quick if we both tackle it. Although these are the lamest shovels ever created."

She'd zeroed in on one word. *Kids.* Why had kids and a wife never, ever entered the equation? "You've got kids?"

"Two. Let me get them inside."

"You can't leave them inside alone. That's dangerous."

"Then you watch them and I'll shovel. I'm not always into the male-female division of labor, but we might be wise to employ it tonight. Can I use your gloves?" He raised his bare hands. "Mine are at home."

She handed over her knitted gloves. "They're small."

"I won't stretch them out. Kids are Mara and Keegan. You can just move my car over there. My office key is on the key ring in the ignition."

"All right."

She climbed into his fairly small car, and two sets of eyes peered up at her from behind. "Hi."

The girl leveled her a flat look with more than a little purpose, just passive aggressive enough to be almost cute. But not quite.

The boy stared at her, eyes round.

"You're Keegan, right?"

"I hafta pee."

"Okay, then."

She didn't waste time on small talk because when a kid his size needed a bathroom, talk was a stupid choice. She pulled into the cleared space in front of the office door.

"We can't park here." Mara pointed to the handicapped accessible sign attached to the post in front of the spot. "It's for people who have special stickers, and we don't have a special sticker."

"I think it's okay right now, honey. The office is closed."

"I'm not honey."

"Mara." Thea climbed out of the car and offered an encouraging look. "When the office is closed, no one with a handicapped sticker is going to need this space."

"It's not right." The little girl folded her arms firmly across her middle. "We would be breaking the law if we stay here, and we should never, ever, ever break the law."

"I hafta go bad! Like really, really bad!"

"Come on, Keegan." Thea stretched out a hand to the little fellow. "Mara, come with me, we'll get Keegan to the bathroom, and then I'll move the car. Okay?"

Thea had never seen a child move so amazingly slow in her life. Mara huffed a breath and climbed out of the car at a snail's pace, while Keegan hopped up and down on the cold sidewalk. "I hope nobody in a wheelchair or a scooter is going to need this spot while we're inside." Mara cast a worried look at the car, then the handicapped parking sign, and then lastly at Thea. "The store over there is open, and so is the hair place. They might have lots of people who need wheelchairs."

"I promise I'll move it. As soon as—" She struggled with Ethan's key, then got it to work when she tugged the door toward her, but by the time she'd gotten the outer and inner doors open, it was too late.

Little Keegan burst into tears, mortified that he'd had an accident, and Mara looked around as if wondering how her life had come to this.

Thea was thinking the exact same thing. At least the crunch of the shovel on crusty snow blocked the sound of Keegan's dismay from Ethan. "I wonder if your dad has extra clothes in the car?"

"He's not our dad. Don't you know anything?"

Clearly not where the good doctor was concerned.

"Well, whoever he is, he's shoveling me out and he brought you two here, so I wonder if the shoveling guy has extra clothes for Keegan in the car."

Mara sighed way too long and drawn out for such a young girl, and then she pointed. "In his office. The lowest drawer."

Obviously this had happened before; it was completely normal for this age. Thea flicked on the lights and led the way back to the office.

She opened the bottom drawer, and there was a pair of soft sweatpants and size-four undies decorated with funny little dinosaurs.

"My favorites!" Spotting the kid-themed underwear seemed to lighten the boy's distress. "I can't believe you found my favorite ones. Yeah!" He slipped off his wet clothes instantly, unworried about naked protocol, and he wriggled into the dinosaur undies and gray sweatpants with no help.

"Good job, little man." She high-fived him and then packed his wet pants into a plastic bag. "Let's go wash our hands, and I expect the shoveling man will be done soon. He was going at that pile way faster than I was."

Mara rolled her eyes. Thea ignored the action.

He said he had kids. Two of them. She'd retrieved two kids from his car. So whose kids were they if they weren't his?

Not your business. You're here short term. Remember? And so, by the way, is he.

On a need-to-know basis, all she needed to know was where to park and how to treat patients with the tender, loving, professional care they deserved.

Mara moved back into the waiting room. She crossed to the window, staring into the nothingness of a black-ink night. There was no missing the sadness on her pinched face. Not when Thea had seen a similar image in the mirror for years. A different little girl, but one just as sad. Just as solemn.

Headlights moved their way across the empty side of the parking lot. Ethan had freed her car. He parked it and left it running next to his, then came their way.

"Eefen's here!" Keegan raced his way, laughing.

Not Mara.

She looked pained, as if seeing Ethan wounded her spirit. She sent Thea a dark look when she caught her watching. "We get to go now." She hunched her shoulders deeper into her raspberry-and-white jacket, making herself smaller. Less noticeable. Another trick Thea had learned at a young age.

"All set." Ethan palmed Keegan's head. He smiled, and the boy grinned back, but Ethan's eyes went sober when he shifted his attention to Mara. "Thanks for watching these guys."

Keegan tugged Ethan's arm. "I peed." He pointed outside. "On the step. I tried so hard to hold it, Uncle Eefen."

Uncle . . .

Ethan hugged the boy to his side. "We'll rinse it off with a bucket of water. You found dry pants in my office?" he asked Thea.

"Mara told me where they were, which was a huge help." She kept her voice level. Too much praise and the kid would scoff. Too little and she'd likely feel overlooked. Skating a thin line seemed to be the order of the day, and Thea understood that line well. She'd lived on it for years.

"Thanks, Mar."

"Mara." The girl didn't look at him as she corrected him. She moved past him to head outside.

Ethan's expression seemed just as troubled as he followed, but when he turned to lock the door, he paused. "Have you eaten?"

Thea shook her head. "No." It was a silly question; she'd stayed to lock up the office at the end of the day. When would she have eaten?

"We're going to the diner. Come with us."

She frowned. "I haven't seen a diner."

"Just this side of Warsaw. Great food, daily specials, lots of folks eat there. I've been told you're not truly part of Wishing Bridge until you've become a regular at the diner."

What if she didn't want to be part of Wishing Bridge? Like, ever?

Then she saw Mara's face.

Mara didn't want to be part of Wishing Bridge, either. She stared at Ethan, then around the dark, snowy lot as if lost. That made Thea's decision for her. "The diner sounds good. Straight down the road?"

"Take a left at the light and go about a mile. It's on the right."

"I'll meet you there." She settled herself into the driver's seat of her now-warm car, not sure what she was doing but absolutely certain why she was doing it. She saw too much of the child she'd been in Mara's pinched features, and if there was anything she could do to help . . . any little thing at all . . . she intended to do it. And she needed to tell Ethan what she'd promised Sara Hilbert. He might be all right with it. He might not. Either way, she'd done it, and if worse came to worse, she'd pay the Hilberts' bill herself.

CHAPTER SEVENTEEN

Thea hit her Bluetooth connection to call Jazz as she pulled up to the nearby intersection. "Hey, I'm going down to the diner to have supper with Ethan and his kids. Can you let Maggie know?"

"The handsome, grumpy doctor has kids?"

"Kind of."

"My interest is piqued," Jazz replied. "There's no such thing as 'kind of' having kids. That's like being a little bit pregnant. You either are or aren't or do or don't. Kids are a tangible where I come from."

"Point taken, and I've got nothin'," Thea noted as she made the turn toward the diner. "But I'm hungry and . . ." She let her voice trail off.

"And?"

The image of Mara's strained face invaded her thoughts. "The little girl looks sad. So sad."

"A troubled kid is reason enough to join the party, my friend. I'll tell Maggie and Kelsey. And this baby is smiling up at her Auntie Jacinda right now, like a real smile. Not one of those half things."

"Amazing, isn't it?"

"I wouldn't have thought so, but yes. It is. See you when you get back here."

Thea disconnected the call, and in a few short minutes she was pulling into a brightly lit street-side restaurant marked Genesee Family Diner.

Ethan had already taken the kids inside.

It was just as well. If he'd been hanging around the sidewalk, waiting for her, she might have made the supper more important than it was. She crossed to the door, reached to open it, and then didn't have to.

Ethan was there. Right there. Pushing the door from within, against a stiff northwest wind. "That wind's a killer."

"It's strong all right. But it used to tunnel down the streets of Pittsburgh when I was in grad school, and it was rough there, too. Although we didn't get the major snow accompaniment you take for granted here."

"Lake effect." He made a face, and she leaned forward as she stomped the snow off her boots.

"I don't even know what that is," she whispered. "Everybody around here talks about it, and I meant to look it up but forgot because we've been so busy. What is it? And should I be afraid?"

"It's what got Kelsey here, and why so many people head to Florida and Arizona for three months," he told her. "Cold air plus the Great Lakes and wind equals massive snowfall when the wind from across the warmer water hits land."

They'd reached the table with the kids. Thea ignored Mara's scowl and slipped into the seat next to her on purpose. "The kids must love it. So much snow to play in."

Mara scowled. "I hate snow."

"I like it a real lot." Keegan charmed her with a grin. "And when we get a s-s-sled, we're gonna go s-s-sledding!"

Mara kept her eyes down and sniffed, loudly. On purpose.

"This weekend," Ethan promised him. "Sunday."

"What if it storms?" Mara turned to face him with a flat look of challenge.

"If it's too bad, we'll have to postpone," Ethan answered as the waitress dropped off waters for the table. "But hopefully not."

"We don't have sleds." Thea had to hand it to Mara. For a fairly small kid, the girl packed a sizable load of maturity and disagreeableness into a compact package. And the grown-up tone of voice suggested a high intelligence, but also disappointment. As if life were more of a chronic letdown, not to be trusted. It was a concept Thea understood quite well. "I don't think your plan's going to work without a sled."

"Arriving tomorrow," he replied. "I ordered them online," he went on. "Red for you and yellow for your brother."

"Gender neutral?" Thea asked.

"When you shop in January, you take what they've got," said Ethan.

"Understood. And I actually like bright colors. They stand out against the snow." Thea spotted the rigatoni special and closed the menu. "I haven't had rigatoni in months. Now I'm psyched."

"What about you?" Mara faced Ethan in challenge. "Did you order a sled for you?"

Thea waited for him to say no, but his answer surprised her. "Sure did. Mine's blue. I picked Superman colors, and did you know that the favorite ice cream blend at Betty's in the summer is Super Hero Blast? Red, yellow"—he drew the words out as he high-fived Keegan—"and blue."

"But we won't be here in the summer."

Ethan started to answer, but Mara turned her back on him and the moment and whatever words he might want to offer. She leaned her fair head against the window, staring out, and when it was time to order, she didn't turn, didn't speak, and didn't acknowledge anything except the dark, cold, windswept night.

Depression.

Thea recognized the signs and the symptoms. She remembered the long, dark days and the horrible nights. She'd never forget the time stolen from her as a young teen, the time bartered away by her horrible mother.

What doesn't kill you makes you stronger.

She had that saying posted in her Pittsburgh apartment, the same apartment she needed to give up. There was no sense paying her half of the rent for the next few months when she could be tucking that money away toward a deposit on a new place once she was situated.

But right now all she could see was the grief in a little girl's eyes. And not just her eyes; her whole being seemed constrained by sorrow.

Ethan ordered chicken tenders for the kids.

Keegan ate two tenders and half of his fries.

Mara stayed turned, face out, lost in her own little world.

"Do you want sauce for your chicken, honey?" The waitress stopped by and noticed that Mara hadn't touched a bite. "We've got barbecue and ranch and honey mustard. And there's ketchup on the table."

Mara didn't move.

Keegan looked up at the waitress, then at his sister, and shrugged. "She doesn't like to eat too much. Maybe later," he added, as if consoling the waitress.

Ethan watched the girl without trying to appear like he was watching her.

From Thea's side, she could see a skewed version of Mara's grave reflection in the window. Slightly distorted by the angle of the light, the shadowed reflection worsened the image. When a tear snaked its way down Mara's left cheek, it was all Thea could do not to draw her into her arms and tell her everything would be all right.

But would it?

How could she know?

The waitress set a steaming plate of rigatoni and meatballs in front of Thea.

She couldn't eat a bite. Not one morsel.

She hated sadness, and she abhorred mental anguish or mental illness in children. A child should be prized and loved and should certainly be the apple of someone's eye.

"You're not hungry?" Ethan had been plowing through a burger and fries. "You must be hungry; you didn't take time for lunch today. Is there something wrong with it? Torrie will fix it."

He started to raise his hand to get the waitress's attention, but Thea stopped him. "No, it's fine. I think I'll just take it to go. I'm not as hungry as I thought."

He looked at her, then Mara, then her again before he motioned her closer. "If I stop eating, I can't help either of them. It's not about not caring." For a moment he looked as desperate as the child, as if hoping she'd understand. "It's about survival."

She glimpsed it then, some of his struggle. He was trying to be a leader for a funny, happy, normal boy . . .

And deal with the gravely distraught older sister who didn't want his help.

A mess.

A wicked mess.

Thea didn't do messes well. In the abstract, yes. She could handle patients just fine. Her wretched childhood had given her a rare insight into children's emotional and mental stresses and how those could affect the whole child. She'd gone into family practice because she believed she could help bring things into focus for others.

But she was wise enough to keep her distance, because Thea had learned the hard way that if she got too close she could pitch herself down that rabbit hole of emotional distress. She couldn't afford that.

A second tear followed the first one in the dark window. And then Mara saw her. Saw her watching.

Their eyes met.

Hollow and hungry, Mara's gaze met hers as if challenging her.

Thea's chest went tight. Or maybe it was her heart. For those moments she didn't hear Keegan's dinosaur chatter or Ethan's responses. For those moments, eyes locked, the clatter of dishes and light-hearted conversations of normal people disappeared, and nothing existed but their shared expressions.

"Can I wrap this for you, hon?" Torrie paused by their table. "I expect it will make a great lunch tomorrow over at the doc's office."

She knew that Thea was working with Ethan? Score one for the small-town grapevine. "It will. Thank you." As Torrie took her plate away, Thea did a mental breakdown of what she was seeing.

Mara wasn't undernourished. That meant she ate enough to maintain health, a good sign.

She was punishing Ethan.

From a mental-health standpoint, that could be for a host of reasons.

She was healthy enough to get by but sad enough to be antagonistic.

Thea remembered it so clearly, how the anger and despondency had affected her. A kid doesn't have the luxury of an adult overview. They can't see the light at the end of the tunnel, and time was an intangible that seemed to stretch on interminably.

Don't get involved. Neither one of you is slated to stay. Play it smart by playing it cool.

"Do the kids have school tomorrow?"

"Mara does. She's in first grade. Keegan's with a babysitter."

Torrie returned with Thea's wrapped-up dinner, a box for Mara's food, and the check. Ethan took it from her and slipped it right back to Torrie with his card.

"I can get my supper, Ethan."

He didn't look up as he shook his head. "I've got it. Thanks for coming out with us, Thea. It was nice."

It wasn't nice.

She'd barely opened her mouth; she'd focused on the quiet child at her side and hadn't even attempted to be pleasant. Were her social skills that backward?

"I'll go in early and open things up so you don't have to rush with the kids in the morning. All right?" She'd slid out of the booth and slung her purse over her shoulder before she lifted the hefty to-go container.

"Great, thanks. And I meant to ask if there was anything you needed the practice to order for you."

She paused, confused.

"You lost stuff in the fire. If you need help replacing things . . ."

Was he being thoughtful or looking out for the business?

She couldn't tell.

She shook her head. "My roommate is sending me a box. I can't handle having too much stuff at Maggie's."

"Right."

"I'm okay with getting by on itinerant supplies for the moment. But thank you."

"Are you and your friend looking for an apartment?"

She didn't really know what their plans were. She shrugged. "We're kind of taking each day as it comes."

"Understandable."

One-word answers. Crisp. Businesslike. Always moving on as if he were the only busy person in the world.

She was about to label him a social egotist when Mara moved. Ethan's attention shifted instantly. His brows lifted. His eyes became hopeful, and his face seemed to lighten.

Then Mara laid her head against the cool glass of the dark window and closed her eyes, shutting him out again. Shutting everything out.

He didn't sigh. There wasn't time to sigh because Keegan's dinosaur was trying to ride roughshod over a stray French fry.

"He's a carnivore." Ethan broke off a tiny piece of his burger. "Try this instead. Meat eaters like meat."

"He loves it!" Keegan laughed as he stuffed the morsel into the T. rex's gaping mouth. "Thanks, Uncle Eefen!"

"Glad to share, little guy. See you in the morning."

He added that last to Thea without looking up and probably wondering why she had come to supper with them and hadn't eat a thing.

She was wondering the same, but at least she knew the answer.

Mara's sadness was pushing old buttons. Lots of them. Buttons she thought she'd disengaged a long time ago. She'd moved on to an enviable career and an education that offered her a wealth of opportunities.

But all that paled in significance, looking into one small child's pained face.

Thea didn't look in mirrors for two reasons. First, because she knew she was plain. If Hollywood were to cast a new Jane Eyre, Thea Anastas could win the part. She understood that because she'd lived the reality for a long time.

The second reason was easier.

Looking in mirrors reminded her of the child she'd been. No hope, no choices, and little chance of success. No matter how far she moved from that child, it was young Thea's face she saw in the mirror. A face of want and need.

No one else got to see that face. She made sure of it. But no matter how many degrees and letters she put after her name, the mirror never lied. Her reflection showed that needy soul, striving for love and acceptance that never came.

Meeting Mara's gaze engaged all those old insecurities. Too many.

She set the Styrofoam box of food on the back seat of her car and drove back to Maggie's. She left the food in the car. She'd take it to work tomorrow, and the overnight chill would keep it fresh. Taking it inside would only raise eyebrows and questions. She didn't want to have to come up with answers; those seemed scarce right now.

Years ago, Mrs. Effel had loved two kinds of music at Hannah's Hope: crooners and old country. She had an old-style record player in the home's dining room, and she'd spin those discs morning, noon, and night. On the wall above the stereo system was a saying by Jimmy Dean, an old country singer who went on to make great breakfast sausage for the masses. *"I can't change the direction of the wind, but I can adjust my sails to always reach my destination."*

"Change your tack, darlin'." That was one of Mrs. Effel's oft-said remarks when girls struggled over just about anything. "If your sails aren't fillin' with wind, you will waste your time bein' dead in the water." She'd point to the sign if she happened to be in that room. "Can't change the wind, but the good Lord blessed us with the gumption to change up our sails. If we're willin' to put in the effort."

Thea heard the words as clearly as if her old friend were there, but if you had no clue which direction to take, how could you adjust your sails?

Which meant she needed to figure out her destination.

CHAPTER EIGHTEEN

"I got the job!" Kelsey set down the phone in mid-January and hugged Maggie, then Jazz, then Maggie again. "Starting the first week of February, I will be a full-time teacher at Wishing Bridge Elementary! I can't believe all this has happened." She paused and faced Maggie. "It's absolutely amazing. I went from a state of such nothingness that I wasn't sure how to climb out of the hole I'd dug. And now I'm a mother, I have a place to stay, and I have a job." She gave Maggie a big hug. "You did this."

Maggie was quick to offer protest. "I did nothing. It's all the school board's doing, and the principal's, of course."

"No, I mean you're responsible for so much of this, Maggie." Serious now, Kelsey indicated her surroundings and her dear friend Jazz. "You saw me that night. You saw the car. And you didn't brush it off. You acted. Oh, Maggie." Kelsey hugged her again, wishing there was a way to explain the fullness of her heart. "You changed my life. And hers." She nodded toward the bassinet. "Things would be quite different if you hadn't made that call."

"And if Hale Jackson were a different sort of man," supposed Jazz.

"There's a sight more truth in that than worrying about an old woman who picks up the phone," fussed Maggie, but she looked pleased, nonetheless. "You girls know it's been good for me and Jeb to have the four of you around. That precious baby is just the thing to get us older folks up and moving, especially in these dark days of winter. I can't say I was looking forward to them, nor was Jeb, but now you're here. All three of you. And the baby, she's a blessing, for sure. And while I'm proud of you for being willing to make the sacrifice, I'm real glad you've decided to raise Hayley yourself, child. Jeb and I have faith in you."

"You've decided for sure?" Jazz had been tugging on her running gloves. She paused and hugged Kelsey instead. "Kelsey, I'm so glad. With so many good things falling into place, it's the right thing to do. Don't you think?"

She did, mostly. Until doubts swept in late at night. But would so many things have gone right if this weren't her destiny?

Jazz picked up on the hesitation. "You're still worried."

"Worried?" Maggie moved toward the baby as she began to stir. "About what?"

Jazz looked like she regretted saying anything. She winced slightly and mouthed, "Sorry."

Could she tell Maggie?

Yes. But even as part of Kelsey longed to explain who she was, fear forced her to silence. Vonnie's story rang in her ears, how she'd been an innocent young woman, taken advantage of by an older man. She'd found her mother's picture in the local weekly paper. But how could she find out the truth behind the assertion? And there was a real possibility that being in Wishing Bridge could put her and Hayley in danger if her father had a criminal past. And yet . . . there was so little truth or dignity in anything her mother had done or said, her words weighed little. How could Kelsey ferret out the truth? She had no idea, so she lied to Maggie, and that felt downright terrible.

"Just normal mother stuff, I guess."

"You know you can talk to us if there's other stuff going on." Maggie looked from Jazz to Kelsey. "I'm known around town for having big shoulders and tight lips. That's a rarity in a small town."

"Or anywhere," Jazz agreed. She faced Kelsey. "You've got friends here. Old ones and new ones." She winked at Maggie. "And we'll all stand by you."

"I know you will. I still can't quite believe you and Thea came and you're both still here."

"God's timing." Maggie lifted Hayley from the raised bassinet and cuddled her to her chest. "God's hand has been in this from the beginning, plain as day. Oh, I know you're not a churchgoer." She sent Kelsey a frowning smile, mock scolding. "You've told us that. But child, if ever there was a perfect intersection of God's mysterious ways, it's here and now. You, coming down that road in the storm. Getting off when you did. And me, chancing to look up at the right moment because of a popcorn stitch in my crocheting that was driving me crazy. I saw you because I was *supposed* to see you, and I believe that with all my heart. For all your non-church-going ways, I think you see it, too. Like that woman who cared for you three gals, and all those other girls at the home in Philly. The one that prayed every day."

"Mrs. Effel."

Maggie nodded when she heard the name. "Your Mrs. Effel didn't give up, and she never stopped praying. We might not always see the answers to those prayers"—Maggie laid her cheek against the baby's soft, sweet face—"but that doesn't mean they're not answered in God's good time."

"But what about our choices?" Kelsey didn't mean to argue, because Maggie had gone the distance for all of them. "Doesn't it come down to the choices we make, Maggie? And how those choices affect us and others?"

"Well, we play our part, that's for sure!" Maggie took a seat in the broad-armed captain's chair at the head of the table. "That free-will stuff isn't anything to take for granted, but it's more than that, Kelsey. It's taking that free will and realizing that, as doors open or close, we make our choices while trying to discern his path for us. Which door to take."

"Kind of sounds like a game show, doesn't it?" Jazz tugged on her second glove. "But my grandma thought the same way, and you couldn't find a better woman. Maybe wandering far away from those old-fashioned basics isn't the smartest thing to do."

"There's common-sense truth in those words, and I've messed up like most, I expect, but the beauty isn't in the achieving, is it?" Maggie asked. "It's in the trying. God wants us to keep trying."

"Even when it's hard." Mrs. Effel used to tell her that. Often. Why had she laid aside the kind woman's wisdom?

"Especially then, and I'd be smart to take my own advice. Getting older doesn't always make you smarter. Sometimes it just makes you more stubborn."

"Bless you, Maggie." Jazz leaned down and hugged the older woman with gentle care. "You have already made a difference in my life, and I love being here. I'm so grateful to have escaped the madness of the city, the dragging of the twelve-hour shoots. And I'm not afraid to spend my time on the trails praying these days, and I can't tell you the last time I did that."

"Your grandma would be proud."

"She would," Jazz agreed. "I hope she is. And I think she'd be sitting here, just like you're doing, encouraging me to find a new path while she rocked that baby."

"It is a delight, isn't it?" Maggie grinned. "You watch for roots on that trail. I don't want you hurt."

"Will do. And you figure out a time for Thea to run those tests she talked to you about. Please?"

"Doctors and nurses and tests." Maggie waved her off with a little eye roll. "They've got bills to pay, and the only way to pay 'em is with patients and tests, I guess. I'll make time. Soon," she promised when Jazz scolded her with a look. "Cross my heart." Maggie turned toward Kelsey once Jazz had gone out the side door. "And whatever it is that's worrying you is best shared. When you're ready."

There had been no time to look further into her mother's records or family since her library visit. Thea had tried to pull up information on her smartphone, but Vonnie was just old enough to be nonexistent on the Internet.

She did find several Nora Hannons, and one of them had connections to Wishing Bridge. She was listed in Florida now, and there were family names listed alongside hers, including two people in Wishing Bridge, New York. That meant she had family here, she supposed, if Nora and Yvonne were related.

Could she find out more without confiding in anyone?

Maybe. But now she had a new job on the line . . . would being honest sweep the job offer off the table? Did she dare risk her new opportunities?

She stared down at her baby, safe and secure in Maggie's loving arms, and for just a moment, she couldn't quite breathe.

She was cared for here. Respected. Nurtured and loved by strangers and friends.

She couldn't mess this up. Not now, while so many dreams were coming true. She retrieved a bottle from the refrigerator and warmed it gently. "I'll pump while you feed her because this sweet little darling needs to get used to a bottle. I don't want her to give you a hard time when I'm gone. And Avis said the best time to get ahead on frozen milk is now."

"Avis would know, and how could this little sweetums ever give us a hard time?" Maggie looked up as Jeb came through the side door with nothing but a slim envelope in his hand. "Jeb, did you forget the things I sent you out for?"

He paused on the top stair. He looked at Maggie with the baby, then Kelsey, then back to Maggie as he held out the mail. "There's trouble."

"Trouble?" Maggie raised her brows. "What kind of trouble, Jeb?"

"This." He held the letter out to Maggie, then realized she couldn't withdraw the letter and hold the baby easily. He pulled the letter out and handed it to her. "You won't like it."

"Do you want me to take Hayley?" The bottle wasn't warmed yet, so Kelsey came forward. "That way you can read it."

"I can read it, all right. It's short enough. And mean enough." Maggie glared up at Jeb. "Who would do this, Jeb?"

He rubbed a hand across his chin. "I don't know. It was in our mailbox with the regular mail. Someone desperate?"

"There are desperate people in this town?" Kelsey sat down next to Maggie and reached for the letter. "Can I help?"

Maggie pursed her lips so tight her cheeks went hollow. "No. Well. Maybe." She handed the letter to Kelsey. "Someone wants to make trouble for you. My guess is they're hoping you leave town, which is wrong by every possible standard, but when I see this drivel"—she pointed to the letter—"and know you've got worries of your own, then a body's got to wonder what's going on. So Kelsey, I was willing to give you time because there's not a thing wrong with needing time, but it seems our time's run out."

She sent Jeb to check the bottle, and when he pronounced it warm enough, Maggie sat back with the baby snugged gently in her arm. She touched the nipple to the corner of Hayley's mouth, and the infant rooted eagerly, content with so little. "Do you have any idea why someone would start a campaign so that you don't get the teaching job? Because I can't imagine why it would matter to anyone here."

Kelsey gripped the letter. *The woman you have living in your house isn't who she says she is. She has no place in Wishing Bridge and should never be considered for teaching our children. This won't end here. It can't.*

Pack her up and send her on her way." The note was signed *"A concerned parent."*

Kelsey's throat swelled tight. Tears were near, but they weren't tears of disappointment. These were tears of pure frustration.

She wanted to crumple that letter. She wanted to cross the room and throw it into the small wood-burning stove.

She didn't.

She set the letter down and faced Maggie and Jeb. "I don't know what's going on. Not really," she added when Maggie arched a skeptical brow. "But a long time ago, years before my mother died and I was put into foster care, my mother told me she was from a small town in Western New York. A town called Wishing Bridge."

"Your mother was from here?" Maggie asked. She and Jeb both looked surprised. "Are you certain?"

"If you knew my mother, you'd understand why I wasn't certain," Kelsey told them. "She lied constantly. You couldn't trust anything she said. She had a false name, a phony driver's license, and a stolen social security number. When she died they had no way of tracing me to family of any sort, and that made me so angry . . ." She hauled in a deep breath and sighed. "I wanted to belong to someone. Somewhere. Someplace. But I didn't, and she made sure my life was messed up before it nose-dived into a couple of rough foster-care settings. And before you feel sorry for me, the placements were rough *because* of me. Not the other way around."

"What was her name?"

"Vonnie. Vonnie McCleary. That's what she called herself. Years ago I looked up the name Wishing Bridge, and I found the town online, but there were no McClearys here. I figured she had seen the name on a sign somewhere and it had stuck in her head. But when I saw the Wishing Bridge sign on the highway, I had to wonder . . ." She paused. "What if I had family here? And if I did, it could be bad because she said my conception wasn't consensual, and that she had gotten stuck with the bad end of the deal."

Maggie gasped, but Kelsey had grown so accustomed to her mother's put-downs over the years, that she could share the story without much emotion now.

"When I was at the library, I found an old picture of her in a weekly newspaper. I printed it out and have it upstairs. Her name was Yvonne Hannon. She wasn't in the Warsaw High School yearbooks; there was just this one single picture of her in the weekly paper."

"If you quit school before senior year, there wouldn't be a senior picture, I guess." Jeb sounded sad, but a little disgusted, too. She hoped it wasn't with her.

"I saw enough to know that it was my mother. But then I saw another woman's picture. She was older than Yvonne, and her picture was in the yearbook. Her name was Nora."

"Nora Hannon . . ." Maggie drew her brows together. "I've heard that name. Not the other one, but Nora's . . . yes. It rings a bell, but it's from a long time back. And if they lived more toward Warsaw, I wouldn't have known them necessarily. Is that why you turned off the highway?" The baby started to squirm, and Maggie set the bottle down to lift her for a burp. "Because you thought you might have family here?"

"No," Kelsey answered firmly. "I saw the town's name on the sign, and I was tempted because of what she'd said. I'd looked up the town, seen where it was, but I hadn't intended to come here. Or stop here. My plans were all laid out, but then everything got messed up, and I had no choice. Please don't hate me for not telling you." She put a hand on Maggie's arm. "I don't want you to think badly of me. I wasn't trying to deceive anyone, but if I suddenly turned up in a town where a man had raped my mother, I was scared of what might happen. No one wants to be visited by the end result of a thirty-year-old crime."

"Oh, child." Jeb didn't stay in his seat. He got right up and came around that table and pulled Kelsey up with him, and then he held her close, like a father would. "How could anyone be mad at you over the stupid doings of grown-ups? This is a conundrum." He loosened his arms and shifted his attention to Maggie. "You think someone here recognized Kelsey?"

Kelsey was pretty sure that was impossible. "No one here has ever seen me, so it can't be that."

Maggie snorted. "When Carol Givens had a child, everyone knew it was a Givens because it either looked like her or Greg." Maggie waved Kelsey's assumption off. "One way or another, we knew. Now, if you look like a Hannon . . ."

"I look like Nora." Could Jeb be right? Had someone seen her and noticed the resemblance, even though Nora didn't live here anymore? "I saw her picture, and it was like looking in a mirror. I don't look anything like my mother, but I look like Nora Hannon."

"There's our answer. And all that nice publicity probably pushed you right into someone's living room."

Her father's living room most likely. A man who clearly didn't want to be outed three decades later. "It has to be my father. Who else could it possibly be?"

"I'm not saying yes or no." Maggie frowned. "I can't believe someone might be willing to mess up your life to protect themselves, but I can't think of another reason why this would happen. A note like this is nothing to be taken lightly. Veiled threats are still threats. I think we need to call the sheriff."

"Oh, no, please." The last thing Kelsey wanted was more drama, especially this kind of drama. She'd shrugged off darkness years ago. There was no reason to invite it back in now, and yet what choice did she have? "Can we keep it to ourselves for a little bit? See if things die down? The thought of sheriffs and people knowing . . ." She winced. "I don't tell most people about my past because I've worked so hard to overcome it. I really don't want the whole world to know what I've gone through. It's no one's business, and I've moved beyond all that."

"It isn't a bit fair," Maggie agreed, but she didn't look comfortable with it. "I see your point, and we'll let it ride for the moment, but a smear campaign like this is nothing to take lightly. And it's not just you now. It's you and her." She kissed the baby's forehead. "Calling the sheriff is most likely in your best interest. And hers," she added, jutting her chin toward Hayley. "Sometimes we have to swallow the bad stuff and put safety first, but I don't suppose a day or two would hurt." She said the words but didn't look at ease with the concept.

"We'll keep an eye out," promised Jeb, but he didn't look happy either.

"I should probably move someplace else."

Maggie rolled her eyes and refused to listen. "Well, that's about the silliest thing I've ever heard. You will not move, at least not 'til you're on your feet, and then you can do what you want, but dear girl, you and this baby are a blessing to us. And while Jeb doesn't hunt much anymore, he's brought home many a meal in the past, and he's a handy man to have around if things get bad."

"You think someone might endanger us?"

Maggie stood with the baby. "I think someone is feeling threatened, and threatened people do stupid things. Sometimes dangerous things. We'll give it a few days since there wasn't an overt threat. I'm not sure we're right to wait, Kelsey"—Maggie looked doubtful to be making that call—"but I'm agreeing because you've worked hard to get where you are, and no one has the right to take that from you or blast your past. But Jeb and I want you safe and sound, so I'd appreciate it if you let Jeb or one of the gals go with you on your walks into town."

Maggie was right. Going out on her own could make her an easy target.

"I hate to inconvenience others, but I'll do it." She faced the older couple. "As much as I love Wishing Bridge, and as much as I want to stay, this might be a sign that I shouldn't try to settle here. Sometimes it's more important to cave than to stand and fight. I want Hayley to have a normal life. The kind of life I always dreamed about, with a place to call home, food on the table, and clean clothes. Not fancy. Just nice. And if there are people here who hate me, or are threatened by me, then that's no place to raise a child."

"Don't you be doubting our sweet town just yet," Maggie declared. "There's a reason we're called Wishing Bridge, because this is a town where prayers get answered and wishes come true. You hold onto that and keep those dreams alive."

Prayers get answered and wishes come true . . .

Kelsey wanted to believe that. She longed to believe it. But she had wished and hoped for so long that disappointment seemed more likely.

Hayley squirmed in her arms. She opened her tiny rosebud mouth in a big yawn, then settled back to sleep with a smile, and that was a wake-up call for Kelsey.

This baby might have been unplanned, but she was not unwelcome. She was not a disappointment. And what if Kelsey's life hadn't been saved in the crazy wildness of that storm?

They both could have been lost, so maybe it was time to stop looking at the negative side of things and start thinking positively.

So much good had happened. Too much to count.

On the mountain of good, why was she tempted to let one spot of bad own the summit? That might be her insecurities talking. "You're right," she replied. "I need to be strong for her and me. If I cave the minute trouble comes my way, what kind of mother am I?"

Maggie's face shadowed. She leaned forward, and Kelsey thought she saw the older woman blink back tears. "It's not an easy road. It's about the hardest one I've walked sometimes, but then I think of Mary, at that cross, and I realize we women are made of strong stuff for a reason. Because when our children carry a cross, we're right there, carrying it with them. Wishing we could help. But it's also the greatest road I've walked, and I'd do it again."

Her face looked drawn and pale. Jeb wrapped an arm around her. "I'd do it again, too." He looked down.

Maggie looked up. She sighed. "Well, then."

Hayley picked that moment to fill her diaper.

Jeb laughed and planted a kiss on Maggie's soft gray-brown hair. "I'll leave that to you ladies while I go get those groceries."

"I've got it." Kelsey carried the baby toward the living room, where they kept diapering supplies on hand. "You got the last one, Maggie."

"And didn't mind in the least, but if you do that, I'll get that Crock-Pot going for tonight. That way Thea can eat when she gets here, and Jazz can eat early, the way she likes."

"You're a kindhearted soul, Maggie Tompkins," Kelsey called over her shoulder. "I don't know what we'd do without you."

"Get on, I expect. But it's more fun getting on together, don't you think?"

Kelsey smiled as she cleaned her infant daughter. "I don't think it. I know it. And me and this little princess are mighty glad to be here," she added, glancing that way.

"Heaven-sent, that's what I call it, so we—"

Maggie slumped, then hit the floor.

Kelsey left the half-changed baby in the crib and rushed to the kitchen. She grabbed up the phone and hit 9-1-1 as Jeb mounted the stairs with two small sacks of groceries.

He dropped to Maggie's side instantly. Fear filled his big, pale-blue eyes. "Mother? Come on, Mother, come on, don't do this. Please . . ." his voice begged. His eyes begged more. "Don't do this, Mother. Don't be leavin' me. I know you got business in heaven, but there's business here, too. Don't leave me. Please."

Kelsey offered information as the operator requested it, and within three minutes the sound of a siren rang up the street and paused in the adjacent driveway.

Volunteer EMTs took charge.

They talked back and forth, bundled Maggie onto a gurney, then maneuvered her down the steps and into the back of Rescue One.

Jeb had grabbed his big flannel jacket and didn't think of a hat until Kelsey thrust one into his hands.

"Jeb, I heard the call." Hale Jackson and another man came through the side door. "Max is going to take you to the hospital. Is there anything they need there? Pills, prescriptions?"

Jeb looked dazed, but he shook his head. "She don't like admitting things are wrong, ever, and she had a beef with Doc Wolinski, so she hasn't been in a long while. She doesn't take any pills except for her vitamins, and she's done all right 'til now."

"My car's right out here, Jeb," said the older man. "I'll stay with you while the doctors figure out what's going on."

Jeb turned toward Kelsey. "I don't like leaving you on your own, considering."

She shooed him on. "Jazz will be back soon. You go. I'm fine. We're fine," she added, pointing to the baby. "Go. Call us and let us know what's happening." She delayed him a few seconds more when she reached out and hugged him. "You take care of Maggie. We've got this. Remember, I've been getting along on my own for a long time."

"And stronger for it, I know. I'll call."

They hurried out the street-level side door, and Hale shut it tight behind them. "That west wind is sharp." He shut the upper door to the kitchen, too. "I'm going to let a couple of folks know what happened."

He pulled out his phone as Kelsey headed for the living room. But first, she slipped the threatening note into her pocket. "I'll get the baby changed and dressed."

By the time she'd cleaned up Hayley, Hale had put his phone away. "I called Ethan's office to let them know."

"Except Maggie doesn't go there."

"She did. A while back. Then she got mad at Doc Wolinski and stopped going."

"Mad at him?" She started to lift the baby to her shoulder when Hale put his hands out.

"May I?"

"Of course." She set the baby in his arms. The paper in her pocket rustled softly, reminding her. Maybe teasing her to tell Hale the whole thing. Had Maggie collapsed because the letter had worried her too much? Was Kelsey partially responsible for this new turn of events? "Why would Maggie get mad at a doctor?"

He laid his cheek against the knit cap covering Hayley's soft head and stayed noncommittal. "Folks have issues, I expect. Things get emotional. And with him in hospice care, and Ethan here on a temporary assignment, that's not boding well for the town. But we'll survive. We always do."

Maggie's house phone rang.

Kelsey went to answer it, then thought twice and let it go to voice mail.

She didn't feel right taking on the role of family spokesperson. She was a visitor, no more, no less, here on the kindness of strangers.

The doctor was leaving. Thea would be leaving. Jazz, too, would leave. For something else, somewhere else, living their dreams.

Kelsey was foolish to consider staying, living in a fantasy world that had sprung up with Hale's act of courage nearly a month ago.

She had a job offer and now a threat.

This was a no-brainer. She needed to leave and bring her daughter up in a place where past indiscretions wouldn't dog her. She wanted her very own Mayberry, and she'd come close here in Wishing Bridge. So close.

But no one had the right to demean or threaten her. Sure, she could stay and fight, and blab her entire life in front of the whole town, but to what end?

Nothing good. Nothing wholesome. Nothing pure. Looking at her baby in Hale's strong arms, she wished she could offer all of those things to a good man like him, but she understood her reality better than most. A wonderful man like Hale deserved the best possible soul mate. There was no denying her attraction to him, and she wasn't blind to the twinkle in his eye when she walked into a room, either.

But he deserved better, and whoever had her in their sights wasn't likely to give up, so she had to. Because it would be wrong to risk anyone else's health or happiness.

Jazz burst through the kitchen door just then. "I saw an ambulance and Jeb in a car riding behind. What's happened?"

Hale explained. When he was done, Jazz flexed her hands. "We'll take care of things here. I know Maggie might not be able to watch the baby for a while, so I can step in there. I might not be experienced, but I can be taught. Hale, what can we do to help? Will Jeb stay there? Will he come back here?"

"I think that all depends on what they find at Rochester General and what happens."

He didn't have to remind them that Maggie might not make it home. It was in his gaze and Kelsey's heart.

"We'll do whatever we can to help, and if Jeb needs to be driven back and forth to the hospital, we can do that."

"He'd appreciate that, I expect. He hates driving in the city, and he tends to think his big old Ford truck can fit into places meant for midsize sedans."

"Hence the crunched bumper."

"Yup." He handed the baby back to Hayley. "Can we keep each other posted? If you hear anything, let me know. And vice versa."

"Yes." Jazz tossed her jacket onto the nearby hook. "Is someone letting the rest of the family know?"

"Family?" Hale gave her a strange look.

"Their daughter. Or any other relatives that should be called. Like those kids Maggie told us about. The ones they adopted. Surely they'd want to know, wouldn't they?"

He looked at a loss for words, then tapped his tongue to the top of his mouth. "Adam and Alexis aren't your everyday grateful kind of people, from what I've heard. I was young, I didn't know them first-hand, but my mother's been one of Maggie's friends for a long time. There's a lot of heartache that goes along with that situation." His frown deepened. "I'll ask Jeb about informing them, but the only thing they'd be wondering about is inheritance, most likely."

"What about Bonnie?" Kelsey crossed to an old family picture on the wall. Jeb was standing behind Maggie, and a young woman sat to Maggie's right. Fair-haired, blue-eyed, she smiled at the camera without a care in the world.

"Bonnie Jean." He shrugged and grimaced. "I don't feel right saying too much, it's their story to tell, but Adam and Alexis never bonded with Maggie and Jeb. My mother said they made Bonnie's life pretty tough, but no one realized that until later. Bonnie was seven years younger than Lexi, and a sweet kid. Always smiling, always laughing; she made everyone feel good." He paused and looked pained. It was a long moment before he spoke again. "And then she just stopped eating. And she stopped laughing. She died last summer. It's hard to believe that something from that long ago affects a person for so many years. The doctor said her heart had been too damaged when she was a teenager, and it just gave out. That's why having you guys here has been wonderful for Maggie and Jeb. You gave them reason to smile and hope through the holidays, and we weren't sure how they were going to handle that. You gals made a big difference here."

Jazz stared up at the photo. Her neck tensed, and then she reached up a hand to the portrait. "How old was she here?"

"Seventeen. And thirty-five when she died."

Jazz's jaw quivered.

"Jazz." Kelsey tucked her arm through Jazz's. "Don't."

Jazz shook off Kelsey's hand on her arm and faced Hale. "Did she ever get help, Hale?" She looked at the framed photo, intense, then back at Hale.

"Off and on, but she'd gotten good at fooling her parents. When she was off at college, she drove herself to get great grades but couldn't bring herself to eat. She came back here, and Maggie realized how bad things had gotten. That's what caused the final rift between Maggie and the doctor. She thought Bonnie should be with a specialist, and the doctor just figured she was being willful. He wasn't one to coddle mental illness, and he was kind of proud of that, so by the time Maggie and Jeb realized that Bonnie was failing, the damage to her heart had been done. And then it was just a matter of time."

Sorrow darkened Jazz's face. "The extra bedroom upstairs."

"The closed door at the end of the hall." Kelsey sighed at the thought of the Tompkins' generous spirits bringing them such pain.

"Yes." He frowned as he faced them fully. "I don't want them to know I told you, and I'd prefer it come from them, but this way you'll understand when no kids come running to see how Maggie's doing. And having you here will make it easier because you ladies care."

Kelsey did care. But Hale didn't realize that someone wanted her gone. She should tell him, and it was on the tip of her tongue to do just that when his phone rang. He answered it quickly, then grabbed his jacket.

"Flu's going around, and we've got two deputies calling in. Gotta run and pick up some extra shifts. You ladies are okay here?"

Maggie was on the way to emergency, Jazz was facing the reality of an eating disorder that had cost a young woman her life, and someone was threatening Kelsey . . . but she pretended they'd be fine. "We're all right. Talk to you soon."

"Will do."

He left quickly, a man with a job. A man who cared about his job, his family, his town . . . and his faith. It was all there, in everything he did.

But right now Kelsey needed to fill Jazz in on the letter in her pocket. If nothing else it might move Jazz's mind from the image of that sweet, deceased woman on the living-room wall.

CHAPTER NINETEEN

Long days followed by short nights made for tired sheriff's deputies. As Hale began the 5:00 a.m. shift, he spotted first-floor lights on at the Tompkins house. Was there trouble? Had Maggie taken a turn for the worse at the hospital?

He pulled into the drive without his lights on. He tried texting Kelsey to make sure everything was all right, but when she didn't respond, his concern mounted. In the dark predawn, he considered his options. He could either call the landline and risk waking the whole house or go to the door.

He went to the door and tapped lightly.

No one answered. To his left, he saw the image of a figure moving around the extended living room.

He tapped again, not wanting to wake people up with the doorbell, then wondered why he was there in the first place.

But he knew why.

He hadn't seen Kelsey in three days of working doubles, Maggie was in the hospital recovering from heart surgery, and Jeb was beside himself. Max had gotten Jeb a room at the inn adjacent to the hospital grounds. All he had to do was walk across the enclosed sidewalk to get to the medical complex, but the fifty-five-minute drive from Wishing Bridge to the hospital made it tough for working folks to visit. Still,

Maggie was where she needed to be to get help, and Jeb was safe and sound.

Hale decided knocking on the door was a futile effort, so he moved to the curtain-trimmed picture window and raised his hand to tap, then paused.

Kelsey, holding that baby.

Chin down, her cheek resting against the baby's head, she was the image of beauty and the picture of exhaustion.

An urge to help swept over him. She needed help, she needed strength, she needed someone to watch over her while she nurtured that beautiful child.

You barely know her. You're not falling for her, you're falling for the circumstances. Young mother with child, no beloved husband. It's the circumstances pushing your buttons. Not the woman.

Hale shut down the stupid voice.

He knew he had issues from relinquishing Michael. He realized that. A guy can't exactly minimize that his wife slept with someone else, had the other man's child, and pretended that child was his for nearly two years.

But it wasn't just Kelsey's need for help that drew him. It was her. The longing, the kindness, the sweetness, the unstated insecurities. He wanted to know her better. A lot better. He wanted time to talk, to sit, hold hands, and maybe more. Maybe a great deal more. He ignored his conscience and tapped on the window.

She turned, startled, and then saw him.

She smiled.

Oh, that smile.

As if she'd been hoping he'd come around, and he had.

She moved to the door and unlocked it from inside. He pushed it open, then shut it quickly to keep the frigid air from intruding. "What's going on? I saw the lights and wanted to check things out."

Kelsey moved back into the warm living room. "I don't know." She gazed down at the baby and shook her head. "She's not sleeping. She's not sick, she just starts crying every time I lay her down. And the only thing that seems to help is walking her around and singing to her."

"Well, that's going to get old real quick," he whispered. "You look exhausted."

She winced. "Not exactly the greeting-card image of a new mother, is it?"

"I didn't mean you look bad." He offered a sympathetic smile. "You're far too beautiful for that, any time of day. But you do look tired."

He shouldn't do it. He knew that. But he raised his hand and cupped it along the curve of her cheek.

The warmth of her skin heated his hand. She gazed up at him, with the sleeping baby tucked against her chest, and something came over him. Need? Want?

He wasn't sure and didn't care.

He dropped his gaze to her mouth and didn't wait. Didn't ask. He simply leaned in and took her mouth gently with his, a part of him wondering what he was doing while another part wondered what had taken him so long. And when he finally broke the kiss, it wasn't because he wanted to, it was because a call came in for backup on an MVA just outside of town. "Gotta go."

"Of course." She looked surprised by the kiss . . . and happy. And not quite so tired anymore.

He started to leave, then turned back for one last, quick kiss. "I'm not usually a kiss-and-run guy," he whispered as he moved to the door. "I'll call you later. Get some rest."

He couldn't stay to hear her reply.

He jogged down the steps and over to the running cruiser.

He felt wonderful.

No, scratch that, he was so far beyond wonderful that he refused to classify it.

Hope blossomed within him, a hope that began a month before when he first met her gaze in that tipped-up car. Something that told him she was here for a reason . . . and maybe he was that reason.

He called her twice that day, just to check in, and each time they spoke, he hated to disconnect the call.

The kiss . . .

He wanted more. More kisses, more time to talk, more time to tend that baby.

Was he being ridiculous?

Probably.

He didn't care. He hadn't felt this way in a long time, and he allowed feelings of faith, hope, and love to come back to life inside him. It was like a new day dawning, a day he hadn't expected but welcomed with anticipation.

Dispatch sent him and Garrett to the Voss farm about five that evening to check out a threatening letter. He met Garrett outside, and they approached the farmhouse together. Garrett rang the bell.

Dave Voss came to the door. He didn't look good. Donna was behind him, and she motioned them in when Dave opened the door. "Come in, boys, it's cold out there."

"Crazy cold," agreed Garrett. "We've had some real winter so far, not like last year."

"That's so true. Can I take your coats?"

"No, that's fine, we might have to leave in a hurry," Hale told her. "So what's going on? Dispatch said someone is threatening you?"

"Threatening to ruin our family is what she's doing." It was Donna who spoke, not Dave. "Bad enough to have sins of the past rise up to dog the heels of the present, but blackmail? Extortion?" She folded her arms around her middle and glared at Dave, then at them. "The apple didn't fall far from the tree in this case."

"May I see the letter?" Garrett asked.

"Come through to the kitchen. The snow on your boots won't hurt anything on the tile floor."

They followed her into the updated kitchen in the back of the house. They sat around a sparkling clean farm table, and Dave handed them a typewritten letter.

> *You don't know me. I am your daughter. My mother was Yvonne Hannon. I am twenty-nine years old, and my mother left town when she discovered she was pregnant.*
>
> *I grew up with nothing. Your other kids had everything. A home, a life, two parents. They had everything I ever wanted.*
>
> *But they didn't know they had a sister, did they? A sister who grew up in foster care because her mother was a druggie.*
>
> *I'm not looking for a father. I'm a grown-up with a child of my own. But I am looking for my fair share. It's the right thing to do. You know it. I know it.*
>
> *I can disappear quickly and no one need know about this, but I can't disappear without funds. It's the least you can do. Figure it's the cost of the college education I paid for myself while you were footing the bill for your other children.*
>
> *A cool $50,000 buys my silence. I'll leave, and you'll never hear a word from Kelsey McCleary again. No one will.*
>
> *That's enough to give me a fresh start for a new life. I think it's the least I deserve, don't you, Dad?*
>
> *I'm staying at the Tompkins house for now, but it would be weird for you to come here. People might see. And then they'd talk.*

I have a bank account through Community Savings. Here's the number. You can do a quiet transfer of funds from your account to mine, and no one will ever be the wiser. Except you and me. And neither one of us has any reason to reveal this.

In fact you have four really good reasons to keep this to yourself. Your wife . . . and your three (other) kids.

The letter was unsigned.

A bank account number was printed at the bottom along with the routing number.

Kelsey. Words escaped Hale. So did air.

Garrett stared down at the paper, then at Hale, but Hale couldn't meet his gaze.

Kelsey.

Hale's heart didn't just speed up. It raced.

He'd known there was something. He'd seen the resemblance, but he'd let himself be fooled by what could have been tragic circumstances. A lone woman, pregnant, trapped in a car, about to give birth, and him, the rescuer . . .

Meant to be?

Destiny?

The descriptors threatened to choke him, but he couldn't get up in arms about that now. He had a job to do, a job he'd always done well. Today couldn't be any different, regardless. "When did this come?"

"Today." Dave looked troubled and embarrassed.

"Is Kelsey McCleary your daughter, Dave?"

He winced, but Dave was an upright guy. He always had been. "She could be, it's true. Yvonne and I saw each other about that time. Donna and I had broken up for a while. It wasn't something I was proud of, and then Vonnie went off when Donna and I reconciled."

"You and Donna had dated before?"

"We were almost engaged, then Donna wanted some time apart. She had finished school and wanted time to think things over."

From the corner of his eye, Hale saw Donna flush slightly.

"That's when I started seeing Yvonne. And then Donna wanted us to try again, Yvonne left town, and I never heard another thing. Until today." He tapped the letter with his right hand.

"We'll need to take this," Hale told him. "If you have a copier here, we can leave a copy with you."

"My printer makes copies."

Donna hurried to help. She took both papers back to the kitchen and handed the original to Hale in quick fashion. "Here. And I'm just going to say that I knew there was something fishy going on with that woman, something not right, just like I told you, Hale." She nailed him with a firm look. "Showing up in town, creating a stir, and then the media nonsense, all while she was after some cold, hard cash. The nerve of some people."

Dave looked terrible.

On the other hand, Donna looked vindicated. Because her suspicions had been borne out? Maybe.

Garrett moved to the crux of the matter. "Dave, are you willing to pay her any kind of settlement?"

Donna's head jerked up instantly. "Pay her? Why would we pay her when Gail Pritchard saw her at the library, making copies of things to figure out who to blackmail? Studying page after page of local people, Gail said. Searching for something. Well, I guess she found it." She threw her husband a look of pained disgust.

Dave worked his jaw, frowning. "I don't like how she did this, but I'm not afraid to take responsibility for my own. I can't tell you how bad this makes me feel, that I had a child out there, going without all these years. And she must hate me a lot," he added, touching the letter. "And resent my family. If Yvonne had told me, I'd—"

"You'd have what?" Donna demanded. "Would you have married her? Instead of me? Made things right?"

Garrett became a voice of reason because Hale wasn't in any condition to act smart at that moment. "Going back thirty years doesn't do us much good, does it?" he counseled. "You guys have been happily married for a long time. Beautiful home, great farm, a wonderful family. I think we all make some missteps when we're young, don't we? It would be a bigger mistake to let something that happened so long ago, when you guys weren't together," he reasoned to Donna, "impact your marriage now." He sighed and tucked the letter into his pocket. "We'll go see Kelsey and let her know that blackmail and extortion aren't allowed here."

"She should be punished." Donna's eyes narrowed and her jaw tightened. "How could our school board possibly allow her to stay in town and teach, knowing this? Knowing what she's done?"

"Well, that's another thing entirely," Garrett told her. "Dave, you think about what I said. I'm not encouraging you to give in to blackmail, but if your conscience is telling you to do something for this young woman, let us know."

Donna didn't look surprised. She looked flabbergasted. "Run her out of town is what we need to do. Give her something? Some of our hard-earned money?" She stared at Garrett and Hale, then her husband. "That's impossible. I want this over and done before word gets out. I want her gone. There's no reason to have our children and friends know about this, David. Think of how this is going to hurt our family. *Our* children."

Garrett raised his hand. "Just something to think about as this calms down. You ready?" He looked at Hale, and Hale couldn't miss the gravity in his cousin's eyes.

"Yes."

He wasn't ready. He was about as far from ready as a body could get, but he almost felt like he should have expected this. How foolish was he to let himself be drawn in so quickly? Her needs, her warmth, that sweet baby, images of an innocence that didn't really exist.

He followed Garrett out, and when his cousin turned his way, he held up a gloved hand. "Don't say it. Please."

"I have to ask because you know her as well as anybody. Is this possibly true?"

He'd walked her to the library. She'd referenced her early life just enough to make him sympathetic. He nodded. "It could be. My mother was friends with Yvonne's older sister. We both saw a resemblance."

"And you didn't say anything?"

Hale flexed his hands. "What was there to say, Garrett? There's no law against looking like someone. Mom got in touch with Nora after Christmas, but she had no information on her sister, so it was a total dead end. But this"—he flicked the Voss house a quick glance and ran a hand across his jaw—"I didn't expect this."

"I bet." Garrett hesitated, then moved toward his running cruiser. "I'll meet you at Maggie's."

Hale didn't respond.

He climbed into the car, used the turnaround, and aimed for the street once Garrett had backed out.

He had to keep his cool. Remember who and what he was—a cop, sworn to uphold the law.

He pushed his earlier feelings into a mental folder labeled *How Could You?* and drove to the village, heartsore.

Garrett pulled up to the curb in front of Jeb and Maggie's house. Hale parked in the driveway. It had been a thirteen-hour day already because they were short on help, and disappointment vied with exhaustion, a tiredness made so much worse by Dave's revelation. Hale climbed out of the car and up the steps, a different man from the one who had climbed them thirteen hours ago.

CHAPTER TWENTY

The doorbell rang as Kelsey finished feeding the baby. "Jazz, can you get that?"

"Sure can." Jazz had been stirring a pot of soup. Even though it was from a bagged mix to which you added browned meat, the rich, beefy aroma filled the kitchen with old-fashioned scents to match Maggie's quaint retro décor. The rumble of male voices came her way. Kelsey readjusted her top and laid a cloth over her shoulder before she raised Hayley up for a last burp.

Garrett came through the door first. He took one look at her with the baby and his face went flat.

Hale followed him, looking as if this was the last place he wanted to be. She started to stand, but Garrett waved her back down. "Don't get up, Kelsey. This isn't a social call. We came by to talk to you about a serious matter."

Jazz had followed them into the kitchen. Garrett's firm tone of voice drew her to Kelsey's side, and Kelsey was glad to have her there.

Jazz folded her arms, looking and sounding every inch the tough girl she used to be. "What are you talking about?"

Garrett didn't look at Jazz. He aimed his gaze at Kelsey, and when she asked him to sit down, he didn't. He continued to stand, they both continued to stand, and then she realized why when he asked, "Who are you, Kelsey?"

Her heart fluttered to a stop, then sped up. She stared at him, then at Hale.

No help there.

Her heart beat faster, making her fingertips tingle. "You know who I am. Kelsey McCleary."

"But who exactly is Kelsey McCleary?" Garrett asked. "And what is your relationship to Wishing Bridge?"

Kelsey's pulse thrummed, but inside something else stirred. A flicker of anger rose up, fed by his tone of voice. And the expression, as if she'd done something wrong. "I'm not sure what you're asking. Hale?"

She looked to him for support or explanation, but the loving man who'd held her in his arms that morning had disappeared. In his place was an unyielding sheriff's deputy, hands clenched. She read disappointment in his face, and that made her chest feel sore, but she was done taking undeserved hits. "What is it you both want to know?"

"Is Yvonne Hannon your mother?"

"How did you find this out when I only just discovered it myself?" She looked from one to the other, because how could they know this? An old flare of self-preservation and caution rose within her, the kind of reaction Vonnie's name inspired.

"You didn't know who your mother was, Ms. McCleary?" Doubt filled Garrett's voice.

Jazz's hand on her shoulder offered support. "So we've gone from Kelsey to Ms. McCleary? And from having food together to throwing accusations? Well, let me tell both of you that when you come after one of the Soul Sisterhood, you get all three, so don't for one minute think you can stand there and browbeat a new mother on my watch, because it's not about to happen. Is it a crime in Wishing Bridge to have a mother? Because we'd all be in jail, gentlemen." The irony in her use of the word "gentlemen" was indicated by her severe tone.

"My mother used the name Yvonne McCleary when she was alive." Kelsey kept her voice flat with effort. "She was a drug-using, partying liar, and she managed to make both our lives miserable."

The baby burped just then, such a funny sound of sweet innocence. But with two big, gruff men staring her down, Kelsey couldn't take her normal joy in such little things, and that made the glimmer of anger inside her burn brighter.

"You knew she was from here, didn't you?" Garrett asked. "When you turned off the interstate before Christmas? People saw you searching for information in the library, Kelsey. There's no use denying it now."

Hale looked away as if he couldn't handle the sight of her, and that did it. Kelsey stood up, handed the baby to Jazz, and faced the two deputies.

"Go." She walked past them to the foyer. "You can't just march in here and start acting like a couple of jerks all of a sudden. I've done nothing wrong. Not one thing. And I may have been a down-and-out kid, but I'm not that kid anymore. I'm an accomplished woman with a beautiful daughter, and I refuse to let anyone treat me like this. Shame on you. Shame on both of you." She aimed her look over Garrett's shoulder to Hale. "Maggie would be affronted to think you would do this in her house."

"Would she be as affronted if she saw this?" Garrett pulled a folded note out of his pocket and opened it in front of her. "An extortion letter written to your father? Dave Voss?"

"My father?" Kelsey stared at him, then Hale, then the letter. "I have no idea who my father is."

"This letter suggests otherwise, and Dave admitted to having a relationship with your mother at the right time," said Hale in a voice much cooler than the one he had used that morning. "You were seen checking out people on a library computer. Making copies of information about local people. And this letter came to Dave Voss today." He held her gaze, and in his look she felt like she had already been accused, tried, and convicted.

"I wrote no letter. I have no idea who Dave Voss is, and if he is my father, this is the first I've heard of it."

"It's got your name on it, Kelsey." Garrett's voice softened as if being nice might help her confess. "And the letter is asking Dave to give you fifty thousand dollars to buy your silence so that his wife and kids aren't embarrassed by his past indiscretions."

"So that's what I'm labeled now?" She moved past Garrett and faced Hale straight on. "Someone's indiscretion? Well, that's a more dignified word than some things I've been called, and many of those at the hands of my very own mother. I will repeat this once, and that is all." She pointed to the letter. "I never wrote a letter to anyone. Not to someone named David Voss or anyone else, and is his wife named Donna?"

Both deputies nodded.

"She came to visit me before Maggie got sick. She kept staring at me as if I were some kind of zoo exhibit. She acted weird, and when she found out I was applying for the teaching job, she got even stranger. I was relieved when the baby woke up and needed me, but you two have some nerve coming in here and trying to intimidate me."

She was glad to see they both looked a little surprised by her onslaught. Good. "Despite the fact that I come from a messed-up life and that I made a major mistake last year by trusting the wrong man, I don't intimidate easily." She didn't blink, and she did not back down. "I'd like to see the letter."

Garrett handed it over.

She scanned the letter before she lifted her gaze to theirs. "You don't know me." She aimed that at Garrett. "But you do." Now she turned to Hale. "You read this and thought I wrote it? You thought I could be that mean-spirited and crude? To extort money from someone who probably got just as fooled by my mother as the rest of the world?"

Now both deputies had the grace to look a little less certain.

"I'm done." She handed him back the letter. "You guys do what you need to do, but I can guarantee you that when you go down to that library and check the computers, you will not find a search for David Voss under my card sign-in. The only research I did there was to see if my mother actually was from here, because she mentioned the name Wishing Bridge when I was a kid. And yes, I wondered if I had family here, but my mother called my conception a rape, so there was no way in the world I was running around—with a newborn daughter, I might add—looking to find a possible rapist in town. Following your line of reasoning"—she crossed to the top shelf of the living-room bookcase and withdrew the letter Maggie and Jeb had received the day Maggie collapsed—"I must have written this letter to Maggie and Jeb, incriminating myself." She handed Garrett the threatening note. "This came the day Maggie collapsed."

"Someone sent them a letter like this and you didn't report it?" Hale asked, and the doubt in his voice was enough to strengthen her resolve even more.

"We decided to wait, because it's not fair." She looked from one man to the other, determined. "I've worked a long time to remove myself from sketchy beginnings. I've done nothing wrong, and I refuse to let someone else's agenda dictate my life. No one has the right to make my past public knowledge without my permission, but it seems someone here is willing to do exactly that." She put her hand on the door and pulled it open. "It's time for you to leave. If you come back to question me again, it won't be without my lawyer present." She pointed to the open door and clamped her mouth shut.

The men exchanged glances, then left.

She wanted to slam the door on them. Maybe more than once. But that would wake the baby, and punishing herself and Jazz with a crying baby made little sense.

Jazz had tucked the baby into the portable crib. She came her way and gave Kelsey a hug she sorely needed as Thea came in the side door off the kitchen.

She'd held it together in front of Garrett and Hale, but now . . .

Now Kelsey let her tears fall, but they were not tears of anguish.

These were tears of anger.

How dare someone use her name to make threats? Why did the sins of her mother seem to dog her? She'd felt so peaceful here, only to run into the hurt and heartache she'd tried to put behind her.

On top of that, she might have a father. This man—Dave Voss— admitted to having a relationship with her mother.

He knew about her now.

Was he guilty of what Vonnie had said? Could he be that person but yet a happily married father with three successful children?

"We'll figure this out," Thea promised when they'd rehashed the entire scenario. "I can't believe that pair of goons fell for something like that. No one who knows you would give that kind of thing the time of day. Clearly a forgery."

"They're required to investigate." Jazz kept her voice calmer. "But they're not required to believe a stupid letter. In the first place, it most definitely fell below Kelsey's skill as a writer. Almost as if the author was trying to make you sound dumb."

Make her sound dumb.

Unskilled.

Teaching in the same wing as her daughter . . .

The sequence of events suddenly became crystal clear.

Kelsey stood. "Who wants to go with me to meet my father, and who wants to watch the baby?"

"I'm going." Jazz stood and crossed the room to grab her coat. "I'm more intimidating than Thea, although I'm definitely gaining experience with babies."

"I'll stay. Take both your phones. Kelse"—Thea moved in front of her—"is this a good idea?"

Kelsey wasn't sure, but she was done letting things happen around her. It was time to take charge of her life, her path again. "It's either this or sit and wait while legal wheels churn. Since I know I didn't write that letter, maybe my father will have an idea who did."

They took Thea's car because it was already warmed up and brushed off, then headed for the address they found on the Internet. When Jazz turned down a long, dark, two-lane road, she paused at an intersection. "Are we sure this is a good idea? Because there's a lot of spots to get rid of bodies out here. And it would be fairly easy under the cover of darkness."

"It's the country; it's supposed to have a lot of secluded spots, Jazz. There." Kelsey pointed to an upcoming farmhouse not too far off the road. "This is it."

Jazz turned into the driveway. She parked the car and got out of her side while Kelsey stepped out onto the dark, slick asphalt. Kelsey stared at the house, wondering if she was being crazy smart or downright stupid, but she was so tired of dim truths, half-truths, and outright lies.

"You okay?" Jazz's voice sounded strong and supportive.

Kelsey hauled in a breath and started forward. "Let's do this." They went up the driveway and across the front walk, then up three concrete steps to a covered front porch. Kelsey steeled her nerves and rang the bell.

It echoed through the house, and it seemed like long ticks of the clock before they heard the sound of footsteps.

A man opened the broad, wooden door. Peering through the storm door, he stared at Jazz, then Kelsey, then did a double take. And then he opened the second door.

"Mr. Voss?"

"You're Kelsey."

"Yes, sir."

He flinched slightly, as if he hadn't expected that response. "Come in." He held the door wider as she and Jazz stepped into a simple and tasteful foyer. "I got your letter."

"You didn't," she told him. "I mean, you may have gotten a letter, but I never wrote any such thing. Can we sit down?" He started to nod, and Kelsey interrupted him. "I'm sorry, this is my friend Jacinda. I didn't feel right coming alone."

"No, that's fine. You were smart to do that. Listen, Kelsey . . ."

She held up a hand as they took seats in an inviting living room. "May I go first?"

He looked uncomfortable, but why wouldn't he?

He nodded. "Please do."

"My mother was Yvonne Hannon. That part of what you read in that letter is true. And if you and my mother had a relationship thirty years ago, then yes, you could be my father. I don't know about that," she explained honestly. "My mother was deceptive, she wasn't faithful, and she wasn't very nice, so I don't know where the truth lies. When I was young, she mentioned this town. It's the kind of name that sticks with you when you hear it."

"It does."

"So when I ended up here because of the storm, I took the opportunity to check out my mother on the library computer. I found her, in a picture with an elderly woman at a nursing facility."

"Crestwood Adult Care."

"That's a place near here?" Kelsey asked.

"It used to be. It's been changed over a few times. She worked there for a few weeks and got on well with the old folks. They liked her sass and her energy. Then she got let go when some of the prescription meds went missing. Not too much later she left town."

"While I was there I also found a picture of Nora Hannon in a Warsaw High School yearbook. I realized I look like her."

"Yvonne's older sister. You've got her eyes for certain."

Kelsey folded her hands. It was time to get to the heart of the conversation, and she wasn't sure how to broach it. Then she thought of Mrs. Effel and those prayers and how the truth was supposed to set you free. And she wondered if that was just an old saying or something rooted in truth.

"Mr. Voss, my presence in Wishing Bridge is making someone nervous. When we received a threatening note at Maggie's the other day, I thought my father might have sent it. That whoever he was, he might still be in town and figured out who I might be."

He frowned. "But I've never seen you before today."

"Kelsey was on several news channels because of the accident and the baby," Jazz told him.

"I know that now," he admitted. "Before today, I'd heard about you and the baby, because it's a small town, but I never saw the video. I'm busy in the barn in the morning and don't care about too much of anything by night."

Kelsey believed him. And that confirmed her suspicions. "Then it was someone else who sent the note saying I should get out of town."

Footsteps sounded overhead before a voice called down. "David? Who are you talking to?"

Kelsey looked at him, then the stairway, then Dave Voss again.

He put his head in his hands for a few seconds as he digested her silent message, then called out, "Kelsey's here. She wanted to talk to us."

"Here?" It was more than surprise that hiked Donna Voss's tone. It was fear. "Did you call 9-1-1? Did you—"

Dave got up and crossed the room. "Come down here. Please."

Jazz gave Kelsey a firm thumbs-up as slow steps sounded on the stairs, and when Donna Voss appeared, Kelsey almost felt sorry for her. But not quite.

She stood. So did Jazz, a true friend.

Donna came down the last two steps. She aimed an angry look at her husband. "Why is she here?"

"To clear up the matter of a threatening note and a letter she didn't write, Donna."

Donna stared at him.

She turned her attention to Kelsey, then back to Dave. "What do you mean? Her name was on the letter."

"Donna." Dave Voss put his hands on her upper arms and held her gaze. "Stop. Please. Don't carry this any further, okay?"

She stopped.

She looked at him, and then her eyes scanned the room as if seeing so much to lose . . .

And then she faced him again. "I didn't want anyone to know about . . ." She hesitated, and when she did, Dave stepped in.

"About my other daughter."

"We don't know that for certain." Donna looked desperate enough to demand a mouth swab test right then and there.

"Kelsey, when is your birthday?" he asked her.

She told him.

He didn't cringe. "That's proof enough right there, although we didn't need it. You've got Nora's look and voice, but you carry yourself tall, like my mother and my daughter Kristen. And your face is expressive, like theirs."

Hurt darkened his wife's face. "You would compare her to our daughter?"

"Donna." He looked sad. So sad. But he also seemed determined, as if he wasn't afraid to take control of the situation. He sat down and motioned his wife and Kelsey to do the same. "You're worried about what people will think. I don't care what they think. Yvonne and I had a short relationship before you and I got married, and I'm not the only man who's ever had more than one relationship in his younger years. And you knew about it, Donna." The furrow between his eyebrows deepened. "I kept no secrets from you. That's how you knew when you saw her, isn't it? Coming to town, the right age, and looking so much like Nora? And a little like Kristen."

The hurt on Donna's face turned straight to anger. "I did what any decent mother would do," she told him. First she looked fierce, then pleading. She reached for his hands. "We've worked so hard to have a good family, Dave. I didn't want it spoiled."

That was about the last insult Kelsey wanted to hear in one day's time. She started to stand, but Dave shook his head. "Stay. Please. I want you to hear me out."

She didn't want to stay. This woman's selfishness wasn't anything she wanted to be part of, but she sat back down.

Dave Voss looked back at his wife. "We've had a good life, Donna. Nearly thirty years of a good life. Beautiful kids, enough money and some to spare, a lovely home, and the farm is thriving. So much to be thankful for every week when we get down on our knees in church. Do you know how it makes me feel to think of what Kelsey's life must have been like with Yvonne? To imagine how wretched it must have been at times, and here we were, safe and warm and well fed and beloved? What father wouldn't want that for his daughter?"

"How do you know this about me if you didn't see the newscasts?" Kelsey asked.

He pointed to the laptop on the desk along the far wall. "I looked you up after Garrett and Hale left. I saw your interview, and I thought about what it must have been like, being the lost lamb."

Mrs. Effel had talked about the lost lamb. Kelsey thought it was just a nice story.

"Jesus talks about a shepherd with one hundred sheep and how one goes missing. And that shepherd can't just stay and watch the ninety-nine easy sheep, because he can't rest until he finds that lost lamb. It's like that, you know." He seemed frank and honest and big-hearted, the kind of perfect father you saw on TV. "With farmers, every baby is important. Not for the money, but because it's life. In our very hands, it's life." He looked at her, troubled. "I would have found you, Kelsey. If I'd known."

He stood and crossed the narrow space and took a knee by Kelsey's side.

"I'd have found you. And I'd have taken care of you because that's what a father does, honey. I would never have abandoned you."

I would never have abandoned you.

Tears pricked Kelsey's eyes.

They shone in her father's, too.

Mrs. Effel used to read that passage to the girls at prayer time, a house full of children brushed off by their parents, thrown into circumstances beyond their control. She'd talk of faith, of God, of how humans might abandon their young but God never would. And how she wanted that kind of love for all her girls.

He took her hands in his. "I'm sorry for what my wife did, and I'm going to ask you to forgive us. Both of us. Me for not finding Yvonne and making sure there wasn't a child, and Donna for letting fear and pride make choices she wouldn't normally make."

"Dave." Donna stood. Kelsey didn't look her way. Neither did David Voss.

He ignored his wife's protest and hugged Kelsey. He hugged her tight, and when he stopped hugging her, Donna had left the room. "Can you give us a few days to sort through things here? I need to see to my wife, but I would like you to meet your sisters and your brother. They're good people, and they'll want to meet you."

Kelsey wasn't so sure that was true. "Let's not jump to conclusions. An almost thirty-year-old sibling isn't always the best surprise."

"You're wrong, Kelsey." Dave Voss put a hand on either side of her face and gave her a smile, a smile she saw in little Hayley's open grin every day. "It is the best surprise because the lost lamb has come home."

Her heart swelled at the quiet beauty of his words. Her throat ached. She pushed down emotion long enough to say goodbye, and then she and Jazz walked out to Thea's car.

When they got inside, Jazz raised her fist to bump knuckles, and when Kelsey did the same, Jazz gave her the quick hand-to-hand acknowledgment and two little words: "Crushed it."

CHAPTER
TWENTY-ONE

You're a moron.

The inner knowledge did little to make Hale's situation any better.

Dave Voss had called the sheriff's office within a few hours of Hale and Garrett's visit three days earlier, letting them know that Kelsey had done nothing wrong, that Donna had freaked out over the thought of an illegitimate child and tried to force her out of town.

Hale knew he'd overreacted. He and Garrett both had, but him more so because how could he have believed that Kelsey was an extortionist?

Because you let old buttons get pushed. You're right. You're a moron. But usually you're a nice moron.

He'd gone by twice to apologize. Both times Jazz had coolly and calmly shooed him away.

His fault, of course, for jumping to conclusions.

Dave Voss showed up at the sheriff's office as Hale was going off duty. He spotted Hale and came his way.

"I've spoken to the sheriff. He said the sheriff's office doesn't intend to take this farther if Kelsey doesn't bring charges against Donna. And I was hoping that you and Garrett could see your way to keeping a lid on the ugliness. Sharing what Donna did would only hurt our other kids, and they don't deserve that."

That made sense to Hale. "We'll say nothing, Dave. I'm glad you got to the truth before things got blown out of proportion."

"Me, too, and that was because Kelsey took matters into her own hands and came directly to me. It took a lot of courage for her to do that, especially under those circumstances."

It had. She'd shown courage under fire, and he'd acted like a judge and jury, assuming she was guilty as charged. "She's a strong woman."

"She is, and I hope she and Kristen will be okay working in the same wing of the school. That's a little weird, I expect, but I can't let anything get in the way of Kelsey's chance for success at long last. If I can make her life easier in any way, I aim to do it. And that baby." His eyes lit up. "I stopped by to see her yesterday, and she's a cute little thing."

She was a cute little thing. Beautiful. Precious. Hale swallowed a lump of self-loathing and agreed. "She's a keeper."

"Thank you, Hale." Dave extended his hand, as if Hale had done something right when actually he'd really managed to do multiple things wrong. "I'm grateful for your understanding."

Understanding? The word mocked him, but he thanked Dave and walked toward his truck.

He needed to see Kelsey. To talk to her. Maggie had come home yesterday, and she was expected to do well following a weeks-long recovery period. She'd give him a tongue-lashing, no doubt well deserved. She'd scolded him as a boy, now and again, expecting him to rise above the roughed-up reputation that dogged several of the Jackson men. And Kelsey would get her shot at him, too, once they let him through the door.

He went straight to his house, put on his farm layers, and headed out back. He and Ben didn't have a big beef holding, just shy of a hundred head, but when the calves started dropping, they had their work cut out for them.

Three new calves had joined the group huddled on the lee side of the back barn. Two little bulls and one heifer. Ben spotted him and came his way.

"Five so far today, with half a dozen more ready. We've got snow coming, so I put them in the barn just in case. The forecast looks like a solid blow."

"What should I do?" Hale might have footed the bill for this enterprise, but Ben ran the cattle end of the business.

"Check that far pen." He gave Hale ear tags to look for. "And don't forget Rosey."

"I won't." He took the four-wheeler to the back pen. It took a little while to separate the cows from their herd, but as he urged them through the fenced channel to the barn, they almost looked relieved to be off on their own.

Once they were in, he went back for Rosey, a good old girl, one of their first acquired cows.

She stared at him, mournful.

Rosey never looked mournful. Rosey was the kind of cow animators created for kids' cartoons, placid and easygoing. But when the big roan-and-white cow looked at Hale, he read fear in her eyes.

He got off the four-wheeler and walked her back to the barn, Rosey following like a trusty dog. When she got inside, she crossed the barn to a quiet, straw-filled area, breathed out a puff of white air, then strained.

Nothing showed.

She bawled softly, then strained again. Still nothing.

He needed to check things more personally, and when he did, he found a bad presentation.

"Rosey's gone bad?" Bennett had come in the far door, and when he spotted Hale, he undid his heavy jacket and flung it on the stall post nearby. "We need to pull?"

"Yes."

Hale hated pulling calves. He understood the necessity, but he was a big fan of Mother Nature. The puller was a great invention, and a beef-farm essential, but the stress on the calf and the mother was tough.

He led Rosey to the chute, but when Ben approached with the sterilized chains, he held up a hand. "Let me try to bring the head around one more time. The feet are there, and if I can bring the nose forward, she might be able to do this on her own."

"Go for it. But if she's been like this for a while and I missed it, we might not have a lot of time."

Hale knew the truth in that. The longer the cow labored with no result, the bigger the danger of a stillborn calf.

He rewashed his arm, lathered it well, then applied disinfectant. And then he groped for the calf, tracing his way up the feet, to the smooth neck, bent away.

Patience. Go slow, feel your way and ignore the ticking clock. Let your fingers guide your brain.

He closed his eyes. Tracing the neck one way got him nothing. A contraction hit full force, squeezing his arm as Rosey strained with all her might, and the big red-and-white bovine was strong.

He held on. As soon as the contraction passed, he traced up in the opposite direction. His stretched-out fingers traced a long, moist triangle . . .

He'd found an ear, which meant the nose must be somewhere close by.

Eyes shut, he focused on moving his fingers forward, away from the ear . . .

His hand touched a nose, then a mouth as another contraction roared through the cow's body. "I've got it." He had to hiss the words to Ben as his arm was being squeezed, and as soon as the contraction faded, he gripped the nose.

Picturing the position his fingers had traced, he pulled the nose down and toward him, drawing the calf's face forward. He had to twist his arm to bring the face around, and when he felt the chin rest on the forelimbs, he withdrew his arm. "We're good."

He stood back, and when the next contraction hit, Rosey presented them with a beautiful rose-and-white heifer, the image of her mother.

Ben tickled the calf's nose with straw. The heifer sneezed, bawled, and scrambled to her feet on unsteady legs.

A sight to see.

Hale began scrubbing up as Ben released Rosey from the hold. She rounded quickly, sizing up her baby, and when the pair began bleating little sounds of satisfaction to each other, Hale met Ben's gaze. "Looks good."

Ben nodded. "Patience wins the day."

Patience. Understanding. Prayer. "You're smart for an ugly guy."

"You got the looks. I got the brains." It was an old joke between the brothers. "Mom went to see Kelsey today. She told her she would help Jazz watch the baby when Kelsey starts teaching next week. That gives Maggie time to recover, and Mom and the supermodel can tag team the baby."

That was good news on multiple fronts. "I'm glad. Then she doesn't have to worry about Hayley while she's working. And Maggie will enjoy having company around while she heals."

"You get to see her yet?"

Ben was the only person besides their mother and Garrett who knew what had happened with Kelsey and the Voss family. "Can't get through the door."

Ben laughed, then indicated the cow with her new calf. "Show the same patience and determination you did here. And as you do everywhere, as long as women aren't involved."

Good advice, but with calves dropping and extra shifts because of the flu outbreak, his chance to beg forgiveness might not happen for a while, and the thought of that didn't sit well.

And then an idea occurred, simple, really. He might not be able to get through the door, but the rules of engagement wouldn't include a ban on candy or flowers. Even the busiest man could handle placing an order, one that just might pave the way toward forgiveness.

CHAPTER
TWENTY-TWO

"Flowers and chocolates." Thea tested one of the dark chocolates the last Sunday in January and sighed happily. "Oh, honey, make our guilt-riddled cop suffer a while longer. He might send more. Our box is getting low."

Beautiful flowers from Hale with a sweet note. *I'm only dumb sometimes. Most times I'm not. I'd love another chance, dear Kelsey.*

And then chocolates, a massive box, which had sweetened his standing with Thea, for sure.

"They are good chocolates," admitted Kelsey. "But I'm focusing on one thing right now. Two, actually. Meeting my siblings this afternoon and starting a new job tomorrow. That's plenty for the day, don't you think?"

"I'd say so!" declared Maggie as she picked out a chocolate. "But our selection *is* running low."

The doorbell rang. Dave Voss had arrived with two of his grown kids. Another moment of truth was at hand.

Her palms grew damp. She wasn't sure if she should answer the door or hide, but Dave had promised it would be fine. And Kelsey believed him. She pulled open the big, solid, walnut door.

"Hi." She spoke softly and motioned them toward the living room. "Come on in." Kristen and her brother came through, but Dave paused to hug her.

A father's hug, something she'd never expected to feel, to enjoy.

And then he kept his arm around her shoulders as they moved to the sitting room. Maggie had gone to rest in her first-floor bedroom, Jeb was doing something outside to give them privacy, and Jazz and Thea were tending the baby in the kitchen.

An awkward silence ensued, then Dave presented his children. "Kelsey, this is Kristen. She's our oldest."

"And also an elementary-school teacher, so that's kind of cool, isn't it?" Kelsey noted. She wasn't sure what to expect from Dave's daughter. Kelsey was the one who had moved into their town, their family, and now Kristen's workplace, and she had no idea how her half sister would react to all of that.

"It's odd how genetics work, isn't it?" Kristen didn't appear weirded out but was definitely cautious. "A fairly unpredictable mix, but I love what I do, and I'm glad you love it, too, Kelsey." She paused and pulled in a deep breath before she added, "And I want you to know I'm really sorry about what my mom did. Dad didn't want us to hear all that, but we could tell something was up, so we pestered Dad until he explained the whole thing."

Kelsey didn't want Donna's misdeeds to overshadow their meeting, but Kristen kept talking. "She was wrong, Kelsey. I love my mother, but she let pride get in the way of decency, and that should never happen. It's not how we were raised, and I'm truly sorry."

"Mom's Mom," said the young man pragmatically. He put out his hand. "I'm Brandon, I'm a biomedical engineer doing research at the University of Rochester, and it's really nice to meet you."

"You, too."

She sat. She looked at them. They looked at her.

Dave folded his hands loosely in his lap. "Kelsey, I went to see Hale and Garrett. It seemed best to clear the air with them. We misled them—"

"Mom misled them," cut in Brandon.

"Well, I went along with it, son. In any case"—he faced Kelsey again—"Hale assured me they'd keep it to themselves if that's all right with you."

"I am perfectly fine with not having people talk about me, us, or my situation any more than they already will. I think mothers can go a little out of control trying to protect their kids. I'd do anything to keep Hayley safe. So I almost understand."

"But when it's more about protecting the status quo than protecting your children, it's a whole different matter." Kristen reached out a hand to Kelsey's arm. "We're not excusing Mom's behavior. If she'd gotten away with it, she'd have hurt a lot of people, most especially you and that baby. Thank you for saying you weren't going to press charges, but we shouldn't pretend it wasn't a serious matter. It was. And I'm so glad you had the guts to set things straight."

"I was scared to death and brought my friend for reinforcement, so there was little courage involved," Kelsey confessed.

"Which only makes the courage more admirable," Dave told her. He smiled and patted her hand. "And do you mind if the kids meet their niece? Because I know they want to."

"Of course." She went to the kitchen, where Jazz and Thea had been shamelessly listening to the entire conversation, and brought out the baby. "This is Hayley."

"Oh." Kristen put both hands to her face, then reached out. "May I hold her?"

Kelsey handed Hayley to her sister.

Her sister . . .

And then she sat down.

"It's a lot to digest, isn't it?" Brandon sent her a look of sympathy. "The one thing I've discovered at the university is that families tend to revolve. Or maybe it's evolve. They rarely stay stagnant, and I've come to believe that's a good thing. Like adaptation of the species."

"You sound like a scientist."

He grinned. "When you see things at a cellular level, and how a tiny change can alter a being . . . not just their life but them as a person . . . then you have a greater appreciation of how life shapes us. We're the person, but what we choose, what we do, shapes our destiny in new ways."

"He's the smart one. Although Samantha's a brainiac, too. Me?" Kristen smiled at the baby, then Kelsey. "I just love working with kids. Seeing them shine."

"Me, too," said Kelsey. "My teachers made such a huge impact on me while I was growing up. They gave me hope, and I knew if I could break my mother's cycle of drugs and poverty and deceit, I could be anything I wanted to be. And what I wanted most was to teach."

"Lead by example." Kristen smiled at their father. "That's a Dad thing, for sure."

The baby began to fuss, and Kelsey reached for her. "It's feeding time, and there is no such thing as patience in a newborn."

Dave stood. He bent and kissed Hayley's forehead. "We'll see you soon, sweetheart. God bless you."

Her baby daughter had just been blessed by her very own grandpa. For real.

A thick knot formed in Kelsey's throat, because none of this had been on her radar six weeks ago. And now . . . her life had changed. She'd changed. Was it all because of that one decision? To turn off the road at that moment?

They said quick goodbyes so Kelsey could feed the baby, but then Kristen turned at the door. "If you need any help with the job, I'm right next door. I'll be glad to offer advice, coffee, tea, and/or chocolate. Whatever it takes, Kelsey."

"I expect I'll be taking you up on that."

Kristen shared a smile with her. "I hope you do."

Thea and Jazz came into the room once they'd left.

"They're nice!" Jazz sounded slightly amazed. "Like real-folk nice! Kelsey, you got yourself a decent family, girlfriend!"

Kelsey laughed softly. "They are sweet, aren't they? And normal. All my life I've longed to be part of a normal family."

"Ain't that the truth?" said Thea.

"Across the board, yes," agreed Jazz. "And now you are."

"Yes. And girls . . ." She faced them both, grateful, but wanting what was best for them. She hated to say it. Dreaded it, actually, because the last thing she wanted was for Thea or Jazz to leave, but they'd already devoted over a month to her. "If you need to go, if you need to get back to your regular lives, I'll be fine. I know I will." She let out a soft breath she didn't know she'd been holding. "But I couldn't have done it without you. Both of you."

Jazz took a seat and crossed her legs. She looked at Thea.

Thea looked at her, then said, "I can't possibly go anywhere right now. It's out of the question. Hillside Medical needs me. The people here need me. And the grumpy doctor and the somewhat grumpy staff need me. I can't in good conscience leave until things are calmer, so for the moment, I'm staying right here. In the snow and the cold and the long, dark nights. Because I can't walk away and leave those folks in a fix. Even stubborn ones like Maggie," she teased as Maggie came into the room. "Who has now promised to come in for regular check-ups. Right?"

Maggie slipped into the firm-cushioned wingback chair while Thea took a corner of the couch. "Promise. For real, this time. I was being downright stupid, staying away from doctors because I got mad at Dr. Wolinski. And mad at myself, and mad at everything, mostly." She paused, then turned toward Jazz. "I didn't know anything about eating disorders when my daughter slipped downhill years ago. She was so good at hiding things."

Jazz nodded in understanding. "We learn quickly, Maggie. The loose tops, the quick smiles, the whole charade."

"I was a young mother, so certain that I could help the world by helping those kids we brought in," Maggie continued. "It never occurred to me that youngsters would be that angry for so long, so me being naïve played a part. I thought I could help them. I believed it was my Christian duty to help them."

She bit her lower lip and frowned, pensive. "I saw it playing out different, that Jeb and I would get our big family and still keep things good for Bonnie. By the time I saw the whole picture, it was too late. Bonnie had been starving herself off and on for a long time. Her heart never fully recovered its agility, they said. She went on to do good things, lots of things." She looked up at the graduation photos of Bonnie on the wall. "But she never regained that strength, and when she felt like things were out of her control, she'd stop eating again. Last Christmas she came to visit and we saw it right off, but it was too late. She'd gone too far, and when her heart gave out it was such a bitter reminder of how delicate and fragile the body's balance can be. We never meant to upset that balance. But we did, wanting to do the right thing."

Jazz went to her side. "Maggie, I—"

"Shush." Maggie took a tart tone but softened it with a gentle expression. "I'm just saying that losing a child is the harshest thing there is, but then to have the good Lord bring you here to us means something to me and Jeb. A long time ago you lost the grandmother who just loved her 'Cinda,' then we lost the daughter we loved . . . well, it works, you see? Somehow, someway, it all works. I think this town is good for you, Jacinda, for all of you." She included all three younger women. "And I think you're good for us. Otherwise why would this have all worked out so splendidly? So stay in Wishing Bridge for a while, or stay forever, but I want you and Thea to stay with us as long as you need, if you don't mind two old folks and their ways. It's the best company I've ever had, and thinking of you gals while I was in that hospital made me hurry to get better enough to come home. To come home to Jeb and all of you. And that's all I've got to say."

"All?" Jazz gave her a frank smile and a gentle hug. "I'd say that's quite a bit."

"It kind of was," Maggie agreed.

"I'm staying. Thea's here for a while. Jazz?" Kelsey lifted the baby for a burp. "What about you?"

Jazz sat back on her heels. She looked around the room, then at them. And then she sighed. "I can't leave."

Maggie breathed a sigh of relief they all heard and felt.

"I can't trust myself in New York. I don't have the skill set to do other things right now, and I feel good here. I feel good for the first time in so long that I can't remember the last time I felt good about myself. About life." She stretched and smiled, long, lanky, and relaxed at last. "I wake up each morning expecting to catch a plane or a train or a limo and go through the primping process and have designers pick apart my figure, my face, my eyes, my hair. And when I realize I don't have to do that, it's like a blessing washing over me. So Maggie, if you're good with it, and you don't mind my struggles, then I'd love to stay here. With you, all of you. In Wishing Bridge."

"I'd say this calls for a celebration, but I've got no energy as yet to celebrate outwards, but inwards?" Her smile brightened her face. "I'm throwing a party! Come here, girls."

The three women gathered around her.

She hugged them one by one. And when she was done, Thea and Jazz helped her up.

"I think it's a good time to have coffee in the kitchen, don't you? I've missed my kitchen something awful!"

"Unless you're more comfortable here," Jazz began.

The doorbell rang.

"No, I think the kitchen's best," said Maggie. "Kelsey, can you get that, please?"

Thea and Jazz exchanged looks but followed Maggie to the kitchen and quietly shut the door.

Kelsey tucked the baby onto her shoulder and crossed the room.

Hale Jackson was standing on the other side of the big, broad door. He looked good. So good.

But she'd seen his expression the night he and Garrett had accused her, just half a day after kissing her. No one needed a man like that. Not her, certainly. She started to turn away, to refuse him entrance, but he called her name.

"Kelsey."

She didn't want to face him, but hadn't her father just complimented her courage?

She turned back. "Go away."

"Five minutes." He held up five fingers. Then he shrugged and almost smiled. "Maybe ten. And then if you never want to see me again, I'll understand. Although it will be hard, because this is a very small town."

She'd noticed that all right.

"Please? I did save your life, as I recall. And not that long ago."

Oh, man. She crossed to the door, tucked a receiving blanket around Hayley so she wouldn't take a chill, and opened the door.

"Five minutes." She kept her voice tight as she moved back to the warmth of the living room.

"Or ten."

"Hale . . ." She turned, and he was there. Right there. Tall and broad and strong, with the most gorgeous eyes and short, crisp hair, looking like every woman's dream.

"I was wrong." He didn't ask to sit or move toward the living room. He stood still, probably because he knew she had a mental timer running. "I saw that letter. I realized it was true, about you being Dave's daughter, because Nora Hannon was one of my mom's best friends when I was young, and the rest just fell into place. I was wrong, and I want you to forgive me, Kelsey. Please."

"You want me to forgive you for thinking I was capable of blackmail and extortion? For thinking I came to town purposely, and conveniently arranged to go into labor in the snow, just to bilk money out of a father I didn't know I had? Hmm." She tapped a finger to her mouth, as if considering, but then he surprised her.

"No. I was right to investigate the case, Kelsey. That's my job. And the job doesn't play favorites. But I was wrong to let the circumstances push old buttons. That was stupid on my part, and I'm going to try to control that better."

Old buttons? "So you were right to interrogate me? Somehow I don't see this as getting better, Hale. And your time is running out."

He reached out a hand. His right hand. And he touched her cheek softly. So softly. And he lowered his voice as he met her gaze. "You asked me once if I had kids."

She remembered it well. The question and his hesitation. "Yes."

"I did. Or thought I did. I was married while I was in the NFL. We felt like we had it all. I had an amazing career, Layla was taking care of the foundation we'd set up to help kids in sub-Saharan Africa, we had a beautiful little boy named Michael. Then I got injured." His mouth drew down. "Everything went wrong. I hadn't realized it was already wrong, but once I was in the hospital, then rehab, I could see it. She filed for divorce the same day I realized I'd never play professional football again."

Who kicks a guy when he's down like that? Kelsey frowned. "I'm sorry, Hale. Really sorry."

He shook his head quickly. "Those are survivable things, Kelsey. I could feel Layla pulling away, and I knew my career was jeopardized the minute my knee came apart on that field, but when she told me that Michael wasn't my son . . ." He pulled a breath. "That the little boy I loved and doted on was someone else's child, my world fell apart. Because in all the hype surrounding careers and lifestyles, Michael was the one true thing I had going for me. Only it wasn't true at all. She was leaving me to go to the West Coast and marry Michael's father."

Kelsey didn't know what to say. What could she say? The thought of someone taking your child away, regardless of blood relations. "Couldn't you fight for him? Because you were married?"

He nodded. "Sure. We could have had a custody war that would have made all the papers, and then the whole thing would have come out, and there would be nothing normal about a little boy's life that wouldn't come up to haunt him later on. Or I could be the bigger person and sign off, and give my son the best present I could possibly give him at the time. A normal life."

Her heart didn't just ache for him.

It broke.

Sacrificial love. The kind of love she'd read about, the kind of love she'd wanted for Hayley, enough that she had been ready to give her child up to ensure she lived a life surrounded by sacrificial love.

"I didn't mean to hurt you, Kelsey. And when I kissed you that morning, I walked out of here thinking my life had taken the best, most unexpected turn I could imagine. All I could see was the promise of a new life, new love, new joy. So when Dave handed me that letter and I saw your name, I saw Layla's deceit all over again and wondered how I could be that stupid."

He paused and searched her face, her eyes, then took her hand. "I want your forgiveness. I was stupid, but not because I was attracted to you. I was stupid for letting those old buttons get pushed. The night I rescued you, I looked into your eyes and I knew, Kelsey."

"Knew what?" She held his gaze, challenging him to say it out loud. And he did.

"I knew you were my destiny. I knew that somehow we were meant to be in that place, at that time. I don't know how or why, but I knew. As if my finding you was an answer to a wish. Or a prayer."

It was both, she realized.

She'd prayed for God to deliver her safely, and she'd wished for a town where folks still loved one another.

Wishing Bridge.

She faced Hale. And then she leaned up on tiptoe and put her lips gently on his. But not too gently. She wanted him to know that a kiss was still a kiss.

"I'm not a praying person, but I called on God that night, Hale. I wished for a place to belong, a place where people still love each other, and then you showed up. And since we're all going to be in this small town together, I think it would be really nice . . ."

He snugged one arm around her waist and drew her closer. "How nice?"

"Crazy nice," she whispered, with her mouth almost on his. "To get to know each other really well. What do you say, Deputy?"

He smiled. And then he kissed her. He kissed her the way he had the week before and left no doubt about his feelings. And his intentions.

"I say I'm the luckiest man in the world, Kelsey. And I'd be honored to start a nice old-fashioned courtship with the local schoolmarm." He grinned when she smiled. "If she'll have me."

"This schoolmarm would like you to know that she's also honored. Honored to be here. And to be courted by the deputy."

"Well, then." He kissed her again, and when he finally broke the kiss, he settled his forehead to hers. "Kelsey?"

"Yes?" She murmured the word sweetly against his cheek, his face. "What, my love?"

He smiled. She felt his lips move and his cheeks lift, and then he kissed her one more time. "Welcome to Wishing Bridge."

ACKNOWLEDGMENTS

First, big thanks to Sheryl Zajechowski for contracting this delightful series for Waterfall Press! And to Faith Black Ross for her insights as my editor. Her keen eye gave the story extra (and well-deserved!) luster. My copyeditor, Laura Whittemore, was literally the best I've ever worked with, and I'm so grateful for her care and expertise. And as always, big thanks to my beloved literary agent, Natasha Kern, for her diligent work to bring great fiction into readers' hands.

And huge thanks to retired NYPD Detective Greg O'Connell, whose diligence in rebuilding towns caught my eye a few years ago. I first heard about Greg in a *New York Times* article, and I loved his story of investing his money into a town, and then helping the town reap the benefits of his investment. His work in Mount Morris, New York, inspired Max Reichert's character in the Wishing Bridge series. Thank you, Greg. I've seen your example carried on in other towns and villages and I can only say, Bravo! Well done!

Sincere thanks to our local sheriffs, first responders, and fire departments, whose dedication and valor can be the difference between life and death for folks in rural settings. And also to the doctors, PAs, and nurse practitioners who fill a huge need in rural settings. Big-city medics are wonderful, but the people in rural districts need good, convenient medical care. You are a true blessing.

I'd also like to thank Carol Garvin of British Columbia for sending me a cute video at the right moment . . . and that video helped put the final pieces of *Welcome to Wishing Bridge* firmly in place.

And I'd be remiss if I didn't acknowledge my readers, because you make this all possible . . . and crazy fun! I hope you love this new, beautiful story of faith, hope, and love . . . and the greatest of these is love.

ABOUT THE AUTHOR

Ruth Logan Herne is the bestselling author of more than forty novels and novellas. With millions of books in print, she's living her dream of touching hearts and souls by writing the kind of books she likes to read. A mother of six and grandmother to fourteen, she loves God, family, country, chocolate, and dogs and lives with her husband on a small farm in upstate New York, where she can be found prepping chicken eggs for local customers—who know not to say too much (or they just may end up in a book).